REVEALED

KATTY'S STORY

BONNIE LACY

FROSTING ON THE CAKE PRODUCTIONS

Revealed by Bonnie Lacy
Book 4 in The Great Escapee Series

To all the tiny humans who were on the Earth for such a short time,
but who deeply affected our lives.

To all humans who struggle with overcoming—I hold you in my heart.

"For I know the plans I have for you," says the Eternal, "plans for peace,
not evil, to give you a future and hope—*never forget that.*"
Jeremiah 29:11 The Voice Version

ONE

Katty Randolph watched her daughter Bea Randolph paint another rainbow above a unicorn. A unicorn with two horns? Some sci-fi or fantasy fans might want to argue the case for one horn. The rainbow hovered in the space above the unicorn, like a sort of umbrella—a covering or protection.

Katty glanced up. There was no rainbow over her. No covering. No protection.

Sigh.

Katty let her eyes travel over the living room walls—from one taped drawing or painting to the next—a zig-zag trail of colorful images. Her daughter's art literally wallpapered the three living room walls. If there'd been a fourth wall, it would have been covered, too. Instead, the pictures traveled on to the kitchen walls, above the kitchen cupboards, and on each cupboard door. She chuckled. The hallway would be next.

Bea was only four years old but already a decent artist. Anything was better than looking at cheap paneling. Pictures covered scratches left by moving furniture, she guessed. Paintings covered holes punched in anger. All of it was old trailer house just-plain-crappy-paneling.

Good thing Katty had sipped from that bottle and wasn't drunk. Otherwise, she knew she'd get dizzy looking at all the pictures. Maybe get sick.

Taking it easy today. Backing off booze, slowly. It might take a while, but she knew she'd been hitting it too hard lately.

Deep breath.

Bea appeared to be deep in her own little realm, so Katty could freely study everything about her. Her perfect, pale skin appeared mostly without blemish and unscarred—well, a small scar was still visible on her forehead from the accident. Thick, dark eyelashes made up for a thin head of curly brown hair. Katty guessed she herself had been that tiny. Definitely not muscular. Some people called Bea skinny, but how could a mom keep a kid healthy on just peanut butter sandwiches and ice cream.

Peanut butter ruled as Bea's absolute favorite. She climbed the cupboards to find a new jar—if there was one.

The ice cream was the fault of their now-grandfather, Clarence Timmelsen.

Katty shook her head and hugged herself. Every time she thought of the paperwork she'd discovered in Clarence's boxes at Hillcrest Nursing Home, she teared up. She should check the dates on those papers the next time she worked. Her heart overflowed when she remembered the day that she found those adoption papers. She was just his paralegal in his new agency—Clarence was the lawyer and Harold the detective. She wasn't his kin.

But according to the words on those papers, Clarence had made her and Bea his heirs—Noell Carpenter, too. Noell was their cousin—almost as good as having a sister.

It was a dream come true for them all, but especially Katty and Bea.

Bea burst from her chair and dangled a wet painting from her fingers. It floated in the air as she blew on it. "Where, Mommy?" She turned toward Katty. "Where should I hang this one?"

"Well." It was getting hard to find a space not already taken. There. She stood and pointed at a small corner wall above the refrigerator. "Will it fit there?"

Bea scrunched her nose. "I was kinda hoping it would be a more 'portant place."

Katty chuckled. "You've used up all the 'portent places, Bea." She pointed. "You used the microwave and the oven." She shrugged. "I guess it's the TV. We'll just have to move the painting when we watch a show, right?"

Bea grinned. "Or we could tape it to the mirror in the bathroom." Orneriness twinkled in her eyes.

This kid.

"Sure. Why not?" Katty stood. "Need any help?"

Bea ripped a piece of tape off the dispenser and stuck it to the paper. "Nope." She checked the roll of tape. "Almost out." She waved the painting at Katty as she passed her. "Don't mess with my paints. I'm doing another one when I get back."

"I won't mess with your paints." Katty blinked. She hadn't painted—or even drawn since …. Fog seemed to part, revealing memories buried deep of her mom shredding her own paintings. Katty had loved painting horses and trees. The day Mom broke her well-used colored pencils in half—crayons, too—and slapped her every time Katty tried to grab one away was probably the last time she used them. She could still hear the crack of the wooden colored pencils—breaking those pencils and breaking her heart.

Oh, there were more—more haunting memories.

Freed from Mom by her new boyfriend, Phil Daynton, Katty ventured to draw again. Just a pencil and paper. The lines that appeared soothed her soul. She didn't even try, most times, to make the lines become anything recognizable. She didn't need to. When she did draw something, it was often a tree—roots and all.

She kept them hidden. No need to put herself through the possibility of someone criticizing them.

But one day, Phil caught her. She'd been so absorbed in what she was doing, she didn't hear him behind her. "What are you doing?"

"Nothing." She'd scrunched it up and thrown it in the trash.

A whisper, now. "No, I won't mess with your paints." A ragged whisper.

She swallowed and glanced at the cupboard door—*that* cupboard. Her booze stash hidden behind cans of vegetables. Bea would never snoop past those. She was always looking for cereal or peanut butter.

Katty stood, hesitated, then walked to the cupboard, but Bea was too quick. "Bea, did you eat your… mac and cheese?"

Back in the room, Bea glanced at the bowl, only half eaten, and wrinkled her nose. "Not hungry."

"You didn't eat very much. There's nothing else for supper." Katty picked it up and walked to the sink. She loved mac and cheese.

Belch.

But not this time. Just the smell. When would this be over? Why was it so hard?

Her own body was her enemy. If she tried not to drink, she got sick. If she drank, it helped for a few minutes, but she still got sick.

Why couldn't she get free?

What did she have to do to get free and have a life like everyone else on this planet?

Why her?

Bea picked up a crayon to start another drawing, and something came over Katty.

Someone wailed from deep within, from way back.

Katty pushed aside the kitchen chair and walked toward one wall. Rows and rows of pictures. Paintings and drawings of everything imaginable. Of trees and flowers. Unicorns. Rainbows. Apples.

"Mommy?" Bea lifted her head. "Do you like them?"

"Uh, sure." Katty swallowed. "I love them." She reached for one. "But…" She slowly pulled the tape away from the wall.

"Mommy?"

"Just a little space for me—for mine." She carefully placed the painting on the coffee table.

Bea's eyes popped wide. "What are you doing?" She stood.

Another painting came off. And another one. "I-I'll only use one wall. I'll only take yours off this one wall."

She couldn't stop herself.

"Mommy." Bea stomped her foot.

Soon, the entire wall was back to the crappy tan-brown paneling. But in Katty's mind, she was already transforming it. She could see in her mind the steps needed. Almost in a trance, she opened the cupboard under the kitchen sink and pulled out soaps and junk.

There.

Towers of used paint cans stacked behind the drainpipe to the sink. Cans and cans. Why had she kept all this? Some were already there from when she and Bea moved in. Some she added after painting Bea's bedroom and the bathroom. Furniture for Bea's room. She had no idea where the others had come from.

She dragged it all out onto the kitchen floor.

"What are you doing?" Bea stood right behind her. "Can I help?" The distraction of big cans of paint evidently calmed Bea.

"M-maybe." Right at the moment, something raged inside her. "It's almost time for bed."

Bea could tell time. She looked at the clock. "It's only 7:32."

"Well, help me carry these to the wall over there." Katty stopped. "Wait. Let's put an old towel or something down first." Hard to be the adult right now. Her insides felt like they might explode—partly from the booze—but fingers of suppressed pain, anger, and creativity pounded her insides to get out.

All Katty wanted to do was paint. No matter how messy it got.

And it might get messy.

Bea walked to the table and picked up her paintbrush—a skinny one that had come with her set of paints. "What are *you* going to use, Mommy?"

Katty dragged towels from the kitchen drawer and scattered them on the floor in front of the wall. "What?" She glanced from the paintbrush to the wall. "I... don't... know."

Brushes.

Make-up brushes. She almost ran to the bathroom, dug out all the make-up brushes she could find, and grabbed at towels hanging on the towel racks.

"My towel? You're going to use my new Daryl & Dumpty towel?" Bea jerked it from Katty's arm. "Clarence and Mrs. T gave it to me."

"Oh. No. I won't..." Katty dropped the brushes onto the floor with the towels and paint cans.

Bea hugged the towel as she watched. Katty could tell Bea was still mad. Her mouth pouted and nose flared. Dang, she was cute.

Katty belched as she leaned over to open the biggest can. Orange. Where on earth? They hadn't used any orange in the trailer. Anywhere.

Didn't matter. Orange it was. The smell of paint—even wall paint—stirred her.

Belch. Sick as she was, she couldn't stop.

She dipped the brush into the paint and swiped it against the wall. Make-up brushes would not work. One small orange stripe. She looked up. On one whole wall.

Voices from her past whispered. "You're so stupid. You can't draw. Your horse looks like a fish."

Katty's face burned.

When her mom began the ranting and abuse, Katty wadded all the papers and drawings up and threw them away. She learned to grab her crayons and colored pencils fast before her mom broke them all. So many times, she'd used stubs just to be able to draw. When her mom's abuse became unbearable, or even worse, dangerous, Katty found an old tree house in an abandoned yard nearby. The house on that lot was falling in, but the tree house was still there in an old tree. She stashed crayons, pencils, and every kind of paper she could find in a corner. Winters were long without that tree house.

When evil Phil came along—her rescuer—he became her savior. He turned out to be her abuser in disguise. He tripped every switch in her. She had been hungry—literally—and he had held out a chocolate candy bar. She had been desperate for love, for approval, for at least appreciation. He gave her that, too.

Until.

Katty grabbed a dishcloth, dipped it into the paint can, and slapped paint against the wall.

Orange popped against the dingy brown paneling.

At first, she'd felt free with Phil. Finally free to be herself. Mom wasn't around and probably was glad to have Katty out of the house.

So she'd started drawing again, back then. Bought a child's set of paints at the store. The rich colors stirred something in her. Made her feel alive.

Until.

Until that night. Phil's druggie buddies were over and they were having a merry time.

She'd gathered her drawings and paintings up but must have missed one, or Phil had snuck one away. Before she knew what he'd done, he taped it to the TV screen, and in a deep booming voice, announced that they had a celebrity in the house. A Master painter. A real ar-teest.

The ones who were still coherent actually looked amazed and agreed with him until they caught on and faked oohs and aahs. Mocking her.

They all had a big laugh over that one.

All except Katty. Shame, shame, shame. The old emotions of fear mixed with new ones of betrayal.

He'd said he loved her.

More orange.

Bea picked up a brush, dipped it in the can, and was just about to swish it on the wall beside Katty's, when Katty flinched.

"No!" Katty's eyes misted over. "No! This is mine!"

Bea dropped the brush onto the floor and backed away.

Katty couldn't stop herself. The smell of the paint. Seeing brush strokes. Hearing a rubbing sound of the now-orange dishcloth against the paneling. "Don't touch my stuff."

Breathe.

She knew she was acting like a brat. But something inside her didn't care. She couldn't stop herself and didn't want to. She needed to be free. Free from the pain, the past. She needed to be free from people in her life who had locked the door to her own personal prison. The voices had played over and over until she couldn't hear anything else.

Glancing behind her, she shook her head. She was more than a brat. She was that slut her mom and Phil had always called her.

She'd treated her own daughter just like they had treated her.

"Bea." Katty set the dishcloth on a towel, closed the lid to the can and wiped her hands on her jeans—well, one hand. The cast still trapped the left one—damn that Phil—tried to ram her and Bea at the convenience store. They should be dead. Both of them.

Bea didn't answer.

Katty turned.

No Bea.

Damn. She always hurt the only person she really loved.

Bea was in her own bedroom or… under the rocker in Katty's bedroom. Her old hide-out.

"Bea, I'm sorry."

Nothing. Not a sound.

The wall called to her, even though she knew she should go after Bea. The ugly stuff inside her right now overruled, and Katty picked up the dishcloth and opened a different can.

Red.

TWO

"Mommy!"

Katty shook her head. Still inside her dream, babies floated in front of her, beside her, sat on her lap. Several babies—four or five—sat in front of her and focused on her face, their eyes deeply engaged and fixed on hers. They saw into her soul, knew her thoughts, knew her past.

Gulp.

Others floated around her, each one looked into her eyes as it flew past. Eyes of every color, every color of skin, some dressed, some ... not. A soothing, warm light poured around and through each baby. A sweet, fresh fragrance wafted to Katty as they moved in and around her. This had to be heaven.

"Mommy!"

"Wha?" Katty tried to move. She peeked one eye open, squinting the other one. The dream morphed over Bea standing in front of her, her little hands on her hips, stomping her foot. Babies perched on *her* shoulders and head. Even a couple flew *through* her. Couldn't be—had to be the dream.

The booze.

Katty rolled onto her back and tried to open both eyes. She had slept on the sofa? She blinked again.

Yup. Belch.

The babies slowly faded into a mist. A couple remained, as long as she focused on them.

"Mommy?" That wasn't Bea. Her mouth wasn't moving. Bea's mouth was … mad.

Katty blinked, her eyes watered. Emotions flooded her mind, her inner being. Emotions from the past, the present, all she'd done, all she'd lived through. Every wrong, every abuse, every wound flooded her.

No.

She shut it down.

"Mommy!" *That* was Bea.

"What, Bea?" She rubbed her eyes and blinked several times. With each blink, her vision cleared, until she could fully see angry Bea in front of her … and painted walls behind her?

Angry Bea. Her eyes were brown, but right now they appeared black. Her mouth pouted. Forehead crumpled. Her foot stomped again. "You took down *all* my paintings!" She stomped her foot one more time, for effect.

Little diva.

Katty tried to sit but just fell onto her side. Someone had pulled the sofa away from the wall, where it had lived from day one. They'd never moved it … u-until now. It stood in the middle of the small living room.

Katty sat up.

Careful.

She finally looked to where Bea still pointed.

The walls.

She slowly rose on unsteady legs. Don't turn too fast. Slow it down. One wall … at a … time.

Swallow.

Every wall.

Every wall had been painted. And not just in one color, like they'd painted Bea's room, all green, trimmed in pink.

These walls. Paintings on every wall. In the orange, but left-over green and pink, but blue and tan and…

What was with babies all over? Clouds.

But… babies.

Her dream.

Some trees and flowers. Bugs? Details of bugs. An enormous tree, painted in a corner, grew across both walls, hovering over more babies. Branches, and the way they grew from the trunk, looked strangely familiar.

And scary.

Katty shook her head. A deep sigh burst from her chest.

"Mommy, why'd you take my stuff down?"

Katty pushed her hand at Bea. "Hush. Shush. Give me a minute."

As she became steadier on her feet, Katty examined every wall, every image. How on earth? She knew this was her fault, but had no recollection of doing it.

Well, she remembered the beginning orange stripe. From there, she'd gone on a search in the cupboard.

Yeah.

She held her hands out in front of her. She'd done it all right. Paint smeared all over her hands—backs and palms. Up her arms. The cast.

But where were Bea's drawings?

Oh no.

But there they were, all stacked neatly … in the sink. Wrapped in plastic food wrap.

Another deep breath. "Here they are. I didn't ruin them. I was careful." She had no idea how she'd managed to take them all down, wrap them in plastic wrap. Plastic wrap was from the devil. When she was sober, the stupid wrap always, always tore off wrong and stuck to itself. She'd wasted more rolls in frustration, throwing them into the trash.

Bea barely reached into the sink on tiptoes and lifted the papers out. "Mom! Why'd—" She turned. "You made a package. You wrapped them like they do watermelon at the store. John does it." She hugged the paintings to her chest.

Whew. Katty would have to buy some watermelon next trip to the store. "Yeah. It's all wrapped up … like … for your baby book."

Bea scrunched her face. "My baby book? I have a baby book?" She looked at the walls. She still appeared mad.

She didn't have a real baby book, but she would now. "Bea. I'm sorry." Katty bit her lips. "I don't remember taking them down." She bowed her head. "I—"

"Mom." Bea carried her stack of drawings and sat on the sofa, glancing from her own art to the walls. Her eyes seemed to study every section of the walls. "Mom. You're good."

Katty pulled out of her fog in time to hear what Bea had said. Oh Dear God. She swallowed and blinked. Breathed slowly, in and out. She gulped. "You … you think so?" She slowly sat beside Bea, wiped her eyes and glanced at every scene on every wall.

"Mommy. You're a good painter." She glanced at the empty paint cans scattered on the floor, then at the walls. "Babies. So cute. So many babies."

How long had they sat there—both Katty and Bea, staring at and studying the paintings on the walls? One pointed at an area and commented. The other nodded and sighed.

Bea made a declaration. "Mommy. We won't ever paint over this."

"I don't know."

Bea patted her stack of papers still on her lap. "We can hang mine … in between babies. And from the tree." She pointed, then sighed. "We need to keep these walls." She popped up. "We need to take them wherever we go. If we move, we have to take them with."

Katty chuckled. "Maybe." She laughed. "Can you imagine us taking the walls off the … w-walls and picking them up? Take them outside?" She pointed to the door. "And—"

"And tie them to the top of our car." Bea nodded.

Katty laughed again. "You're determined."

"Yes." Bea seemed so grown up at that moment. "De-ter-determined."

"Bea." Katty sucked in a deep breath. "Bea, I'm sorry for being such a bad mommy."

"You're not a bad mommy." Bea blinked. "You're a good mommy. Right?"

Katty shook her head. "I don't mean to be bad." Her eyes landed on several empty shooter bottles scattered about the paint cans on the floor. *Breathe*. "I need help. I can't quit drinking. I want to be a good mom. I quit, but then I start up again. I just can't stop drinking that … those …." She pointed.

Bea stood, carefully placed her drawings on the sofa, and picked a tiny bottle up.

Katty unconsciously flinched. "Bea."

Bea didn't stop. She picked up another one. Smelled them and gagged. "Mommy—"

"I know." Katty shook her head and tried to stand. "They stink … to you."

"But how can you drink these?" Bea wrinkled her nose.

This girl. Older than her four years. Wiser. "It's hard to explain." Katty breathed in and out slowly. "It's called an addiction. My body wants what's inside those bottles—needs it."

"Oh. Kinda like when my body," she pointed to her chest, "when my body needs ice cream?"

Katty closed her eyes and shook her head. Tears rolled down her cheeks. She smiled, but it felt like her face cracked. "Kinda. No. Maybe." She chuckled, but crumpled back down onto the sofa. "I can't do this anymore. I want to quit, but I want to drink. I can't be a good mommy to you." She looked up at the walls. "I can't find me anymore. I stop drinking sometimes," she said, then shrugged. "But either I hide it or go back to it. Both. I do what I don't want to do and I don't do what I want to do."

Bea sat beside her. Reached for her hand. Put her head against Katty's arm. Her little head covered with messy, curly hair.

Katty leaned in and covered Bea's head with her own. "Somehow. There's a way. Somehow."

Later that day, Katty found a plastic shopping bag and shook it open. The words in bright red letters on the outside stopped her. "Thank You Thank You Thank You, Please Reuse or Recycle This Bag. We Care."

Katty smirked. "I'll bet you do. I'll bet you care." She shook it out again. "All you care about is if I buy more stupid booze." Talking to a plastic bag, now. Okay.

She picked up the tiny bottles and empty paint cans. Each one clanked as it fell in. Clattered. That sound. It both made her want to drink and want to throw up. Surely that wasn't possible at the same time.

She swallowed.

Breathe.

Tears filled her eyes again. Was there any end to tears and crying? Seems she could cry at the drop of a hat … bottle. She used to be so … strong. Or was it just stubborn? Or avoidance? Mom used to smack Katty across the face if she ever caught her crying. "Suck it up, Buttercup. Nobody ever wiped away *my* tears."

Katty could still see her mom's face, her eyes. She'd even forgotten what color her mother's eyes really were—brown? Green? They would always be black. Black eyes, full of hatred and anger. Evil.

That's probably how Katty had attracted evil ex-boyfriend, Phil. His eyes always appeared black, even though they were blue. She knew his were blue. But somehow, when he was raging and abusing her, they started out sky-blue, then gradually turned all dark black.

Mom's eyes.

Phil's eyes. And now he was nowhere to be found. He'd tried to kidnap Bea before. Where was he now?

Breathe.

She shook the contents of the shopping bag down to make room for more. She had tons of bags. Her legs were stiff, heavy. Her hands and arms wouldn't move. All she wanted to do was sleep, not go get more bags.

She groaned as she tried to straighten. Sleeping on her bed was never wonderful—the mattress was so old. But sleeping on the sofa was even worse. As she slowly stood, eyes on the painted wall inches away, stared back at hers.

Eyes.

Baby eyes right in front of her. Above and below. On the next wall and the other wall.

Blue eyes. Green eyes. Brown eyes. Different tones of those colors.

Katty backed away and stumbled on another paint can. It rolled away, almost trying to distract her from the eyes, but it didn't work. The eyes, the baby faces, drew her—lured her.

Some were just smears where eyes should be on a face. Someone had finely detailed others with eyelashes and pupils. Staring at her from all three walls. Accusing her, blaming her.

They seemed to float at her from every wall. Taking form from the flat images on the wall, filling out, and flitting toward her, their eyes wide, fingers pointing—

"Mommy?"

Katty jumped.

Bea opened the door, stepped inside and dropped the mail right where she stood. Except for one piece of mail, still in her hand. She waved it in front of Katty's face. "What's this, Mommy? Toys?"

Bea walked toward her, still waving the catalog right through the babies. They peered at her, then fluttered in and around each other and Bea. One big baby angel party with Bea in the middle.

Katty gasped and sat down hard, almost missing the sofa behind her.

"Mommy."

The babies.

"Mommy?" Bea sat down beside her and shoved the catalog at her. "Lookie these kits—these building sets." Bea shook the pictures in front of Katty's face.

Babies floated in at the same time.

"Can I have one, Mommy? Just one?" Bea knew they never had any money. "Just this one."

The biggest set.

"Maybe for Christmas, Bea. It's coming soon."

Katty blinked as a baby flew past her face. Bea didn't seem to see it. How much was hallucination and how much was real? Probably all booze related. Babies were just nightmares come alive. She blinked again—longer—moving her eyeballs while she kept her eyes closed.

"Mommy?"

"Bea, I can't buy anything that big right now." She opened her eyes. Bea wasn't paying any attention to her. The catalog was open to the Daryl & Dumpty pages.

"What, Mommy?" Bea glanced up. Her brown eyes oozed sweet love.

Katty was crazy for sure. She now heard voices—baby voices calling her "Mommy." She was seeing things—babies floating all around her and Bea. Bea had no idea just how crazy Katty might be. A visual of her own mom morphed over Bea's face. That ugly stringy hair. Black eyes for brown ones.

No.

Not even close.

Couldn't let that happen. Not going to let that happen. Not gonna become her mom. She glanced over at Bea.

She'd give her own life to not become who her mother had been.

THREE

Phil slammed his fist into the old wooden studs without thinking.

"Stupid idiot!" he growled. People were still upstairs at the antique store.

He held his breath as dust filtered down from between the floorboards above him. Amazing the owners hadn't discovered him yet.

This was getting old, hiding out. Unbearable.

He'd been down in this moldy, damp basement since the accident. Well … he'd snuck out at night a time or two. Just for fresh air. And to relieve himself. He knew his time here was limited. At some point, someone would see his footsteps and find his bathroom.

He and Lex Forte, his cohort in crime, had discovered and explored the hideout weeks ago. Easy to break into the basement. They'd agreed that if things went bad, they should meet here. Simple to slip in and out for supplies. They'd stockpiled some snacks and water back then—even a couple bottles of booze—hiding it under some old, smelly blankets.

But he hadn't seen Lex since that day he'd attacked the deputy. Phil hoped he had gotten away somehow, but since he wasn't down in this basement now, Phil guessed he was in jail. And right now, getting a shower, medical attention and three square meals sounded kind of good.

Kind of.

He winced as he sipped from the plastic water bottle. Something inside was injured—deeper in—not just his nose, because it was uncomfortable to swallow. He had hardly talked since the accident, so that might be affected, too. Could barely tip the bottle up to get the last drop. Stretched his neck too much.

Whiplash? Slamming into a windshield could mess a guy up.

No way I'm going to a doctor or the hospital, but in a perfect world ...

He tossed the empty bottle into the corner, but cringed when it popped as it landed.

"Damn!" Holding his breath, he listened.

Phil needed to find another place, or at least clear out his trash, in case the owners came downstairs. The pile was growing with water bottles, an empty whiskey bottle, and snack wrappers.

A granola bar wrapper jumped.

Damn. Surely not.

No windows in this part of the building. But even in summer, this building had to be cold and drafty.

He might be getting jumpy.

Needed to get out of here—for good.

Not overwintering down here.

"I'd die." Damn. He touched his finger to his lips, glanced up. He'd never been a quiet man.

Needed to get that little girl and run. He'd give her a good home—better than that bitch Katty could. What a crappy trailer. White trash.

The wrapper fluttered on the floor across from him. Snakes or mice didn't scare him. He'd watched how his dad's cult members had sacrificed them when he was a kid. He'd done plenty of that himself, but he didn't like to think he was sitting in their bathroom, either. Or that he'd slept, them crawling all over him.

"Well, enjoy the crumbs, little fella."

The gentle flutter erupted into a skitter as the terrified mouse —or maybe rat—ran along the base of the wall and escaped into a crack.

"Damn."

Hadn't seen that crack until the mouse showed it to him just now.

Goosebumps.

What else lived down here?

Something passed over his arm. A sensation of air movement.

No open windows. No way for air to move. One wall of the room Phil was in remained open studs, so he could see into the adjacent room. A couple walls were old brick—nasty things grew on it. He wasn't a science buff, so he didn't have names, but he was getting a stuffy head and headache to what was probably mold. The fourth wall had visible studs, but boards covered the other side.

Must have been a bug—an ant or a cockroach.

He shuddered and struggled up off the floor. The quilt seemed to have a mind of its own as it jumped with him.

"How on earth?"

Too loud!

He jerked the quilt away, but it caught. Threads and frayed edges tangled around the keys attached to his wallet.

A chair skidded across the floor above him.

Crap!

Stupid, stupid idiot.

Only place to hide was under those moldy quilts. If the owners came down here, it was over. He flipped his gun's safety off and held his breath. Felt for his knife in his boot.

Holding his breath, he cut the quilt from his keys, but they rattled.

He backed away from the wall to the center of the room, body tense, gun stretched toward the door to the hallway. Then to the rat hole. Back to the door. Above him, to the ceiling.

Either the rat, or the people upstairs, might get shot. He moved, guarding both the door and the varmint hole, and backed into a … something.

Phil swung around and tripped over a stack of wood on the floor, making it tumble and clatter. He almost fell, but managed to keep his balance.

He squinted and peered into the darkness, but he couldn't see anything.

What had he backed into? A pole?

Something solid.

With substance.

Without thinking, he reached his hand out and touched … something hard.

He couldn't move. Something wheezed in and out against his face. Breathing.

Sweat trickled down his back, underneath his shirt and down his sides. A distinct odor—sewer, dead, sulfur—made him almost puke. But more than the smells and sounds.

Terrifying evil.

Something so evil, he could feel it. He had touched it.

His insides quivered. He withdrew his hand and rotated.

Rat hole wall.

Quilt.

Door to the hall.

Eyes.

Bloody yellow eyes, up as high as the ceiling.

Looking down at him.

Just eyes.

Phil was tall—six feet, five inches—but those eyes were … up high.

He shuddered and tried to back away.

Upstairs, a chair screeched across the wooden floor, again.

The eyes turned black, rimmed with yellow. Wet black eyes. They reflected what little light was available.

Terrifying, but fascinating.

They had to be alive—there was light from within.

They blinked.

"Shit!"

He crouched. He'd experienced evil before.

Never like this.

A deep chuckle.

Phil froze.

"So, Mr. Daynton. Your eyes are opening to other realms —other possibilities." Something growled and breathed into Phil's face. "You're not the only duck in the pond. You think you know everything about evil and what it can become."

Something flicked Phil's ear.

Phil jumped and recoiled. He stepped away, waving the gun and holding his ear.

"You never play fair in *your* world, and I'm here to show you just how one-sided life can be—from my world."

Something flicked Phil's other ear.

Back and forth, left ear, right ear, until Phil landed hard on the pile of lumber he'd just knocked over. The gun skittered away.

"Flicking your ears is such a small thing. I will show you and teach you things your dad never even dreamed of. And *he* was evil."

Something clawed along one wall and laughed as Phil rubbed goosebumps along his arms.

"What should I flick next?"

More than eyes appeared.

A demon. Those eyes, huge curving horns. Slimy scales. A

tail tapped the floor behind, almost like the demon was deciding what to flick next.

Phil stepped back. No.

It stepped closer, face inches from Phil's. Too close. Damn, it stunk. Feedlots smelled better.

Raising its hands, it lifted one talon and gently scratched Phil's nose.

Phil shuddered. His nose was already swollen. Painful. Bleeding.

The thing grinned, leaned closer. Cocked its head one way, then the next. Looked at Phil's nose, then stared into Phil's eyes. And drew back its hand, eyes never leaving Phil's.

Bam!

Voices from upstairs echoed. Phil couldn't open his eyes. What was wrong with his eyes? He rubbed them and cried out. His head wanted to explode. He blinked. Gently, he touched his nose, his mouth and tried to see his hand.

Blood.

How long had he been out?

Phil groaned and tried to sit up. Only each board slipped under him, making a lumber landslide.

No sinus infection had ever felt this bad. He touched his nose and came back with blood. Both ears stung, but something had bludgeoned his face with enough force to knock him off his feet and on his butt.

His face exploded in pain. Felt like his eyes and nose and mouth were re-arranged. The accident had already traumatized his head, but now he was sure something deeper was messed up.

Rustling in the corner distracted him for a second.

The rat?

More scratching on the opposite wall and then skittering up and down along the support post in the middle of the room.

Impossible! Nothing was visible except for the goosebumps along his arms. He'd experienced plenty of evil in his day—his dad's cult, many engagements with demons—but always through human hosts. Never directly from—

A chair scraped against the old wood floor upstairs, then footsteps tapped across the length of the store.

For the first time, when he heard the main door slam upstairs and keys rattle in the lock, he yelled, "Come back!" He gulped. "Don't leave me!"

FOUR

Deputy Mark Scott parked his cruiser in front of the Polk County Sheriff's Office in Osceola, Nebraska.

He'd served at one other department before this one. Small town, same as here. Not enough help. Pay was okay for his needs. But good people.

He liked Osceola the best, so far. Businesses had suffered, just like everywhere else, he guessed. Tough to make a go of it— housing was scarce, shopping minimal, dating was nonexistent. But small towns were where he wanted to live.

"Hey Mark." Chantelle Rodean, the department dispatcher radioed in. "I saw you pull up. We just got a complaint from a block away. Seems a jilted lover won't let go." She giggled. "The caller said her ex-boyfriend is sitting outside her house on the curb, throwing paper airplane love letters at the house." She snorted. "We should all be so lucky."

"Maybe. So is he just a nuisance or is he really doing harm?" Mark shook his head. High school stuff.

"Well, the caller said he is attaching rocks to the airplanes. He already broke a window."

"Okay. What's the address?" Mark sighed.

When Chantelle gave him the information, he nodded. "I know right where that is."

She laughed. "Isn't that right---"

"In our backyard. I have a feeling I know who it is, too." Mark backed out. "On my way. Thanks Chantelle. Keep your cell keys handy."

She was laughing as they clicked off.

Mark remembered being so love-sick over a girl in the class above him—he had to have been a sophomore. Maybe even a freshman. He'd get stuck watching her in the hallway and miss his next class.

As he turned the corner, flashes of growing up appeared in his mind. Growing up with a mostly absent, alcoholic dad.

He'd done the big town thing. Left home, right out of high school, for Omaha, Nebraska. He'd been so cocky. Thought he knew everything. He wasn't a tall kid, but he had a big attitude. Some girls thought he was cute, too. He played that up.

How his mom had let him leave was crazy. Her own life of healing from marriage to an alcoholic must have totally absorbed her. His dad had already died, but Mark was sure—at least now he was sure and knew a lot more—that his mom had more than she could handle trying to heal, but all his dad's bad choices had chased her down. He'd left debt all over the place. From the short time Mark had been a deputy, people's lives became an open file. He knew all the junk, so he could guess at what his mom had dealt with. Probably why she was so tied to her Bible study ladies.

He turned down the next street over and drove slowly, peering between houses and trees.

There.

The guy—a kid really—was literally sitting on the curb surrounded by balls of paper. While Mark watched, the kid lobbed one off. It hit just shy of the house. He threw himself back onto the ground in frustration. Mark rolled down his window and could hear him cussing. It looked like, instead of paper airplanes, he was now loading a ball of paper with a rock to make it go farther.

What on earth?

Get a job, kid.

Job hunting in Omaha was humbling. Nobody wanted to hire a kid. Looking for a job meant Mark needed money back then—he desperately did. His mom didn't have money to support him and he didn't want to live at home anymore. He wanted to try everything, spread his wings, sow his oats. Play the game of life by himself.

Right after moving to Omaha, he found a job at a movie theater, selling popcorn. He had a bomber of a minivan, filled with all his stuff in the world, which covered the back seat. Even slept in his car. He figured he could live on popcorn and when it was his turn to clean a theater, he could watch the movie for free. In reality, he never got to watch a movie for free and it was disgusting to clean a theater after a two-hour movie. Popcorn all over the floors and seats. Sticky pop spills to mop up. Nacho cheese didn't clean up easily from the seat fabric, either. It was his responsibility to clean up after all the jerks who watched the movie and didn't give a rat's behind about the mess they left.

Working at the theater had been the beginning of his freedom, but also the beginning of his personal stupidity. The crowd that worked there seemed pretty cool at first. One guy, Peter, went out of his way to befriend him and, as Mark looked back now, he knew exactly why. The guy needed a scapegoat, a fall guy. But even more so, Peter wanted a slave. He wanted someone he could push his own responsibilities off on, someone he could blame for his own failures. The guy had the supervisors all faked out and didn't care what lies he had to tell.

Mark couldn't figure out why Peter even wanted to keep the job—it was only a low-level position in a movie theater, for heaven's sake.

Until.

One evening after the last showing, Mark had walked into a drug deal between Peter and some thug who didn't work there. Probably a set-up. Mark didn't know the guy from anyone, but he'd never forget the goosebumps that ran up and down his body when he caught them. Right in the middle of the transaction—money exchanged for drugs.

Both had slowly turned their faces toward Mark. There was no fear visible, just gotcha grins.

It should have been the other way around.

Gotcha.

But Mark had no other connections, other than Peter and a girl named Tara.

Now there was a strange combination—her name and her personality. She was tiny—skinny was a better word—had curly blond hair that framed her small face. Big blue eyes that could hypnotize.

And hypnotize him, they did.

Mark fell hard. First time. All the girls who chased him in high school never affected him like Tara had. He would have cut off his right hand and all his toes if she'd asked him to. They'd all three get their work done fast—Peter, Tara and Mark and sometimes a couple of employees from a convenience store next to the theater—then party in the parking lot after the boss had left for the night. Good thing it wasn't an all-night theater or else they'd just party inside as they cleaned.

No respect.

No standards. Well, except the ones Tara maintained. She had high standards—meaning she didn't mess around on her current boyfriend or girlfriend. She didn't do booze—it was bad for her health and her skin. But she loved her pills.

She'd walk up to Mark, those blue eyes intent on his, her rounded lips pursed, hips grinding, and lift his chin—she was taller than Mark. She'd plant a kiss on his lips and slip a pill inside his mouth. The first time, he'd choked, making her laugh out loud.

His face still burned from embarrassment today, as he remembered.

It only took that one time for him to get ready: see her coming and get his own lips ready for hers and the pill. He never knew what she was going to slip inside his lips, but he never turned it down. Uppers, downers. He didn't care.

He lived for that kiss.

Now that he looked back, it turned into a kiss of destruction. She didn't care about him at all. She knew she had power over him, that she could have slipped a knife into his chest when she kissed him, he was that in love with her.

He stopped at the stop sign and made a slow turn left. How to handle this probably drunk, love-sick kid.

By the time his uncle found him, Mark was hooked. Hooked on Tara and hooked on pills.

A real mess.

Even now, sitting inside his patrol cruiser, he chewed the inside of his cheek. Shame still ate at his insides. He'd been so stupid.

He pulled onto the street as the kid threw another paper ball. Pray, Mom. It felt like he was looking at himself back then. Seeing his own stupidity.

He'd deserved time in rehab.

Instead, Mark had served time in Uncle Ted's rehab: work, save money, be accountable, obey curfews, attend Bible study. Up at dawn to run, then work-out. Uncle Ted was ex-military, so Mark lived in a detention camp pretty much. After a work-out, they'd cook breakfast—always eggs and bacon, toast. No strawberry jam from his mom. Mark never knew where it went after Mom visited. She'd plant it proudly on their kitchen table. After she left, it disappeared.

No sugar of any kind, unless it came packaged in one of

God's wrappers, like a banana or apple. Coffee only on Sundays before church.

Church for Uncle Ted was pounding on Mark's door at 6 o'clock a.m., pack up fishing poles, and worship at the lake as they fished. Best day of the week. They'd drag everything home and clean fish for the freezer. Shower. Crash.

Best church ever.

Uncle Ted didn't preach, he lived.

Mark would sometimes wake earlier than usual on a workday and walk to the kitchen past Uncle Ted, who was reading his Bible. The man apologized for cussing. It always happened when he was trying to fix the old mower. Meals never started without a prayer of thanksgiving and blessing to God. And a day never ended without Uncle Ted praying. He never apologized for praying.

Mark would never forget his first night with Uncle Ted. He'd climbed into bed, still uneasy about his surroundings and living there, when Uncle Ted knocked on the door.

"Yeah? Come in." Mark pulled up his sheet.

Uncle Ted didn't say a word but walked in, knelt beside Mark's bed, and bowed his head. He placed one hand on the Bible on the bedside table, and the other on Mark's hand, and prayed.

Even now, emotion flooded Mark when he let himself go back to that memory. He swallowed and wiped his eyes, aware of the fact that he was pulling closer to the kid.

He parked a house away. The kid hadn't seen him—yet. Lights were still on in the house. Someone was trying to tape paper or something up inside to close up that broken window opening. It slid down. Two people, side-by-side, stood there like they could see him.

He slowly got out of the car and held his finger up against his lips and tried to shush them. As he walked closer to the kid, he could hear him talking to himself. Muttering.

Calls like this always seemed safe, harmless. It was easy to relax. Kind of like rescuing a kitty from a tree. Or a school visit with kindergartners. Nothing's gonna happen. It's just a kid. I don't need backup. Easy to miss something. Mark made himself scan the neighboring houses and the rest of the street. He put himself on high alert and reminded himself that Daynton was still on the loose. He inched closer, each step cautious as he strained to hear what the kid was saying.

"Dang." Kid shook his head. "I lose a girlfriend *and* a best friend. She'll never … hiccup … come back now." He spied Mark's boots and slowly followed up to his face. "H'lo Officer." He tried to get up, but slipped back down to the curb.

Mark relaxed just a bit. "Steady, Bud."

"That's just it. I asked her to go steady. And, I never drink. Never." He looked at the house. Mark did too. A young face ducked. "But I just wanted to … we've been best friends for years."

Mark wanted to chuckle. Years? The kid was maybe sixteen years old?

"But we kissed." Kid ruffled his hair and bent into the fetal position.

Wait. That was a problem?

"I read in a book somewhere—maybe Shakespeare—that a guy went to sera-sera … sing to his girlfriend."

Oh goodness. Mark knew the rest. *Don't laugh. Don't laugh.* Who on planet Earth was still this pure in heart. Young love.

"So, we had a report that there was a window broken. Was that you?"

The kid hung his head. He peeked up at the house. "She'll never let me come over again. We used to talk till her mom kicked me out. Best friends." He shook his head. "Broken."

Mark leaned over and helped the kid stand. As they both straightened, a woman and a young girl stepped onto the sidewalk and walked toward them. The kid tensed, but he stood straight, or as straight as possible.

"Mac." The woman spoke, keeping the young girl right next to her.

"Uh, Mrs. Upton, Ma'am." Tears rolled down his cheeks. "I'm so sorry to have broken your window." He glanced at the girl. Her eyes were on her mother. "I'm so embarrassed." He looked at Mark.

"You can do this Buddy. Do the right thing." Seemed to Mark that he was speaking the very words that Uncle Ted would have spoken right now. *Do the right thing.*

"I'll pay for the window, Mrs. Upton. Every dime." Kid swallowed. "And I won't bother you again, ever."

"Oh, Mac. I don't think we need to take it that far." Mrs. Upton smiled at Mark. "Spencer here has something to say."

The girl stepped forward. She was blushing. Did anyone do that anymore? She stopped right in front of Mac and pulled his hand into hers. "Mac, thank you for singing to me tonight." She shook her head and let her hair fall in her face. She almost whispered. "It was beautiful."

Mac blinked. Again.

"Why don't you come inside and we'll talk about the window." Mrs. Upton stepped between the kids and put her arms around each one, herding them to the house. She stopped and looked back at Mark. "We won't press charges, Deputy." She grinned. "Thank you for your help."

Mark tipped his cap and nodded, half grinned. He watched them all the way up the sidewalk and into the house.

Life had a funny way of reminding a person why they were on the Earth.

FIVE

Katty stuffed a twenty into her jeans pocket and tiptoed past where Bea was watching TV. They had pushed the sofa against the wall again. Tried to straighten the room, clean up the painting mess.

The painted walls still made her jump. Seeing the paintings all day brought on more agitation. Everywhere she moved in the living room and kitchen, a baby seemed to watch her from the wall. They accused her. Scared her. Triggered her to want to drink.

A perpetual zigzag of toys, crayons and papers littered the floor. Dishes in the sink. Phew. Trash stunk, too. There weren't even any poopy diapers anymore. How could just napkins and cereal boxes smell so bad?

How long had it been since she'd emptied … ?

Those walls again. Babies again. Clouds. Eyes. That tree. Gah. What had she done? Smell of fresh paint didn't mix too well with the other smells, either.

Katty leaned over the back of the sofa and whispered. "Sweetie?" She propped her chin on top of Bea's head.

No answer.

The TV shows these days. YouTube. At least this show had something educational—science. The guys were a little loopy, but Bea liked it.

Whispering, again. "Bea? Mommy's gotta go to the store quick." She held her breath. Sometimes Bea didn't hear her and she could scoot out to the car without being missed.

"Can I come?" Bea pointed the remote at the TV and shut it off.

Katty sighed. Not this time. "Honey, jush shtay here and I'll be right back."

Bea growled. "But I wanna come." She brightened. "We need cereal."

"Good try." Katty laughed. Bea was one smart kid. "No, we don't. I jus bought some… the other day." She tickled Bea, wrestled the remote from her tiny hand, and clicked the show on again. Bouncing behind the sofa, she sang, "I'll bring you candy!"

Bea nodded and clapped. "Bring me candy, Mommy!" Bea bounced along with Katty. "Candy necklaces! Please?"

Katty belched. Breathe. Shouldn't have bounced. At least Bea bought in—maybe. "Candy necklaces, it is." Katty brushed the hair off of Bea's forehead and kissed it. "Smoochy, smoochy. I'll be right back. Jush stay here and watch your shows. Okay?"

Sugar, sugar, sugar.

Bea was already off into the world of science. Tornadoes today: trees ripped from the ground, roofs torn off homes, debris everywhere.

Black holes tomorrow.

Katty slipped to the door, glancing back to make sure Bea was still sitting down and not following her. The walls rushed at her, morphed over Bea. The babies and the tree danced.

No.

Door lock didn't work anymore. Breathing out slowly, she made sure to close the door quietly, but securely.

She rushed to her car and jumped in, grabbing her keys from under the car mat at her feet. Best place to hide keys. As she dangled them from her fingers, her attention returned to the trailer door lock.

Oh yeah. The trailer lock hadn't broken. She'd lost the key somewhere. She and Bea had even dumped her purse out onto the carpet, and Bea helped dig through the mess.

No key.

Bea had grabbed for an empty shooter bottle amongst the mess, but Katty was faster and intercepted, distracting her with gum from the bottom of the bag, just in time. Dang, that kid. She was always one step ahead. She loved tiny things, and those bottles were… pretty, especially when filled with the delicious yellow liquid.

Dang, she needed one of those cute little delicious bottles right now.

Soon.

Now.

SIX

"Mommy?" Bea jumped off the sofa. "Don't go, Mommy!" She rushed to the living room window just in time to see the car turn out of the trailer court.

She blinked.

The noise of the TV show blared in the background.

But there was a sound louder than the TV.

The sound of her own heart—beating faster and faster.

Her breath stuck in her throat. Her tummy felt empty. But she wasn't hungry.

She blinked again.

"Mommy?" The word came out in a whisper.

Even though the show on the TV blasted loud, an empty quiet blared louder. Nothing moved, everything stopped.

Bea didn't understand, but she knew.

She didn't guess what it was or how it worked. She just knew.

She was alone.

Again.

SEVEN

Mark breathed in the aroma of homemade pizza as his mom set it before him on the table. "Mom, that smells so good." Homemade crust—almost homemade bread. Cheese and lots of it. He knew she loved black olives, but *he* didn't, so little black dots only covered a fourth of the whole pizza. How much did she think he'd eat? Ground beef and pepperoni. Mm-mm.

Mom smiled. "It's so good to have you for supper. I know how busy you are, dear." She sat and folded her hands and bowed her head.

"Uh, sorry." He removed his cap and bowed his head.

Quiet.

Mom peeked up. "You want to offer the blessing, Son?"

"S-sure, Mom." He swallowed and sucked in a breath. He would never refuse her, but he didn't enjoy praying out loud. Help, Lord. "Dear Lord, thank you for this food. Please bless it. Thank you for Mom and her hospitality." He glanced up at her— she was moving her mouth along with his words. "In Jesus' name, Amen."

"Thank you, Mark." She lifted a spatula and served his pizza. "One or two?"

He held up two fingers. "Two. Yum. It's been a long time since I've had your pizza."

"It's been a long time since you've been over." She bit her lip and shook her head. "I promised myself I wouldn't do that."

"Do what?"

"Complain. Whine about how long it's been." She scrunched up her nose. "I know you're busy."

"It's okay. But yeah, we've been busy. Understaffed. Sheriff interviewed a gal today, but I don't think she's graduated yet, so not sure when she could start—if she is even qualified."

"That'd be interesting to have a woman." She cut a bite of pizza. "It might be good to have a woman there to help with searches of some prisoners."

Mark immediately thought of Katty and blushed. He checked Mom's face. Was she referring to Katty? They rightfully needed a woman sometimes to search prisoners or to interrogate a sexual assault victim. Chantelle, their dispatcher, had done it once, but she wasn't qualified to do it.

"Hey, did you ever get your exhaust fan checked in your bathroom? I could do that while I'm here." He swallowed a bite. "If you haven't been able to get it done."

"No. I haven't. I have a ladder, but I wasn't too sure I should climb up on it."

He pushed his chair back.

"No! Finish eating. It will wait." She looked down at her pizza and cut a bite.

She was the only one he knew that cut pizza bites with a knife and fork, like she was cutting roast beef or steak. She seemed content, even though he knew she had been through stuff in her life. Her face relaxed as she poked at the bite and opened her mouth.

Bite in. Chewed.

At that moment, another face morphed over hers.

Uncle Ted's face chewed and glanced up at Mark. "What?

You don't like steak?" Uncle Ted cut another bite. "Best food group—steak."

Mark stared, hypnotized, as his uncle continued to chat and eat.

"We need to get gas today for our trip to the lake. Poles ready?" Uncle Ted looked up, his eyes questioning, and his face morphed into Mom's again.

She tipped her head and smiled. "What, Son?"

Whew.

"I … uh … was just thinking about Uncle Ted." Mark cleared his throat. "I miss him. Lots." He wiped his mouth and picked up his plate and utensils. He walked to the sink. "He … taught me a lot."

She stood and followed right behind him.

He turned to face her. "I wouldn't be alive today, if he wouldn't have taken me in."

Mom blinked. Tears filled her eyes.

He hugged her. "Uncle Ted was a good man." He felt her nod against his shoulder. Again. Heard her blow out a breath, felt it against his neck. He released her. Nodded. "Time to check that bathroom fan." He headed to the utility room and found the stepladder.

"Oh, let me help you, Mark."

He stopped and grinned. "I may be short like you, but I think I can handle this." He started toward the bathroom. "Do you have the vacuum and a cleaning rag?"

"I do." She chuckled and dragged the vacuum out of the closet. Found a rag and dampened it and followed him.

Bathrooms. Whether the master bath or the public one, they were always spotless in this house. Crazy. She was only one person. He was only one person. So, his bathroom couldn't get any dirtier than hers, but he marveled at how clean it was. She loved her decor with flowers, though. Flowery curtains. Flowers on towels displayed. Flowers growing on the wallpaper. Pink.

Everything was pink, and everything was in its place. He knew from living with her in the past that she was meticulous. Oh, the fights over his messy room.

Ladder in place. He flipped the switch. Loud, but it started. "I think you need a new fan motor. Sound pretty rough." The cover was too clean. "Mom, did you already get up here?" She wouldn't look at him as she handed him the screwdriver. "You did, didn't you? It's too clean." He laughed. "Yup. Guilty. Good thing we might have a female deputy soon, because we're gonna have a female prisoner."

"Who, me?" She chuckled. "That new female deputy might turn out to be pretty cute."

Dang. Always the set-up. Matchmaker.

Mark laughed again and handed the cover down to her. "You want to shut it off? Yup. I think this one's done." He unplugged, removed it and handed it to her. "I can take it with me and find a new one someplace." She handed the cover to him. "We can leave it off." He thought again. "Right. It might take me awhile to get back here. I see where you're going."

Cover back on. Fan by his cap. Ladder put away.

Mark hugged her. "Thanks, Mom. Pizza was outstanding, and thanks for the leftovers. They always come in handy. Much appreciated." He patted her back and started to release her.

Phyllis grabbed on. "Dear Lord, please take good care of Mark. Keep him safe. Give him wisdom. Bless everything he puts his hands to do. And please bring forth his life mate—Your chosen woman—in the name of Jesus. Amen." She released her hold on him and backed away.

"Amen." He hooked his cap on his head and took the container from her. "Thanks, Mom." Long deep breath in. "And God bless you and all you do. Tell your Bible Study ladies thank you too, for praying for the department. We appreciate it."

She beamed and nodded.

"No, really." He was going there. He needed to. "We feel it.

Sometimes I have skitters on my arms as I start my car at the beginning of a shift. And I know you've had Bible Study that morning. Guy says so, too." Well, that might have been a stretch.

"Oh, so good to know." She wiped her eyes.

He glanced at his phone. "I better get to work. Night shift."

"Bye, Son."

He turned at the door. "Bye, Mom." He stepped outside, then remembered the fan. "I forgot the fan."

She shook her head. "No. I can do that. I'll let you know when I have the new one."

He nodded. As he walked down the sidewalk to his car, he smiled. He knew she'd install that fan—or try to. He also knew he'd have to share his leftovers with whoever was on that night. But, most of all, he knew that Mom and her ladies prayed with the right heart. Well, except for the life mate thing.

That might have been all Mom, making sure he got the right girl.

Her chosen one.

Back in his cruiser, Mark did his usual rounds. Around the square, past the convenience store, Hillcrest Nursing Home, the hospital. All seemed pretty quiet. Hillcrest staff moved several residents outside in the rose garden—beautiful evening to sit outside. Some wheelchairs. Some walkers. Good for them. He tooted his horn. One resident waved—Harold. Staff all waved. Others not. He shook his head. Had to be hard. Mind clear— body shut down.

Across the highway, past the convenience store again. After that, he zoned. That wasn't safe. A cop should always be focused, but he also knew every driver did it. He must have zoned along a couple of streets. He had driven down every street in Osceola many times—the whole county. They all looked the same. Same houses. Same trees. Sometimes the same vehicles parked outside. Unless it was the school or there was something remarkable about the property, he just drove on by. The remarkable might be a motorcycle or unique vehicle. Maybe a dog barked as he drove on by.

Was this the fifth time? The fifth time he'd driven past the trailer court? Or around it? Maybe through it?

Fifth time. Yep. He'd zoned out again.

He blew a deep breath out and lifted one hip, then the other. Shuffled himself around. Sat up taller—well, that was always a struggle. Focus.

Back to the trailer court.

Hoping for a glimpse of Katty or Bea.

He'd hear about it from the other deputies. Chantelle had already blabbed to Guy about the previous shift. Her voice projected over the cruiser radio, like she sat right next to him in the cruiser, on the passenger seat, "Well, I counted three times. Right? Three times!"

Guy had chuckled in his low, big ox rumble.

Enough.

It wasn't his fault. There must be a beacon on the top of Katty's trailer that drew him in.

There was also a cute little girl named Bea, living in that trailer. She possessed a gigantic piece of his heart, too.

Too?

Like … *Katty* had a piece of his heart?

Hmm. What did he see in her? She was … she might be an alcoholic, and a neighbor had reported her for child abuse. There. All official.

But when he looked at her, he also saw huge brown eyes that pleaded for love and help. Maybe that was all it was. He loved to help others.

Yeah.

There was more. Lots more.

Yeah.

He guessed Katty had a piece of his heart.

Around the trailer court circle again.

Past the last trailer and out to the street. Katty's trailer was always visible in his rearview mirror. He'd have to warn her about the loose piece of siding near the roof.

He shook his head. Her car was gone. They must have gone to see Clarence at Hillcrest Nursing Home.

Or the grocery store.

Either way. Nobody home.

EIGHT

There he was again.

Bea ran to the front door and pushed the screen door open. "Hi!" She waved. He didn't see her. The cop car drove past their trailer and on around the trailer court.

"Depdy Scott." He didn't hear her. "Please come back, Mr. Scott. Depdy Scott." She let the door close, walked to the window. And wiped her eyes. Her tummy felt funny. Like she might throw up.

But not.

It felt like … like it did every time Mommy left to go out.

Go out.

Go out?

Go.

She knew what that meant. She knew that meant get dressed, shoes on, brush teeth. Then … get in her car seat and wait for Mommy to buckle her in. Bea held her breath. She hadn't told Mommy yet that she could buckle it herself.

Go.

To the store, to get more peanut butter and Fruit Loops.

Go.

To see Clarence and play with Mrs. T while Mommy worked. Get ice cream.

But go out?

That.

That was when Mommy got dressed up in her good jeans and a pretty shirt that showed too much of her boobies. When Mommy smelled funny—her soda smelled funny. When Mommy wouldn't let Bea take a sip of her soda.

That. Go out.

Bea had spent many hours sitting in the bathroom, watching Mommy draw black lines around her eyes and flutter her eyelashes in the mirror after she put mascara on. Bea knew what mascara was. She had picked it up once and started to put some on her own eyelashes. Never again. Mommy was already Bad Mommy, that day, before Bea had picked up the mascara. But when Mommy grabbed it back ... never again would Bea touch it.

Mommy's face was always pretty, even without make-up, but that day, her face turned into Scary Mommy. Eyes black. Mouth mad.

Bea blinked as she thought of that day, back then. Even now, she could cry.

Deep breath.

Even now.

Jerahmael stood tall and majestic, just behind Bea.

"Mommy?" Her tiny voice sounded small against the noise of the television.

"Mommy?" She stood at the window, her nose against the glass, for a long time—in Earth terms. The glass fogged up where she breathed against it. He knew she was awake, but he also knew his tiny charge well and she didn't stand still very long —usually.

But, today.

This moment.

This moment, he wished he could be that human and take her in his arms, sit down with her and hold her, comfort her.

Jerahmael couldn't see the future, but he had a feeling that this little girl, this tiny human, would become someone to reckon with as she grew up. He'd seen it before—when tiny humans had sensed Father's presence so intensely—broken limbs had healed and hard hearts softened.

He thought of the many creatures on Earth that hatched from precious eggs. If someone had tampered with the eggs—even to gently hatch out the baby bird, chick, snake, or fish—it would die. They had to do it on their own, building strength after each season of pecking or breaking forth.

Peck.

Rest.

Struggle to peck some more.

Rest.

This little girl, little Bea, would need that season of resting, of healing, but right now, she needed comfort.

Father.

Sensing the Father's presence, Jerahmael opened his mind and heart to Him.

Sweetness.

Father's love for his creation always brought Jerahmael to his knees.

Receiving His download now, Jerahmael reached for Bea's shoulders, letting the Father's message and love flow through him to Bea.

Her eyes flickered and blinked. A tear tracked down her cheek and onto her shirt.

Tears.

His own flowed now, onto his robes.

Such love. Such sweetness.

Tears were a substance all their own. Salty. But the fragrance was precious, sweet, but not like flowers.

Wholesome.

He glanced down at Bea, again. Her tears were the sweetness of rain, of … her tears were the fragrance of Heaven.

Bea stepped from the living room window, past Mommy's paintings on the wall, down the hall to Mommy's bedroom.

There.

She pounded on the window, only Depdy didn't hear her. She followed into the bathroom. Other trailers blocked her sight until she just caught the back end of the car through that window.

Back in the kitchen, then at the front door again. She pushed it open wide. The door made funny noises and didn't close on its own. Bea had to step outside to grab it, but once she was outside, the car drove out of the trailer park and onto the street.

Away.

Bea stood there for a long time. Maybe he had seen her and would turn around and drive back.

Maybe.

She held her breath and stood still. Her eyes followed the street—up and down, back and forth. She glanced at the deck, at the faded flowers in the pots there.

Where Mommy's car was always …. Only it wasn't there. It was gone.

She choked. Couldn't breathe. She swallowed and breathed a deeper breath. That feeling again … like she might puke.

Only—

A flutter to her right caught her eye.

She looked.

Nothing.

Something to her left.

Nothing there.

She shook her head and started to go inside, reaching for the door.

Wings, like a bird. A gi-gimongous bird. Where Bea had stared at Depdy's car driving away, more wings slowly appeared.

The only thing with wings that big was Clarence's angel. "Michael?"

She shook her head. If Michael was Clarence's angel, then this couldn't be him. Michael lived with Clarence.

Wings.

Depdy's car was still driving away, but wings fluttered in front of it. Closer to her.

Bea sat down on the deck step. Her hands covered her mouth.

A smile and twinkly blue eyes appeared, but soon hair, ears, and clothes showed. His clothes were different, somehow, like a big bathrobe. She scanned every part of him. A strap crossed his chest to a belt. The leather belt held a sword.

Her eyes flew to his.

A sword?

She stood and stepped back, without thinking—back into the empty doorframe.

But his eyes weren't mad or scary.

They were … happy. Twinkly. Was he a good angel? Mrs. T had warned her. Mrs. T knew the difference, but she wasn't here right now.

Bea stared at his eyes, his whole body—head to boots.

She wanted to hug him.

He nodded … but she hadn't said it.

He nodded again.

First one step.
Another.
Deep breath.
He felt real.
Real skin. Real arms around her.

NINE

Mark had been on duty for many evening shifts and night shifts in his career as a deputy with the Sheriff's Department, but tonight was already one of the worst.

Some citizens thought all the sheriff's department did in a small Nebraska county like Polk would be to rescue cats from enormous trees. Or redirect traffic around a farmer driving a huge combine on the highway, because no alternate route to the field was available.

Or just drive around town … like he was doing now.

He shook his head.

If they only knew.

The minute he had checked in with the sheriff's department, a report of domestic abuse came in. It appeared to be settled now —Guy and the Sheriff had been dispatched to the address. The wife had called in after her husband threw a sledge hammer at her and missed. Thank God the man was a poor aim. It might have been a homicide instead.

Thank God.

He'd stuffed the leftover pizza from Mom into the refrigerator in the break room, knowing that when he got back, some-body would have eaten it. None for him.

To add to his misery and stress, every time he reported back to the department, the other deputies asked if he'd seen Katty Randolph.

No, not tonight.

Don't ask again.

And if they said one more time, "Go get her, son!" he'd have to … well, he wouldn't draw his gun, but he might have to put salt in the coffee. The convenience store offered a buy 7 cups of coffee, get one free promotion now anyway, so he'd still get his caffeine. Let those dorks sputter when they sipped their first big gulp of that dark goodness laced with salt.

He tapped the steering wheel.

But it was true.

She was all he thought of.

If she'd been home, what excuse would he have given her? No one lately had filed a complaint about anything.

How did the sheriff's department think they knew he loved Katty when he didn't know?

Did he?

What *was* it about her? What kept him thinking about her, planning dates with her? And Bea.

Katty might like to go to eat at that new Mexican place.

He turned into the small city park and followed the road. A car was parked by the playground equipment, and three kids chased each other up and down and around the walkways and the slides, like little monkeys. He guessed on his next round through the park, they'd be heading home.

He drove past the huge leaning tree.

Next, the pool. Then the old Boy Scout cabin.

He followed the road around the outdoor picnic enclosure toward the exit—an older lady sat reading a book at one of the picnic tables. She waved. Everybody ventured out tonight.

Katty might like to take Bea to the park. He'd go down the slide with little Bea. He'd seen kids try to climb up that old leaning tree—it leaned at just the right angle to get them started —but they could only go up so far. Bet Bea would try it with him.

He stopped at the stop sign and waited for a car driving past on the street. Noted the license plate, the make and model of the car, assessed the driver—Mrs. Bertrand? She owned the consignment store. She waved.

He was always vigilant, always assessing each driver and their intentions.

Flowers along the exit still bloomed bright orange. Couldn't miss those.

What if he just took Katty and Bea on a walk around the nursery out by Benedict? Katty loved plants—she had some potted on her deck. Every time they had dispatched him to check on her or … her neighbor filed a complaint, they always sent *him*.

Each time, Katty opened the door, saw who it was, stepped outside and plucked a leaf from a plant. As they sat on the chairs to talk, she'd squeeze it, sniffing it the whole time.

What he wouldn't give to do that today.

Check on her.

Get dispatched to her trailer.

Talk to her.

Tickle Bea.

Katty's injuries from the accident a few weeks before turned out to be mostly her left arm. Still in a cast. That couldn't be easy with being a mom and all. She had worried about Bea, but the hospital had kept her overnight—two nights even—then released her. She'd breathed in smoke, but they felt confident that her lungs looked clear.

Thank God.

Mark grinned, despite himself, when he thought of Bea.

Cute, tiny thing. Ornery. Her brown eyes twinkled and gave her intentions away every time.

Crossing the highway, he noted any out-of-town cars at the convenience store. Nope. All 41 county vehicles—not that any of those drivers were angels.

Huh. Gas pumps were already replaced and in use.

Hard to comprehend the accident just weeks before. Why would a man who seemed so intent on kidnapping his own daughter—getting her for himself, for whatever reasons—ram headlong into the car she and her mom sat in? He might have killed her and almost succeeded. Why would what's his name— Phil Daynton—do that?

He had destroyed the car and the old pickup he'd been driving, but he almost killed Bea's mom.

Katty.

Maybe that's what his intention had been all along.

Kill the mom and kidnap his daughter.

Mark shook his head.

The more he learned on this deputy job—yeah, the technical stuff of guns, protocol, the department itself—the more he grew horrified by the things people actually thought of doing. He should be used to it by now.

But maybe that was it.

People didn't think. They just reacted.

That bastard, Phil, obviously didn't have a brain cell in his head.

And he was still on the loose.

Where had he found to hide? How many hiding places might there be in a town the size of Osceola, Nebraska? Maybe the guy was in Mexico right now. His cohort in crime, Lex, definitely was in jail at the department, waiting to be transferred out.

Mark drove at a slow pace through the convenience store gas lanes. Just to be snarky. He loved to make kids inside nervous.

The kid had seen him, ducked his head and elbowed his friends —as if they were stealing. Maybe they were, but it worked. They always rushed to the cashier, paid, lined up outside—like a police line-up—and waved at him.

Funny kids.

The renovations after the accident—especially the gas pumps —had taken time, but the store was back in action. Some repairs still needed to be completed on the building, but things were coming along fast. He didn't stay and gawk every day … like some people. So progress seemed obvious.

Back to Phil.

Mark's mind reverted to when he used to play hide and seek with his little cousins. They squeezed into the smallest corner in Grandma's house, or crevice between bookshelves, or in closets and might never have been found until somebody's tummy growled and they all raided the kitchen for cookies.

Where had Phil found to hide out?

Mark shook his head. He would kill the man if he ever caught him hurting little Bea, which had apparently been the man's plan all along. Yes, he seemed to stalk Katty, but his actual target pointed to Bea.

Again, if people in the area knew what really went on in their region, *Polk County News* would be twice the size newspaper that it was now. Mark knew of every crime, every case all across the land, but especially in Polk County. It would shock people to know how much went on.

Here he was again, driving past the trailer park where Katty lived. Did that make three times tonight? Four?

He declared himself crazy and called into dispatch to tell Chantelle he was going on break.

Katty's car wasn't home, anyway.

"Did ya find your girl, Mark?"

Damn! Chantelle, too?

Why did they keep teasing him about Katty?

"I'm heading to Shelby, to the convenience store. Need anything?" He put his blinker on at the highway and stopped. Good to do business all over the county. Pizza wasn't available at the convenience store yet, anyway.

"Naw. I'm good. Fixed a big pot roast last night, so I snagged some meat for a sandwich."

He turned onto the highway. "Dang, that sounds good! Okay, well, let me know if you need anything else. Soda? Chips?"

"I'm okay. Thanks." She always did her job and did it well. Never messed around on the clock. "Oh, by the way." She chuckled. "Guy ate your pizza."

"What?"

She clicked off.

Mark shook his head. He kinda planned on it. Guy couldn't leave a bite of Mom's pizza alone—ever. Guess Mom planned on it, too. She always made too much. Guy was a big guy and always put it to good use.

Now. Pizza had worn off. Time for food.

Of course, the convenience store was busy.

Of course … always Katty's luck.

Not even a parking place.

There. A car's back-up lights flashed on.

She gave it room, but mainly to get the space. She could feel another car hovering behind her. Checked her rearview mirror. Yep. She flipped them off and stood her ground—or rather, parked her ground. She couldn't lose that parking space.

The car kept backing.

Damn!

She shifted and her car lurched *forward*.

"Shit!" She stomped on the brake just in time to avoid hitting it.

Then backed up again. "What do they want … the world?"

The car finally cleared the parking space and drove on.

Katty glimpsed an arm swinging out the driver's window, third finger waving.

"Same to ya, jerk!" She quickly shifted into drive and claimed her space, only to have her foot slip off the brake, making the car bounce up over the curb.

"Mommy?"

"Not now, Bea."

Reverse. Reverse. Brake on, then put it in reverse and back off the curb.

She backed up carefully and made sure the car rolled down off of the curb and slammed it into park. "There. I didn't kill anyone."

"Mommy?"

Bea's voice sounded hoarse, breathy. Well, why not, with all the screaming she'd done earlier? The whole day had been a mess. So what if Katty had taken Bea's paintings and drawings down? So what if Katty had made a mess of their house—it was terrible anyway—so what? Bea had been a little stinker and, well, Katty hadn't been … she blinked. She … bad old days were back.

Bad Mommy was back.

"What Bea?"

No answer.

Katty stretched up to check Bea in the rearview mirror.

What?

She turned around, her good arm flopped over the back of the seat. Bea wasn't teasing her. She wasn't even *in* her car seat.

She couldn't have …

Katty faced the windshield.

Damn, she was going crazy!

Right. Right. She'd left Bea at home, watching Daryl and Dumpty.

Whew.

Opening the car door felt like an elephant was pushing against it from the outside. Tougher than usual to open today—especially with the cast on her arm. She kicked at the door and shoved with her other hand, when a car pulled in on her left, just missing her door.

She slid off her seat, stepped out onto the concrete, as the woman driver hurried in front of her on the sidewalk. "Didn't you see me?" She slammed her car door. "You almost hit my leg!"

The woman barely acknowledged Katty, except to mumble, "Then watch when you open your car door. You should've checked behind you … *before* you opened your door."

A moment of silence.

"Bitch."

The woman jerked to a stop. Her shoulders rose and fell. Chin jutted out. But not a word spoken. One more deep breath and she stomped into the store.

Katty wanted to scream at the woman. Scream every dirty, filthy word that had ever been flung in her own face.

Stop. Stop the words. Stop the thoughts. Stop those voices.

Stop everything.

Katty put her hand to her forehead. She had to have a fever. A breeze made the wet spots on the back of her shirt cold, which on most days would have felt good.

Not today.

And … Bea was home alone.

Katty held her breath and slowly blew it out.

Mom used to leave me home alone when I was that age, so … I guess I can do it, too.

And don't forget her candy. Don't forget Bea's candy.

She shivered as a soft gust of wind lifted her hair off her face, like an oscillating fan had just turned her direction. Almost sounded like the buzz of her phone on vibrate.

Only, it sounded like, "Mommy?"

Damn. She *was* going crazy. How long do crazy people live?

As she stepped onto the sidewalk, she stumbled. She pushed herself off the hood of her car and stood for a moment, moving her shoulders up and down and breathing, hoping she wouldn't see anyone she knew. She patted her bun. Good thing the popular hairstyle was messy these days, because she guessed that's what hers was.

A man pushed the door open from inside and spotted her. He stepped through and held it for her, even though she was a few steps away.

"Thanks. Uh. Thank-shou." She put on her sweet girl smile and nodded. "Have a nice day." Only the man didn't hear. He was almost to his truck.

Breath test. She coughed into her hand. Not great. Not terrible either. Booze was never a good breathalyzer.

As she entered the outside door, an old lady pushed the inside door open and her cane bounced against Katty's foot. Her plastic shopping bag bumped against her leg.

Bag ladies.

Katty grabbed the door handle to hold it open for her.

"Why, thank you dear." The lady smiled.

Katty's sweaty hand slipped from the door handle and it closed on the woman's cane, making the lady falter and fall backwards. She tried to keep her balance—taking a step back—but her heavy shopping bag threw her off.

If it hadn't been for the tall cowboy following her—catching her—she might have fallen.

"S-sorry, lady." Katty belched and swallowed. *Get inside the store and get the bottle, or find a bathroom—one or the other ... fast.*

"It's okay." The old lady shook the bag she carried. Plastic and glass clattered. "I'm on a mission to save lives."

"Well … good for you." Katty didn't have time for this. She was on a mission, too. To save her own life and possibly Bea's. "S'cuse me. I gotta get a move on into the store." She squeezed past the lady, making sure she didn't trip on the cane. That would not be good to trip and fall on the floor. It was hard enough to stand, much less walk today. Tripping and falling would get her in huge trouble.

Two deputy sheriff cruisers drove up and parked out on the edge of the parking lot. Sure. Bring in the sheriffs. The deputies. Come on. All she wanted to do was get her little bottles and go back home.

Be a good momma to Bea.

Where was Clarence when she needed him?

Damn him! Going off and getting married. He had always been there for her. He had started it all—or rather stopped it—stopped her drinking and abusing of Bea.

But he was busy now.

Clarence had his wife.

Katty had no one.

Well … there was Phil Daynton, Bea's dad. Maybe he was all Katty deserved. And some dad he was. He had chased them down so he could kidnap his daughter—and not for the usual fatherly reasons. He made babies and turned around and—

Finally. The old lady was out of her way, and Katty could get her booze and leave.

Damn lady. So slow.

The cowboy was watching her, but she didn't care.

Screw him.

Screw everybody.

A department cruiser pulled into the Shelby convenience store from the East just as Mark pulled in from the West. Guy had taken a break at the same time. His dark skin glistened like he'd run a sprint. Dude should be a movie star, with that skin, his dark glasses and that build.

Mark waved. Couldn't help it. He always waved.

Guy did not. Guy was too cool. He grinned, though.

They parked their cruisers side-by-side, facing opposite directions, along the farthest outlying area of the parking lot. Out of the way of semi parking and gas pump customers. Out of the way of anybody. But ready for take-off if needing a rapid departure.

Mark got out, stretched, and twisted. Good to move after sitting in the cruiser—five times around the trailer park.

Guy pushed Mark from behind as soon as he stepped out of his car. "Your mom's pizza was great."

"You ate my pizza!" Mark pushed him back, but forgot to prepare for the neck hold.

Dang.

Guy got him every time. Finished with a knuckle noogie. Easy for him to do. He stood a whole head taller than Mark. Guy had brothers and a sister. Mark did not. Maybe that was a good thing—he didn't have to get beat on, like Guy was doing now. But then, he wasn't great at roughhousing with Guy. At least he'd had cousins.

"Ow." Mark rubbed his head. "You need a kid to do that to, not me."

"Why do I need a kid when I have you?" Guy's grin flashed white teeth—but only for a second. Had to look stern and cool to the public.

Mark knew better.

Guy could be a slob along with the rest of them.

A truck driver stepped down out of his truck and nodded.

Guy's playful stance disappeared into a very intimidating posture.

Mark wanted to grin, because he did the same thing that Guy did at the same time. Without thinking. He tucked the grin down and adjusted his belt and gear as he walked to the store.

An elderly lady with a cane opened her car door. "God bless you, boys." She tossed her cane into the car, along with her bag that clunked and clattered like glass and plastic.

"Thank you, Ma'am." Guy's deep voice boomed. "God bless you too."

Mark knew what Guy was thinking, because he was thinking the same thing. He guessed the lady was old enough to buy booze.

Must have neighbors to share some with, because it sounded like a lot of little bottles.

Once inside, a big man stood at the checkout counter, so Katty stepped in line behind him. Bits and pieces of their conversation floated down to her.

"Yeah. I thought so too, but the team …"

Seriously? Football?

Katty cleared her throat.

Again.

The man turned and looked down at her, tapping his meat jerky package on the counter. He grinned. No teeth. Yuck. How did he eat that stuff? As he turned back to the cashier, she caught a whiff of several days of sweaty body odor.

She swallowed again. Had she eaten?

"I know. The first half was crazy, but they dropped the ball after half-time." The man chuckled. "Get it? Dropped the ball?"

Really? Ha ha.

The entrance door opened.

Deputy Scott.

And that big black cop.

Shit!

She kept her back toward him as he walked to the beverage bar.

"Come on. Come on." She wanted to say it louder. "Excuse me. I need to get my stuff and get back to … wor … uh, Grandma."

The man turned and grinned down at her again. Back to the cashier. "Dude. Have a nice day. Good luck with this one." He chuckled as he walked past Katty and out the door. "Right. Grandma."

Her turn. "Good morning!" Gotta stay chipper. Katty made herself smile. Somebody always used to say that when you smiled, it made people wonder what you've been … well.

When Katty stepped up to the counter, she pointed to the display of shooters … only it was empty. "Wha? Where are they?" Everyone and everything around her disappeared and the empty shooter display shifted to front and center. "What'd you do with them?"

"First of all, it's eight o'clock in the *evening*. Second, that old lady came in and bought 'em all." He adjusted his ball hat as he tipped his head toward the parking lot and slid his hands into his pockets. "Said she was saving people's lives or something." He grinned.

He knew. It'd been awhile since she'd been in, but he'd been the cashier almost every time. They used to even talk about partying together sometime. It never happened. Thank God.

His words finally cleared the drunken fog, and Katty blinked. "You mean you're *out*?" She tapped her fingernail on the counter.

A woman working the food takeout line glanced up.

Katty blew out a breath. Her face felt like a dragon was

breathing fire inside … until she saw the cashier's fingers flicker from his pocket.

He slowly drew a tiny bottle of booze—a shooter—out of his pocket. She could barely see it, because he had his hand cupped around it.

She lowered her voice and unfolded her money. "How much?"

Deputy Scott had his back to them still.

Ice chinked as a kid refilled the ice dispenser from a bucket.

The cashier held both hands up. "Ten."

"Ten bucks! That's robbery."

A man at the checkout, across from them, raised his head. His eyes darted from Katty to the cashier, helping her.

She slid over a twenty, her small hand covering most of the bill.

The cashier dropped two bottles into a chicken takeout box, folded the flaps closed and pushed it to her, quickly stuffing the money into his *own* pocket.

Her eyes bounced up to his.

He shrugged and shouted, "Who's next?"

Katty swallowed and slid the box under her arm and walked to the door, easing past a kid holding a couple energy drinks.

"Those look … good. I need to try one … next time." Katty blew on her fingers, like the chicken box was hot. The kid didn't act like he'd even seen her.

A guy entering the store held the door for her. She tapped the box. "Hot!" She giggled. "Chicken's hot today."

"Oh-oh." He reached for the box. "Here. I can help you cool off. Uh, cool *it* off."

She gave him a dirty look.

Users. All guys were users.

Hugging the box to her side, she opened the car door, jumped in, and slammed the door on her foot. *No. No! Not today! Did this whole day have to be screwed up?* She pushed the door open and rubbed her foot.

Deputy Scott was paying. She had to get away before he saw her.

Turn the key.

Start the car.

Shut the door

Back out slowly and pretend she was right where she needed to be.

That life was grand.

That she was going places.

Well … she was.

She was going straight to hell.

When Mark entered any convenience store, his eyes always darted from person to person—facial identification, what they carried, how they walked. Kind of like one of those movies where an actor moved digital interface graphics over reality— layers of data. Gambler, wife beater, murderer. Whoah. He'd have to remember that person.

He loved those movies.

His nose sampled the air—how they smelled. Listened for change in pockets clinking against a gun. He had a great imagination. Might not be good as a cop, though. Facts, always facts.

He nodded to people sitting at the tables.

Some faces seemed familiar.

Some he knew. "Hey, Wild Bill. Whatchu doing in these here parts? I thought you never got off the ranch."

Bill chuckled. "Well, I was a good boy today, so the wife let me out and I decided to spread my scent a little farther while I have the chance."

Mark laughed out loud and shook his head. The guy was funny. "Bill. Bill."

A man sharing the table piped up as Mark walked away. "Yeah, well, don't get caught sniffing anybody's butt, because that cop there will slam you in jail."

Mark shook his head again and wiped his eyes. Reminder: don't engage too long. Guys like that had no mouth shut-off. They could talk all night.

He made the rounds back by the beer coolers. Kids liked to sneak one out—hide it in their backpack or purses. Purses were huge these days.

All clear.

Feed the growling stomach.

He stepped to the order station.

The woman opened a takeout box. "What can I get you tonight, Deputy?"

Chicken tenders were always good. "Could I get the chicken tenders?" He held up two fingers. "Three."

Guy chuckled behind him. "You sure? How many fingers you holding up?"

Dang. He always looked.

Deep chuckle behind.

Mark licked his lips. The green beans looked good, but he always dripped them on his shirt. "Maybe just the potato wedges." He tucked his fingers into his pocket. He was a slow learner, but he learned.

"Anything else, sir?"

"Nope. That's it. Thanks."

She folded the box closed and handed it to the cashier. "Next."

Cup holder for soda was empty. A kid scrambled to fill it. "Sorry, Sir. I'll have it filled in a jiffy, Sir."

"No rush, Bud. Thanks." Mark checked who stood in the booze aisle while he waited. Empty.

"Okay, Sir. There you go." The kid held out a cup—the largest size—to Mark. "Let me fill the ice for you. We've been busy today, so it's almost out." The kid climbed on a small stool and dumped a bucket of ice into the dispenser tank, and slid the lid back on.

"Uh, thanks." Big cup. That would be a ton of soda, but it was nice of the kid to help him out. The ice clunked into the cup. Then soda. Caffeinated soda tonight.

Convenience stores should consult police for help in designing their stores. He always wished the soda fountain bar was situated so he could observe the store and not the wall. He checked behind him as the pop fizzed into the cup.

Busy place tonight. That only meant that it'd be busy for him and Guy later on.

Lid on. Straw in.

He walked toward the cashier and glanced out the front windows of the convenience store.

Katty! Getting into her car.

His chicken dinner.

She slammed the door on her foot!

Had to pay.

Checkout line was long.

A woman appeared to be contesting the price of … bananas?

He looked outside again.

Katty backed out.

"Hey, isn't that … her?" Guy sniffed. "Love is in the air."

She had to have seen him. He sucked up some soda.

A group of kids entered the store, loud and rowdy, pushing each other into displays.

One backed into Mark, and he reacted by squeezing his cup of soda.

The lid popped, and soda gushed.

"Hey! You got me all …" The kid spouted off, cussing, until he saw who he talked to. And what he'd done.

Guy stepped beside Mark. "Didn't she see you?"

Katty squealed the tires on her way out of the parking lot and turned onto the highway without stopping, right in front of a big pickup.

Honk!

Mark stood, staring out the store window, dripping soda.

TEN

Honk!

Hooonnnk!

The pickup driver following Katty's car blasted his horn. Awful squeal of tires on the highway.

She cringed!

He barely stopped his truck from rear-ending Katty. Lots of truck in her rearview mirror.

She could almost hear the words his mouth had to be spewing and feel the daggers his eyes were shooting at her back right now. The sound of his horn vibrated every cell of her being. Her head might explode.

Shouldna done that.

Shouldna pulled out.

Shoulda waited at the stop sign.

Damn! Katty slammed her fist on the steering wheel and glanced in her rearview mirror.

The pickup looked to be inches from her bumper. The guy finally backed off. Only now the cop cars at the convenience store were visible.

She had seen that pickup coming, but didn't want to stop. She was running away. Or running to.

She'd die either way. What was the difference whether she got killed in an accident or drank herself to death?

Mark had been there.

What on earth had she been thinking?

"Mommy?"

"Shut up Bea!" Bea wasn't in the backseat. Katty knew she was at home. "Shut up Bea!" she screamed. "Shut up everybody. Shut up, Mom! Shut up … voices."

She withered with each outburst.

"Shut up voices." She whispered and blinked—wiped tears away. Her vision blurred from the tears, or the booze, or neither. Or both.

Her car swerved off the highway, onto the narrow shoulder. She caught herself and steered it back onto the road, only to over-steer past the center line into oncoming traffic.

Honnnnk!

She quickly over-corrected back onto the shoulder.

"Mommy?" Many voices this time. Not just one. Many voices blended together, almost harmonizing. Baby voices, kind voices, mean voices. Mom's voice. But always the baby voices.

"Please, please stop." Katty cried out. Again, in a whisper, "Please stop."

She sobbed as she pulled off at the next intersection and slowed to a stop. Deliberately, with every bit of concentration she could gather, she shifted into park and took her foot off the brake.

Tears flowed freely. The dam burst and she could no longer hold the sobs back.

She was such a mess.

Honnnnk! The rush of the truck racing past shook her car. Shook her.

"Stop!" She screamed. "Please stop!"

Only one thing that might soothe this mess.

She would never kill herself. She had to be a wonderful mom to Bea.

But something to cure this madness?

Shooters. Where?

Take-out box. Into the cupholder. Her hands shook as she picked one up and tried to open it.

"Settle down. Calm down." Deep breath. She wiped her eyes with the back of one hand, willing herself to breathe and calm down.

Staring at the tiny bottle, she braced herself. She tried again to open it, wanting so badly to hear the tiny ripple of the cap tearing open.

But it didn't. She couldn't even open the very thing that would calm her down.

Again.

It wouldn't open.

She dropped it back into the cupholder and grabbed the other one and tried.

It wouldn't budge.

She threw it hard against the passenger door.

"Damn! Damn! Damn!" Screaming, she groped for the other one.

Where?

It had slid down between the seat and the console.

She tried to squeeze her hand down. Then leaned over to reach under the seat.

Sirens.

No!

People turned their heads to see what the noise was all about.

Katty's tires had burned a patch of rubber when she gunned out onto the highway.

People pointed and shook their head.

Mark wanted to shush them all, to tell them to mind their own business. To …

"What we gonna do, friend?" Guy's deep voice spoke close behind him.

Mark wanted to smack him. Anybody but her. Anyone but Katty.

He pushed his food at the cashier and dug into his pockets.

"No. No. I got this. Go do your job, Deputy." The cashier shoved his food back to him. "I got this."

He grabbed it, gave Guy a withering look, and ran toward the door.

The minute he started the car, he tossed his food across the console and made sure his drink was secure. Nothing he could do about his wet shirt.

"Damn, damn, damn." Mark pounded on the steering wheel —emotion he'd never admit to exploded in his chest. He checked the perimeter and pulled out onto the highway, gas pedal all the way down.

He radioed in. "Chantelle, I'm west bound after a no stop and run."

"10-4."

"Car visible a mile up ahead, on the side of the road. Highway 92/81 and T Road. Pulling over." He read the license plate, although he knew it by heart. "Plate number 41, no. Sorry. It's letters. Nebraska plate, CLSGRL. Charles, Lincoln, Sam, George, Robert, Lincoln."

"10-4."

Mark pulled over behind Katty's car. She appeared to be hunched over the steering wheel.

Hat on. Car in position, nose forward.

A thought pierced his mind. *This could end badly. What if ...*

He willed himself to stay on task. "Approaching the driver's side of the car."

"Uh … 10-4." Chantelle always added. "Stay safe." Kind of not regulation, but he never cared. She knew he was stopping Katty.

Another cruiser pulled up quietly behind his.

Guy. He nodded from inside the car. Backup.

What if …

Again, he cut that thought off.

Clean it up. Police protocol.

"Hello … Ma'am, Katty." Protocol. "Did you realize you pulled out in front of a pickup, almost causing an accident back at the convenience store?"

Head down. Hair disheveled in a bun at the top of her head. Hand in her lap. Well, one was. The other had moved quickly to cover the cupholder.

Whew.

Yeah.

"May I see your driver's license, please?" His voice sounded raspy. What was wrong with him?

She nodded, leaned forward with her body, and reached over to the passenger seat. Opened her purse.

He flinched.

She wouldn't have a gun.

Would she?

He'd had someone pull a gun on him before, but this was different. Wasn't it? He had totally let his guard down with her. Dangerous. He'd heard stories …

She pulled her purse over on top of the cupholder and found her billfold. She was getting good at using that cast arm, too. Barely peeked up under hair that was falling out of the bun.

God help.

He glanced back at Guy, then squatted down to her level. "You okay, Katty?"

Red, puffy eyes. Black mascara smudged underneath. Orange paint along her hairline?

She handed her license over and stared at him for what seemed like a long time, then shook her head. "No." She glanced ahead, out of the windshield. "I think I'm going crazy."

"Is Bea ..." He stretched up to see in the backseat.

"No. She's at ... with ... I just made a quick trip." Katty wiped her eyes. "I haven't been gone long."

Damn. When he'd driven through the trailer park, Bea had probably been there. Alone. She was four! He knew too much. He knew Bea. If he didn't know Bea, he wouldn't have questioned Katty about her child. He was definitely in too deep.

He tapped the license against his hand, glanced at Guy again. "I'll be right back. I need to check this in."

She nodded. That was it. Just nodded.

As he gave Chantelle the information over the radio, he felt Guy behind him, watching him. Good thing, too. Keep him accountable, because right now he was edging over to no-man's-land—where either he might be a legit cop by the book, or where no cop should ever go.

"A-okay, Mark. Checks out. Isn't this ..." She stopped herself. Knowing. Good woman.

"Thanks, Chantelle." He walked back to Katty and handed her the driver's license and paperwork. "I'm only going to give you a warning." Hesitated. "You must have been in a hurry to get back ..." All wrong. Never suppose. Never assume. Never cross the line between work and personal life.

This was so messed up.

She wouldn't look him in the eye. Kept her purse on top of the cupholder.

"Um, how's the arm? Uh. Never mind. Sorry. I'll let you get back to Bea."

All wrong, again.

Katty nodded. "Yeah."

Hesitated again. "Be safe." He walked back to the squad car and got in.

She seemed in safe driver mode—blinker on, check mirrors, slowly pull onto the highway.

He—totally the opposite—was a mess.

Mark swallowed the lump in his throat, knowing Guy was behind him. He'd hear it all now. From Guy *and* back at the department.

Guy pulled up beside him—window down. "Tough day." Guy's deep voice. "Tough." He nodded, saluted, his finger to his head, and swung around to travel in the other direction.

And that was all.

Mark pictured her face. She'd been crying.

Her expression. Her eyes. Painful.

She was breaking, and he knew it.

What could he do?

How could he help her but not lose his job?

He looked up, her car now a mile away.

And Bea. She hadn't been in the car seat.

Bea, home alone, just like Katty had said.

Every time he'd driven past the trailer court—even through it—Bea had been at the trailer.

Alone.

"Bea!"

What? Bea jumped. She hadn't heard Mommy drive up.

"Mommy."

Mommy walked right through the angel.

His eyes never left Bea's eyes.

Angel. Mommy walked right through his body.

He had hugged Bea.

He was real. As real as Mommy.

But Mommy had walked through him.

Bea knew words: around, beside, past. She knew through.

"Why is the door open? What did you do?" Mommy moved the door back and forth. "Good. I thought you broke it and you'd be in so much f'n trouble."

She was back.

Her car stood there in the driveway.

Bea cupped her hands to her mouth.

The angel! Was he hurt?

Only he still stood there, like … well, he was grinning. He was all there … kinda.

Mommy walked past Bea. She smelled that funny way. She slammed something on the kitchen table behind her. "Come on, Bea. Close the damn door."

Mommy talked naughty. Bad words.

"Oh, yeah. I forgot your candy."

Bea looked to where the angel had been before Mommy walked *through* him.

Candy?

His eyes.

Blue.

Not happy.

Not mad.

Just …

"Bea! Now!"

His lips smiled.

His eyes smiled, too.

He slowly nodded.

He was real.

Even now. When she couldn't see all of him anymore.

He was real.

ELEVEN

Katty stretched and yawned. Pulled her comforter up under her chin and wiggled her toes underneath. Fall was here, and it felt good to snuggle under more covers. Plus, the trailer was always drafty.

The morning always started out okay.

Then Bea woke up.

They grabbed breakfast and dressed—exhausting. The brief car ride drained Katty—from their trailer to Hillcrest Homes— just *that* had drained her.

Bea drained her. "Mommy. Mommy. Mommy."

And now, at Hillcrest Homes, going through Clarence's old boxes drained her. She was always exhausted.

Stacks of unopened cardboard boxes taunted her from along the wall. They teased her. Tormented her. When she unpacked one, three more appeared. The contents seemed important: paperwork either from Clarence's first stint in prison when he became a lawyer and helped inmates and guards with cases, or from his dad's business dealings, while they incarcerated Clarence.

She inspected every paper, every note and clipping, to make

sure she filed it correctly. That it was important enough to keep and not throw away.

Those new filing cabinets would fill up fast.

Life had changed for Katty with her job. She had gone to school to be a paralegal—on Clarence's dollar—but learned so much with Clarence, and now Harold. Starting up a proper business, even a small one like theirs, surprised her at how much work there was to be done. Clarence, being a lawyer, could do many things that others, without a law degree, couldn't. He just had to tell her what to do. She had driven to the next town, to the newspaper office, and put in a "doing business as" ad. What on earth was that for? It seemed stupid to her, but apparently, it made it all legal. They set up an LLC, which he had to explain to her, too. She learned so much with them—Clarence the lawyer and Harold the detective.

Their little detective agency had grown since they'd put up a shingle—as Harold called it.

Katty had to admit that it was nice having Mrs. T, Clarence's new wife, babysit Bea. They played together, took walks together, watched TV. Bea always seemed different after she'd spent time with her. She was more obedient and respectful. Still ornery, but almost more fun.

Katty looked up from the box. They were right in the next room. She didn't have to run Bea somewhere to a babysitter, then rush to work. She didn't have to watch her time, so as not to be late, to pick her up again. Probably was unusual to rent two rooms in a nursing home, side-by-side. Worked really well—an office with desk and chairs at a small conference table, and a bedroom with ... beds and their stuff. Two bathrooms, which came in handy, too.

Also, this room, this job, turned out to be a blessing from day one, when Clarence had convinced her to apply for the paralegal course.

She herself had accomplished nothing with her life ... except Bea.

In high school, her grades had been decent, but never good enough for her mom.

"You'll never amount to anything. You'll always be a filthy scab on my life." Her mom's voice still cursed her, from wherever she lived now—hell, probably. "My mother always said that to me, and that's all you are, too. A scab. I should have gotten rid of you when I had the chance."

Even now, as those words rushed through her memory, they drained any shred of confidence and self-worth that Clarence had built up in her—straight into the toilet. Katty could almost feel Mom's hand slapping her cheek. Time travel child abuse.

Clarence had been the only reason she'd been able to pass those classes.

But she'd done it.

She glanced up at the wall beside her. Her certificate hung right beside his licenses and permits. She had a degree.

Screw you, Mom.

She patted her jeans pocket. The little bottle hiding there looked a lot like a lipstick bulge. Or change. She'd spent time in front of the mirror earlier, checking to be sure. Just knowing it was there—

Clarence and Harold burst out laughing.

Inside joke.

Those two.

Harold was a dear friend—family, even. A major half of this little business.

The Timmelsen and Dexter Agency.

Katty glanced at the walker sitting on tennis balls in front of Harold. He wasn't the street detective anymore, but he *had* been. Because of that, he brought many contacts with him—from notorious to notable.

Lisha Hall peeked into the room and grinned. "Y'all need refreshments?"

Oh yeah. Katty needed what was in her pocket. She could almost feel that burning liquid flowing down her throat.

Clarence stood. "Sure, Lisha." He walked over and held out his arms to hug her.

She swung her hand to smack him on his cheek, but stopped short of touching him. "How are you, Mr. Ornery?" She stopped. "Oh. Yeah. Forgot to knock, as usual." She hugged him, then pounded on the door loud enough to bring Bea running.

Bea peeked and saw who had knocked on the door, ran straight for Lisha, and jumped high—knowing Lisha would catch her.

Lisha groaned, but caught her, having practiced it every time Bea was at Hillcrest. "How are you, my little Snuggle Bug?"

Bea nuzzled into Lisha's neck. She raised her head and kissed her cheek. "Fine."

Lisha set her on the floor.

Bea walked away, back to the bedroom with Mrs. T, but turned. "How are you?"

"Oh!" Lisha pounded her ample chest. "Listen to yo manners." She straightened up, primping, arranging her dreads tied up in a bun. "I am fine, thank you."

That woman.

Bea started back to Mrs. T.

"Wait." Lisha pushed her cart into the room. "Anybody want juice?" She winked. "Water? Coffee?"

Bea ran back. "I'll take juice." She glanced over her shoulder at Mrs. T in the next room, then to Lisha. "Please?"

What? Bea hardly ever said please or thank you at home.

Lisha laughed. Her belly jiggled. "Yes, Ma'am." Lisha poured a small cup half-full and handed it to Bea. "When you git all that gone, Sugar, you can have more." She glanced around the room. "Anybody else?"

"Naw. We just had coffee," Clarence chuckled. "No, thank you, Ma'am" He stuck out his tongue at her.

She did it back.

"Kat? Need anything?"

"Su-sure. I'll take some coffee."

The room air sucked away as everyone waited.

"Please." She rolled her eyes.

Lisha placed the full cup on the desk beside Katty.

The aroma wafted up. "This isn't your … uh … usual nursing home brew, is it?" She lifted the cup close to her nose and breathed it in.

"Nope. Made it just for you, my love." Lisha leaned over Katty, wrapped her arms around her, and planted a kiss on her forehead.

Oh, please never stop.

Wrapped in that huge warm hug, Katty could conquer the world. Even win over booze. Believe she might even be worth loving.

She blinked. Not crying here.

Sigh.

"Okay, loves, I'm onward." Lisha pushed the cart out the door.

Oh, the smell of that coffee. Katty lifted the cup and breathed it in. If all she had to do was sit and sniff and sip. But no. So much to do. Katty leaned over the next cardboard box—breathing intentionally, slowly—one breath at a time. Blow out. Breathe in. Hold on to Lisha's love and presence. Hold on to what that woman oozed.

Would Katty ever be able to affect another person like that?

Back to the box.

Inside, more documents. Words on the top document drew her interest. A lawsuit against the prison. Interesting. Was that even possible? That would be like a lawsuit against the government. Could they ever win? She sat back in her chair slowly, reading.

Wait!

Could she sue Phil Daynton?

Her head popped up.

What if? What if she … why hadn't she ever thought about that before now?

Life was so cluttered, so confusing.

She peeked at Clarence and Harold—deep in a discussion about the whys and why nots of putting ads in The Polk County News for their new agency.

Harold was winning. "How will people ever know we're here?"

There would be time to ask about suing Phil when Harold went back to his room.

Then again, if she sued Phil, she couldn't squeeze blood or money out of someone who didn't have an ounce of goodness in him. Phil was made of cold, hard evil. Having blood meant a person had to be a living being. Phil was a demon.

Another question bugged her.

Should she stay in her trailer?

Noell Carpenter had asked her and Bea to move in and share her enormous house—they'd only recently found out they were family—well, Clarence had adopted Katty, Bea, *and* Noell as his own. But she and Noell were cousins. *Real* cousins. She didn't understand all that once or twice removed stuff.

Didn't matter. She had family.

What if she'd been able to grow up in that big beautiful house—cluttered to the ceilings, now—but still beautiful? What if she'd gotten to have a sweet grandma like Noell had? Someone to sing to her like Mrs. T did to Bea? She'd never known family, except her mom and dad, and they were outcasts, probably because *they* were so evil.

Why did some people seem to have all the luck? Some

might have been born into it. They didn't have a thing to worry about. Every day of their life, someone cared and provided for them.

Well … Noell's mom had drowned.

What would have been worse: a mom drowning and then growing up with a sweet grandma and grandpa, or having a mom and dad who were there, but just plain evil?

She'd been unlucky enough to be born into evil.

There was nothing fair about it.

Katty stood, the document still in her hand.

With Phil still on the loose, it crippled her from deciding to move. Lex was in jail, thank God, but Phil was still free to stalk her and Bea. He had almost killed them several times.

Until they locked him up, or he was dead—she'd never be free. Bea either.

Even now, she shivered.

"Katty. You cold?" Clarence stood and stepped to the thermostat. "We can adjust this." He smiled and held his finger to his lips. "Shh. We're always doing that to keep Mrs. T warm." He barely moved the dial, then smiled at her. "Let me know, Hon. Okay?"

She nodded. "Okay."

Clarence was the only person in this world who would not only change the thermostat for her comfort, but would literally die for her.

"Twinkle, twinkle, little toe." Mrs. T sang in her soft voice, a smile in her eyes.

Bea collapsed in a giggle. "Not a toe." She sat up. "It's a star." She sucked in a deep breath and sang. "Twinkle, twinkle little star." She wiped her eyes. "It's a star, not a toe!" She laughed again, rolling next to Mrs. T on the bed.

"Oh. I thought it was a toe. I'm sorry." Mrs. T chuckled and stroked Bea's cheek. "My Baby Bea."

Bea blinked, but knew. Mrs. T was the only person she let call her baby. No one. Not even Clarence. Well, maybe Mommy. Depended on if Mommy was Bad Mommy or Good Mommy.

Maybe Lisha.

Bea rolled closer to Mrs. T. They curved into each other, Bea in front and Mrs. T around her back.

Tiny shivers skittered through Bea as Mrs. T combed through her tangly hair with her fingers. Bea wiped her eyes.

Something—

"Father, we love you." Mrs. T always prayed. Always. When they snuggled. When they laughed, or when they sang, or when they ate. All the time, she prayed.

"Da-da, ma-chon-di-a." Mrs. T prayed.

"Is that baby talk?" Bea rolled over so she could see Mrs. T's face, her mouth. She watched her lips as they moved.

Mrs. T didn't stop stroking her hair, and her eyes were open. But she didn't stop speaking that baby talk either.

Mrs. T just shook her head and kept on talking. Funny words. Bea watched Mrs. T's lips and moved her own mouth at the same time.

Funny words came out of her own mouth, too.

Bea sat up, her eyes wide. Her mouth said funny words again. "That's not baby talk." She whispered, glancing to where Mommy sat. "What is it?"

Mrs. T took a deep breath and blew it on Bea. "It's angel talk. God talk." She pointed behind Bea. "See, angels come when we speak angel talk."

Bea slowly stretched to look behind her. "My angel." Back to Mrs. T and pointed. "My angel is here." She paused and watched him. "He has nice eyes. He wears a bathrobe, like Michael does. I like his hair, too."

"Yes."

"But how did he get here? He was at my house." She remembered. "Mommy walked through him and I thought he … he died." She cupped her hands over her mouth. Back to her angel. "I thought you died."

The angel smiled and looked at Mrs. T.

"He wants me to tell you he's okay and people do it all the time. Only special people see them. You see them." Mrs. T tapped Bea gently on her nose.

Bea smiled, but then frowned. "Mommy can't see them if she walked through him." She faced her angel. "How did you get here, Angel? You were at my house."

Angel smiled and looked at Mrs. T, again.

Mrs. T seemed to listen to him. She chuckled. "He says to tell you he *flew* here." She grinned.

Bea's eyes popped as she thought about that. She glanced from Mrs. T's face to Angel's face, then out the window. "Y-you mean he flew … l-like a bird? Like … that bird?" She pointed.

They all looked.

Angel nodded.

Mrs. T nodded.

"Wow." Bea nodded.

Katty put down the paperwork.

Bathroom.

Nice that Clarence and Mrs. T's bedroom had that private bathroom, and the office had one, too.

Katty opened the door. Industrial pine was strong this morning. The lady just cleaned. Naw. It always smelled that way. Cleanest place on the planet.

She finished her business and stared at herself in the mirror as she washed her hands. Those eyes staring back accused her.

They accused her of what they knew she planned to do, immediately after she dried her hands.

Her head swiveled from side to side. The battle was on.

"No, I won't."

"Yes, you will."

She should either give in and drink herself to death, or … go to rehab. That thought made her cringe. She'd heard awful stories of clinics that drugged the patients so they didn't have to deal with them—like drugged veggies. She'd watched a documentary on some facilities costing tons of money, but people still overdosed and died.

Back to the mirror. Those eyes.

She leaned closer, searching deeper underneath. Under the accuser. Under a layer of control that was ever thinning. Under the layer of anger.

Fear lurked there.

She blinked.

No.

Not here.

She belched and quickly swallowed.

Not here.

Her fingers flew to her lips.

She belched again.

Just a little sip might settle her stomach.

Always worked before.

Her fingers trembled as she fished the tiny bottle from her pocket. Good thing she was right-handed, because the cast on her left arm didn't bend right. Holding the bottle in her left hand, she broke the seal with her right. Bea's colorful drawings on the cast made her pause.

That little girl.

Deep breath.

One more glance in the mirror.

She should stop for that little girl—her Bea.

Breathe.

Or was there another little girl that Katty should stop drinking for?

Everything stopped as time seemed to wait for her decision.

Will she drink?

Will she be strong?

Slowly, she brought the bottle to her lips. Seemed almost like there was another arm that helped her tip that bottle.

Closing her eyes, she breathed in the whiskey's fragrance. She sipped the golden liquid. Another drink. And another.

She held the bottle away from her. One sip left. Better save it. She capped it and shoved the tiny bottle into her pocket again. The warm liquid didn't even burn anymore, like she remembered.

It hit her stomach.

She belched.

Had she eaten?

Belched again, and she wiped her mouth with the back of her hand.

Breathe.

Again.

Clarence and Harold burst out laughing from the office. Some joke.

Her fingers were tight against her lips, as if they could prevent the whiskey from bursting out of her mouth.

Breathe.

The nausea soon eased.

Hand down by her side.

Back to the eyes in the mirror.

Oh God.

Those eyes.

She couldn't let the world, Clarence and Harold, Mrs. T, see.

Or Bea.

Couldn't let her see.

Mask on.

Bea snuggled back down against Mrs. T.

Angel never moved. He sat right next to the bed. His eyes moved from her to the room, the walls, then back to her.

Her eyes wanted to close—so sleepy—when another angel appeared next to the window. A big angel. He was taller than the window and he had a stick … or a gun.

Wide awake, she sat up and pointed at him. "Who's that … there? He has a stick. He's dressed like Hiccup in that movie. That train your dragon movie."

Mrs. T lifted her head. "You mean his armor?"

"Do you see him?" Bea pointed. "Does *he* have a dragon?"

Mrs. T laughed. "I don't know. We can ask him sometime." She wiped Bea's hair from her eyes. "And, yes. He's always there." She slowly sat up. "One is standing there by our door, too."

Bea's eyes felt like they'd popped. His shoes. Coat. His stick. "Wait. Is he holding a—"

"Sword?" Mrs. T nodded. "That's a sword." She pointed at Angel. "Your angel has one, too."

Angel held it up.

Bea reached for it.

He shook his head and grinned. He blew at Bea.

She sucked in a deep breath and pointed. "My angel has a sword, too."

Another angel appeared by the door between the two rooms.

Swords.

Armor.

Shiny.

Big.

Taller than the wall.

Her angel was smiling at her and looking all around them. The others were more serious and stood like they were ready for a fight.

Bea lay back down and watched.

"Want to finish our movie, Bea?" Mrs. T aimed the remote.

Bea nodded.

Mrs. T punched start, and the music played, penguins toddled, but Bea couldn't take her eyes off the angels.

Mommy sat back down at her desk after going to the bathroom. A huge angel eased into the room behind her.

Bea slowly sat up.

"Mommy's angel is … big." Bea stared at his feet and on up his robes and armor, his sword, his shoulders and up to his head. "He has a hat."

Mrs. T nodded. "It's called a helmet, Bea. It protects his head."

"From what?" Bea looked at Mrs. T, then back to the angel. "Does he fall down a lot? Or get in accidents, like Mommy and me?"

Mrs. T took a long time to answer. She looked at the angels, then closed her eyes. When she opened them, all the angels bent a knee, heads down, and knelt.

Something changed. Something was different in the room. It wasn't scary.

She wasn't laughing. Nothing was funny.

She wanted to cry, but she wasn't sad.

She turned and faced Mrs. T.

She didn't ask lots of questions like she usually did.

Bea then slid off the bed and stood by her angel, watching him and the others.

She bent one knee, the same knee they had bent—their left one—and knelt down beside her angel on her right knee.

He and the others hit their chest with their right arms.

Bea did it too.

Mrs. T hit pause on the TV remote.

Somebody else was in the room.

When Katty returned to her desk, Clarence and Harold were discussing a court case.

They had set up a sitting area by the window, with a small table between the chairs. It made the nursing home room seem like a real law office. Not very private for Clarence and Mrs. T, though.

Mrs. T.

Katty had a hard time calling her that. She'd always been Mrs. Hatly. Katty stuttered every time she saw her—starting with Mrs. Hat, when she'd catch herself—and spit out something like Mrs. Hat-T. They'd both laugh and Mrs. T would hug her, saying it didn't matter.

But it did. It was important to Katty to say it right. Mrs. ... T was Clarence's new wife.

Mrs. T had moved into his rooms after the wedding. Super convenient for them. She had been sick for a while, with him going back to prison. Must be comforting now, knowing the nurses were right down the hall. Convenient for him, too. Short commute.

Super convenient for Katty, too. Mrs. T always insisted that Bea come and play while Katty worked. The door remained open between the two rooms, but Katty tried to get Bea to respect the fact that the other room was their private bedroom.

It never failed, though. When Katty and Bea arrived, Mrs. T pushed her walker through the door and welcomed them. She'd ask if Bea could play, which always got Bea excited and made Katty smile.

Mrs. T was so cute in her pinkness—a pink headband held back her chin length grey hair, and there was always pink somewhere else—whether a bow around her neck, or a pink shirt under her sweater, or pink socks. So cute.

Katty picked up the empty box and set it on the floor. That one could go to the dumpster.

She felt Harold watching her as she organized papers on the desk. She peeked at him.

He smiled his tender smile. He knew. He knew what she was thinking and how she felt almost more than Clarence. He wasn't a detective for nothing. He knew the signs, too.

There was something between them … like, what was that saying … they were on the same wavelength? She felt him. Nothing creepy or sexy. He just hugged her without touching her. He brought tears to her eyes when he did that.

Whew.

Somehow, things felt different between them all. Yes, Clarence had gotten married and Mrs. T had moved to his rooms, but something felt … off.

Probably her.

Bea giggled from the next room.

Katty had also gotten over checking on Bea every time she heard her laugh or talk. Mrs. T assured Katty that Bea was fine and no trouble. They even took naps together, if Katty worked longer than usual.

It had grown quiet one afternoon, so Katty peeked in on them and Bea had snuggled beside Mrs. T, with Mrs. T's arm around Bea's waist. Katty watched them like that for what seemed like hours. Didn't need to take a picture with her phone—it imprinted on her heart for forever.

The days when Bea's little girl voice and Mrs. T's old lady voice blended in song were the best. Songs like Jesus Loves Me and This Little Light of Mine.

Like earlier this morning.

"This little light of mine, I'm gonna let it shine." The two voices blended sweetly. Katty picked up another box and placed it on her desk and stopped, listening. "This little light of mine, I'm gonna let it shine, let it shine, let it shine, let it shine."

Both men seemed to listen, too. They stopped talking and sipped their coffee.

"Won't let Satan blow it out." One voice sang the word blow, but Bea's little voice gave a puff of air for the word blow.

Harold closed his eyes. "So cute. Reminds me of my own kids when my wife, Vera, taught them that song."

Wow. A mom that would teach a kid sweet songs …. She gulped and blinked back tears.

Help me, God.

Her emotions spiked right now. Near breaking.

Katty wanted more than anything in the world to be a wonderful mom and she didn't even know those songs to teach Bea.

Memories wafted in from when she used to get fixed up to party. She and Bea had danced to those party songs—not the words that a four-year-old should have been singing.

Clarence nodded and folded his arms. "Yeah. I was little when Mom died, but I remember her teaching me that song. Pretty sure it was Mom, before she died."

Was Katty the only kid whose mom had beat her senseless and driven away the only boy she'd ever liked? Was her mom the only one who cussed and swore her way through the day, mostly at Katty? "You're such a little trash heap. What a tramp. You couldn't …" She didn't want to remember all the awful things Mom had said. She didn't want to even speak them out loud because somehow that made them even more true.

"Mommy?"

Katty's head popped up from inside the box. "What Bea?"

Neither Clarence nor Harold appeared to hear. They were in some conversation about the law and how it didn't always serve the public … or something like that.

Bea didn't answer. She must have forgotten, or Mrs. T took care of it.

Ahh. Notebooks from prison. Dated with month, day and year. Way back to … 1959. Some even farther back.

"Mommy."

"Just a minute, Bea." She picked a notebook up—it was a regular spiral notebook, like she'd used for note-taking at school. "So, Clarence. Did you journal your prison stay?" She flipped through the pages. Lots of notes. Lots of reading.

"What?" Clarence glanced her way, distracted by her interruption, but when he saw what she held in her hand, he stood and reached for it. "Oh, you found my journals from the first time in prison." He opened it. "That'll make for some good winter evening reading."

"Mommy."

Katty walked to the doorway to their bedroom where Bea had been playing. "What Bea? Mommy's working. What do you want?"

Bea didn't answer. She sat on the bed watching TV with Mrs. T all snuggled in beside her, under a quilt. Some show on the TV. Her eyes drooped, almost ready to close for a nap. "What Mommy?"

"Did you call me?" Katty tried to burn the impatience out of her voice. "What do you want?"

Bea shook her head. "I didn't call Mommy." She pointed to the TV. "Look at the penguins, Mommy. They are sooo cute." Like the little girl in the Monsters, Inc. movie. Bea was sooo cute.

Katty pointed behind her to the desk in the office. "But I heard you call. You said, 'Mommy.' I'm sure you did. I heard you."

Mrs. T shook her head. "No. She's been here the whole time watching … penguins with me. She didn't call."

"Oh." Katty shrugged her shoulders. "Okay. Sorry to bother your movie."

She walked back to her desk and sat slowly on the chair. It creaked under her weight. Clarence and Harold flipped through the notebook she'd handed to Clarence, pointing at some words here and there. Commenting on something Clarence had written. She glanced into the next room. She could just see Bea snuggled back into Mrs. T as they watched the movie.

Mrs. T smiled at her.

Sweet woman. Sweet, sweet, sweet. Take notes from her and live like her, and maybe something might rub off instead of the crappy junk she had inside right now.

Yes, from her mom, but so much was her own.

She must have heard wrong. Sounded just like Bea.

She glanced down at her bag. Felt her pocket. Only a little sip left.

Must be the booze making her crazy—hearing those voices.

That was it.

She was going crazy.

TWELVE

Phil held his breath. Checked each wall.

He had to get out of this rat infested basement. No more sleeping under moldy quilts on the floor. It'd be better to sleep outside under a bush or on a slide or—

A slide!

The park.

It might be getting cool at night, but he could get a blanket from the car. Or find one hanging on someone's clothesline.

If.

If he didn't get caught. He had seen deputies parked by his getaway car and call in his license plates. They might have already towed it.

If they had, he could watch for somebody's clothesline. People aired out blankets. Hung sheets out to dry on clotheslines. He could become the bedspread thief. Sneak around at night and steal bedspreads and blankets. He could have his own little tent in the park, complete with bedding.

Visions of sheets hanging from that old slide for a tent made him laugh.

Too obvious. But funny.

The owner of the store left for the day again. Somehow he'd made it thorough the day. So boring. He hated the daytime waiting out until the owner left for the day. His phone had died a day ago. No one could find him or hear it ring by now. Nobody called him anymore, anyway.

Someday.

He'd been living as a vagabond, a bum, for too long. Time to get his own place again. He didn't need much. Just a bed. His own coffee cup again. A place to charge his phone.

That wasn't much to ask.

Money. And he needed money.

He had lived the high life back when Warden was in charge at the prison. Prisoners were clueless about what Warden had built into that prison for his own personal space. He had opened the purse strings wide to renovate several apartments for his thugs—of which Phil was a loyal member. Tax dollars at work. Beautiful woodwork. A fireplace. Kitchens with all the appliances anyone might need—including a wine bar with a wine refrigerator. Two or three bedrooms for guests. And he figured Warden had entertained many guests through those years of his reign.

His own time of living there. He shook his head. The sensation of having his own key and after each day of work—well, it wasn't work to rule in his own little kingdom at the prison. Just being cruel with the power they had given him was all he had to do. Make sure the inmates he was in charge of decided to toe the line. Make double sure that the guards kept control.

Every day, he'd insert his key to his apartment, hear the click, and push open the door wide to reveal such splendor. His favorite feature was the fake view. There were windows, but higher on the walls. Natural light was important. But, lower on certain walls were windows, but instead of mountain views, in reality, they had prison buildings and fences. So Warden installed windows that framed moving landscapes. You could push a button on a remote that changed the view from mountains to seascapes and anything in between. It was exactly like looking out a window and watching the trees wave in the breeze. Deer even appeared if you watched the mountains long enough. Or seagulls hovered above the water as waves splashed against a shore.

Must have been expensive.

Oh, those had been the days.

Wonder what they used those apartments for, now that Warden himself lived in a regular cell. Phil didn't like to admit it, but the corrupt always got caught. The corrupt always paid for their deception. It might be the next generation that actually served the time, but their crimes always caught up with them.

Phil didn't sense the demon anymore today, but he knew from experience that you never trusted demons or any knowledge you thought you had of them. They always—always—pulled a fast one. Never, ever trust your instincts when it comes to demons.

Sigh.

He sounded like his dad.

Time to make an exit from the bad basement.

Easy to leave. He had nothing with him here.

The small hallway in the basement led to the back door, but Phil turned the other way. He'd explored the basement several times, but had found nothing that interested him. He didn't want to cause suspicion when the owner might come downstairs. Seeing boxes moved or things strewn about would do just that.

The stairway to upstairs.

He stopped, his hands on the railings. Maybe explore upstairs. Do a quick walk-through before he left these digs. He might find something. If they left a cash drawer open. Or if anything was of value to him. He might even find a new coffee cup.

He stepped quietly, even now, after hours. Just in case. He knew the owner had left, but you couldn't be too certain.

Just like the demons, a person had to be careful and discerning.

Big space upstairs.

He could breathe here. He sucked in several deep breaths. Even though he had bruised his nose badly, it still felt good.

From where he stood, Phil paused and cased the store. Lots of antiques. He guessed some were valuable. But he wasn't here to steal furniture. He might explore, but he needed to find a spot in the park or someone's backyard for the night.

Huge pillars divided the space into two store fronts. He tapped one. Metal. Impressive. Had to be original. Magnificent building. If Phil was an entrepreneur—well, he was one—just not of the legal sense, he might want to renovate buildings like this one had been.

He stayed toward the back of the store until it started to get dark outside. Munched on a leftover doughnut. It'd dry out and go to waste, anyway. He might as well eat it. A little coffee left in the pot. He found a cup to his liking in a little kitchen area and poured himself a cupful. Just right. Still warm—kinda.

Too bad the bedstead there didn't have a mattress on it or he might have slept there every night. Only, too hard to put things back in order in the morning, to make sure no one suspected his presence.

Ooh. Pie. Three pieces left. Looked like apple—his favorite. Dang. He found a fork in the kitchen display. Wow. Genuine silver. Must be fancy since it had the maker's imprint. Ate the pie right out of the pan. They'd never know. Unless they counted pieces. Unless they had invited someone in for the next day to share a piece with them.

Phil shook his head.

They'd never know.

This pie, though, had been made in heaven. The apples were

tender. Crust so flaky. If he'd had a proper grandma, this would have been the pie she would have made. Only he'd never had that kind of grandma, or mom even. This pie would break all records and take awards.

Without realizing it, he slowly sat in what must have been the owner's chair because he heard it scrape the floor. He knew that scrape sound, except he'd always heard it from below, in the basement. He chewed in ecstasy, savoring every bite. Damn, it was good. Best pie ever. It'd have to qualify for the state fair or something. Whatever these country people did.

Oh, crap.

The pie plate was empty. No way. He'd eaten the whole pie? Crap. Crap.

Oh well, he'd be gone and no one would ever suspect.

They'd know their pie had been eaten, but they'd never know he'd been the one who ate it all.

Cars were driving the square and honking. Must be a high school football game night or some sort of event. Kids were hollering and honking.

He had no idea what day it was. Friday? Thursday?

He eased up to the front of the store. It was dark anyway. No one could see inside. He stuffed the pie plate into an antique stove. Nobody would find it there. Heh. The store owner might think they had a ghost. Well, they did. Kinda.

Another carload of kids drove past the store. Oh, the opportunity to play. He slipped onto a display chair in the front windows and quickly sat before the next car drove past. Props. He needed … he rushed into the store and grabbed a top hat from a dresser.

Perfect.

He sat again and messed up his hair. Probably already messed up. And on with the top hat. Crossed his legs and straightened his back. Sat like a mannequin—stiff-backed and head at an odd angle.

Only his eyes moved.

One car drove past, and no one noticed. They were yelling and screaming and acting … well, probably just like he used to act. Truth be told, he probably never acted like that because his dad always found out and disciplined him at the cult meetings. Only took once.

Next car. One face looked his way.

Nothing. No response.

These kids had money to waste gas like they were rich. Round and round the square, they drove. Chasing each other. Squealing tires.

Leg cramped. He switched. Nobody cared, nobody was looking.

Next car. Same face looked. She pointed. Pounded her friend and pointed.

Oh shit. She noticed. Maybe.

They all drove around again like a merry-go-round.

There she was again. And this time everybody looked in the store window at him. They were laughing and screaming. Pointing.

He grinned. Couldn't help it. They were such idiots.

More screaming and honking.

The car stopped and started to back up, only another car was behind them.

They waved.

The car sped on before any kids could hop out.

Next car.

A deputy squad car.

Oh shit!

Only the cop wasn't looking his way. He was after the kids.

Phil could barely see the deputy pull them over in the next block.

He ran. Threw the top hat off onto the bedstead. Didn't matter. He didn't care.

He knew that deputy.

CHAPTER 13

When Katty spent time at Hillcrest, working for Clarence, watching Bea with Mrs. T, something rubbed off on her.

Hearing Mrs. T sing with Bea—Bea always came home singing those songs and others she learned.

Clarence made Katty feel like she mattered—not only to him and Mrs. T, but she mattered to the universe. She made a difference in the world. He scolded her when she scoffed at him—scolded her gently, but firmly. He made her feel like she really mattered—at least to him, to them.

Harold hugged her. Literally put his walker aside and held out his arms. Same with Clarence. They held out those long arms, and she knew as she walked into their embrace that she'd tear up and cry. They always made her feel like she was their most treasured possession—their one and only daughter or granddaughter who they doted on and loved. Who they would do anything in their power for.

Clarence taught her about law, about the right way to file his papers, about math and finances. He always talked to her with respect. If she didn't understand something he said, he would take a deep breath and back up to where she'd gotten lost and go at it again—only with a different illustration until he was sure she understood—until he was sure she felt confident in taking that next step.

One day, it was all about answering the phone. The phone rang, and she expected him to answer it. It was his phone. His rooms. He lived there. She rarely let Bea answer her own phone. If she saw it was Clarence on the caller ID when it rang, and Bea was close by, she'd hand it to Bea to answer. She knew it made Clarence happy to hear Bea's little girl voice answer. A fun surprise.

So when Clarence started to want Katty to answer his phone, it knocked her back. Her mom had never let her answer as a kid. The only time Katty had answered, it turned out to be a preacher from one of the local churches. He and Katty had a wonderful conversation until Mom came in the back door from the garage and found Katty talking on the phone. She grabbed the phone from Katty, pushed her into the TV, and yanked the phone out of the wall.

End of conversation.

End of answering the phone for Katty.

Guess Mom didn't want to talk to preachers.

"No, Katty. When the phone rings in here, in our law office, you answer." Clarence had been very firm about that. "You have many jobs here, like I do. You are my paralegal, my receptionist, my secretary. There are many tasks you do and they can all have a name." He picked up the phone—still the kind connected to a jack in the wall—and handed it to her. "Pretend it rang."

She hesitated, looked at the phone, then up at Clarence. She smirked and took it. "Hello?" She gave it back. "Nobody's there."

He squinted at her, slowly shook his head. "Play the game. There's someone calling about enlisting us to sue a neighbor." He handed the phone back to her.

One eyebrow cocked, Katty took it back. "Hello?"

By that time, Bea had slid off Mrs. T's bed and come in to see what new phone game they were playing. "Can I play?"

Clarence took the phone back and shook his head at Bea. Sat for a minute and Katty knew he was summoning his patience. "Ring!"

Bea reached for the phone, only he wouldn't give it to her.

He brought the phone to his ear. "Hello? This is The Timmelsen and Dexter Agency, Katty speaking. How can I help you?"

Bea giggled. "You're not Katty." She pointed at Katty. "Mommy's Katty."

Clarence growled, his nostrils flared.

Bea pointed. "Clarence is mad."

Knock, knock.

"Juice anyone? Coffee?"

Bea ran to Lisha as she knocked at the door. "Clarence is mad, Lisha."

"Oh, he is, is he?" The nurse pushed a cart just inside the door and held out her hands.

Bea jumped.

Lisha caught her and held her close. "Is he being mean to my Baby Bea today?"

"No. He'd being mean to Mommy, though." Bea grinned as she hid her face in Lisha's neck.

Little brat.

"I… I'm just trying to teach Katty, here, some telephone manners." His voice was loud at first, but with each word, he seemed to consciously tone down the volume.

"I don't think I'm doing it right." Katty grinned. She stole the phone from him. "Ring!" She fluttered her eyes and pursed her lips. "Hello?" She sighed dramatically. "This is The Timmelsen and Dexter Agency. How can I help you?"

Bea scrambled down from Lisha. "You forgot to say your name. This is Katty." She giggled. "Only I'm Bea. Not Katty."

Laughter exploded in the room.

"Help me, Jesus." Clarence looked like he wanted to cry. He wiped his eyes and looked at Harold. "What are we gonna do with these girls?"

Harold couldn't answer. He was bouncing in his wheelchair. Laughing.

Even now, many months later, when she answered the phone, she grinned at Clarence. She knew he was listening. He knew she was grinning. Their eyes would always meet.

The funny thing was that people frequently commented that she always sounded so chipper on the phone.

If they only knew.

Today, it hadn't been all about that hidden sip of booze.

Bea's little girl voice singing with Mrs. T's old lady voice was so sweet. "This little light of mine." Or "Twinkle, Twinkle Little Star."

Sweet.

Moments like that made Katty a better person. Made her want to quit all drugs and booze. Made her feel like she actually could. Like she had the strength to really do it.

At home, she wanted to cook a meal for her and Bea—even if it was only a roasted chicken from the grocery store. Those were delicious and she and Bea could eat on one for two days. Most times. Chicken with a box of mac and cheese. Sometimes they cooked spaghetti. Bea loved spaghetti. Katty did, too.

Even tonight.

"Hey Bea?"

No answer.

Katty snuggled next to Bea and tickled her. Daryl and Dumpty was her favorite TV show. She was immersed. "Tickle. Tickle, tickle."

Bea giggled, but pushed Katty's hand away.

"Bea. You want spaghetti for supper?" Katty waved the can in front of Bea's face.

"Mommy." Bea pushed it out of the way. Back to TV.

"I'll turn it off."

Bea straightened. That got her. "Yeah. Spaggety. Yes." Back to the show.

Even though it was canned, it was better than cereal. Maybe.

And maybe she'd try to be better at not using the TV as her babysitter. Sit down with Bea and read to her. They had an entire collection of Daryl & Dumpty books. Even coloring books.

She looked at the walls. Her drunken painting spree. That tree always got her. Where had she seen that tree? It felt so familiar. She should remember it.

Katty knew she'd failed at work—in the bathroom. But what could she do? If she drank, it made her feel better. It settled her stomach. If she didn't drink, she needed a drink to settle her stomach.

Damned if she did. Damned if she didn't.

But in spite of that, today there was a feeling of peace. Like everything would be alright. Maybe she would actually kick the booze.

Someday.

Maybe.

CHAPTER 14

Mark opened the squad car door.

Stupid kids. It was too early to be this wild. Screaming and yelling.

His shift had just begun. Night shift.

Again.

His turn.

Again.

Not excited about doing the nightly cruise all around the town and county.

Especially after last night. Uniforms were expensive, but he was glad that he owned more than one. His baptism in soda had made his shirt and pants stick to him all evening. It was always good to get home and shower, but especially after last night. He kept one clean set in his locker at the department, one on his body, and one was in his washer right now. He guessed the kid who backed into him had learned a lesson.

Hopefully.

Daynton was on the loose—somewhere—and it might be up to Mark to run into him. What if … tonight?

He'd love handcuffing that man to a pole. He'd leave him

there all night for the rats to chew on his ankles. That man had caused too much injury and pain for Katty and Bea.

The accident at the convenience store a few weeks ago nagged at Mark. Those thoughts, those visuals, wouldn't leave him alone. After Phil rammed into Katty's car, Katty had been desperate to rescue Bea, knowing they both might die, but willing to take that chance for her daughter. Then the gas tank exploded. Hardest thing he'd ever done was to hold Katty tight from running into the smoke and fire—not letting her run to her daughter. Yeah, firefighters were there. They trained for just that kind of incident.

But, dang.

He'd never had kids. Only loved one woman and he declared almost daily, he never would again.

Until now.

Tough decision: to keep Katty away from the car and safe, or to rescue Bea, himself. He couldn't be in two places at once, although he'd wished many times to be able to do that on this job.

Those tough firefighters almost saved Bea until old man Clarence pushed into the car—more than willing to die trying to free her.

They had declared Katty and Bea okay at the hospital, although Katty sported a cast on her broken arm, and Bea came home with bandages on her forehead, but both were okay.

Thankfully. Miraculously.

That jerk, Daynton, had to be close by.

He should have died.

Deserved to die.

He'd been willing to kill Katty and his own daughter.

Bastard!

Mark's phone buzzed, and he checked it.

Mom.

Not now. He tapped his phone to silent, flicked on the flashlight, and walked up to the car. License plates had checked out with Chantelle. Daddy's car. Didn't really need the flashlight. The only shadows visible were *under* the stopped car, thanks to a street light directly above. But he loved to intimidate kids by shining the light in their eyes.

From screaming and yelling a minute ago, to everyone in the car sitting quietly, halos on their heads. From crazy kids to compliant children. Driver's license checked out with Chantelle, too.

The girl in back spoke up. "Didja … did you see the man in the store window?"

"Excuse me? What?" Mark aimed the flashlight at her.

She blinked and lowered her eyes. "Did you see the man in the store?" She pointed behind them. "Back there."

Another kid. "Yeah. At the antique store."

"My mom goes in there. Wait till I tell her about the man in the window."

Mark shook his head. Hyped up on something. "There was a man in the antique store window?" He leaned back and looked. Antique store. Huh.

All he had to do was ask, and it all broke loose again. All five of them talked and yelled at once.

"Enough." Mark barely raised his voice. Immediate silence. "One at a time." To the girl in the back. "You. Talk." He sounded like a general. "What'd he look like?"

"Well, he." She swallowed. "We were driving around—"

"And the man in the window moved." Her friend interrupted. "He laughed."

"No. He smiled."

They all broke in again.

"He switched his legs."

"He jumped up."

"No, he didn't!"

Mark pushed his hands at them to quit.

He leaned back and peered toward the antique store again.

Dang if it might be true?

Daynton?

Damn!

The whole day had been boring, and that was probably why Phil took such a stupid chance.

And he thought those *kids* had been stupid.

He was stupid.

Stealing apple pie and coffee.

That was stupid.

Sitting in the display window up front?

Over the top, stupid. Just as stupid as ramming that old pickup into Katty's car. He should have just waited for them in the park—a guarantee that they'd be vulnerable. Snatch Bea before Katty would even know it. She appeared so drunk these days, she'd never realize it until he and little Bea were a couple states away.

But no. Anger boiled and became the dictator. That Dictator controlled emotions buried deep and governed when to release them. Emotions of anger and victim mentality exploded. No one would ever control Phil again, tell him what to do or what not to do. Things they had forced him to do as a kid in the cult. Never again. Not his dad, and never Katty. Ever.

He took the stairs down to the store basement two at a time and leapt down the last four. He stumbled over a chair and slammed into a stack of boxes.

Dishes clattered inside the boxes. The stack leaned away from him. He frantically pushed against the other side too hard and the entire stack tumbled onto the concrete floor. Boxes broke open and dishes, cups, and plates shattered.

The noise from that many boxes of dishes breaking was deafening. Dust clouds billowed. Somebody should have washed those dishes one more time; the stench of old dirt, old mold, and old food drifted to Phil's nose.

Belch. His empty stomach revolted. When had he eaten an actual meal? Enough of those stupid snacks. He needed a steak dinner or good old roasted chicken wings with trimmings. Grr. His stomach spoke loud and clear.

Right now, nothing he could do—about food. And especially about broken dishes. As if he cared.

He wove his way around the mess and other boxes back to his room, grabbed his gun, and tucked it in his jeans waistband. The rats could have the rest of the snacks. He'd eaten most of them, anyway. Damn those stinky quilts. Never again would he sleep in that muck.

He pushed open the door into the hall and slammed it.

Good riddance antique store. Good riddance store owner. He'd never have to worry about being quiet again.

At the end of the short hallway, he stopped. If that cop was working with the big black cop, he'd be in trouble. The back exit door had windows that let him see what might be behind the store. He jiggled the latch and shoved the door open. Former bank, now city offices, to the right. No cars or trucks. To the left, not so sure. Offices? Then a new bank. That new building probably had alarms of every sort—motion sensors, entry alarms, sound sensors. They might have forgotten to turn them on when the tellers left the building.

Fat chance.

Nobody seemed to be around.

Wait.

A guy appeared to be walking his dog in the alley.

Phil slipped back into the hallway, keeping the door mostly closed. The latch would be loud tonight, with as quiet as the back alley seemed. Maybe the guy was more interested in what he watched on his phone than if his dog took a leak. The dog jerked the leash, dragging his owner to an overgrown patch of small trees. Good. Keep that dog busy sniffing out a critter. It lifted its leg and peed on everything but the man's foot. The man seemed oblivious to whatever the dog was doing. Bet he'd notice if the dog peed on his foot.

"The half-time show is brought to you by… " The whole town could hear the man's phone. Some kind of event—football, probably. Voices. Ref whistles.

Hurry, dog.

Finally, the dog pulled the man away from the trees, toward the street.

A car rushed by, almost hitting the dog. The dog lunged at the car, dragging the man. Still, he didn't lift his head from watching his phone. Must be a great game. The car could have killed him and his dog.

Phil waited until they walked on down the hill, toward the creek. He pushed the door open.

Squeak!

Stopped. Dang, that was loud. Pushed it open a little more. Same squeak. Louder. Stopped.

Damn! Would he forever have to be quiet, to be undiscovered?

Probably. Especially if he continued in the same calling.

Being a criminal.

A kidnapper.

When he was a little kid—maybe Bea's age—he'd wanted to be a helicopter pilot. Fly those enormous birds. At the county fair, a pilot gave rides in his helicopter. He'd begged and begged to have a ride, but Dad wouldn't do it. Phil knew he had some money. He'd just seen a drug deal between his dad and a dealer. Saw it all the time. But Dad would never let him have a ride. Said it was dangerous. Phil had stood there, refusing to move until it became dark and they quit giving rides. Take-off. Landing. The sound of that engine. Huge blades turning. The wind on his face. Smell of the fuel.

Just one ride. But no.

Phil pushed the door farther open, and this time it didn't squeak.

He stepped out and pushed the door closed fast until he caught it before it slammed. Now he knew. Shut it fast and it didn't make a noise.

A car full of kids slowly turned the corner past the bank. Same kids as at the front of the store. They seemed quiet now.

He slipped against the building wall.

The cop car might be right behind them.

Damn! There he was.

He had to get out of there.

Back in the basement. He ran through the rooms to where the dishes were, stepped and fell onto them. He sprawled over them, trying to get a balance, but the dishes kept sliding under him. Every time he put his hands down to push up, the dishes sliced into his flesh. He could barely see in the limited light, but red blood against white dishes was easy to see.

Damn! He left a trail.

Finally, he found his footing and raced upstairs. He ran toward the front windows again. The black cop pulled in front just as he got to the entrance door. Phil ran to the back of the store and found the steps up to the old opera house. These were easy to climb two at a time until he turned and ran up the last set. He'd been up here before, but things had changed.

Upstairs, panels blocked his way to the front stairs from the opera house. A maze of panels. They faced every which way, blocking his path. He ran around another one and froze.

A huge Frankensteinian monster roared and grabbed at him. The eyes and mouth lit up.

A little girl scream erupted from Phil's throat.

Damn! If anyone had entered the building, he'd be toast.

And worst of all, he'd peed himself.

All down his leg, his shoe, and onto the floor.

Back in his squad car, Mark reported to Chantelle. "Somebody broke into the antique store. Kids saw a man sitting in the chair in the window."

"In the chair?" Chantelle started to laugh, but must have realized he was serious. "Okay. He what?"

"I'm driving around to the back. The front seems secure." He turned down the alley behind the bank. "Thanks."

Seemed quiet.

Phone buzzed again.

Mom.

Again.

Not now.

He let it go. He needed to check the building.

She probably wanted to share something from her Bible study group. They always prayed for him and the department. He was definitely thankful, but—

Buzzed again.

Damn!

He tapped it. "Hi Mom. Hey, just following up on a... doing a building check, so could we talk tomorrow?"

"I just wanted to tell you I love you and I am proud of you. That's all, Son."

His head dropped to his chest, hand fell to his thigh, phone still on. He raised it to his mouth again. "Mom. Thank you. So much."

"You're welcome. Now I know you have to go. Love you, Mark." She tapped off before he could reply.

"Love you, Mom." He hoped she heard him. Somehow.

Wasn't life like that? When you thought you didn't have

time, someone or something interrupted with a gift or a precious word, and everything changed.

Deep breath.

Back to work.

Nothing. All quiet.

"Hey, Mark." Guy radioed in. "I'm out front. Seems quiet." He started to laugh. "Are you sure they saw somebody?"

"They all saw him. One, two, three—five kids! Especially one girl in the back. She said he moved his leg and smiled at her." Mark parked, got out, and flicked on his flashlight and checked the back of the store. "Getting out to check the back. The other girl riding in the back seat saw him, too. The kids were really loud and excited, but all seemed to agree there was a guy, in the chair, in the window."

"Okay. It might just be their imagination." Guy's car beeped. He stepped out, too. "I'll check the front."

Somebody screamed. A woman?

"Did you hear that?" Guy jumped back into his car. "Calling for backup."

"Yeah! Sounded like a girl screaming." Mark pulled his gun and ran to the back of the store. Door unlocked. Was it always unlocked? Small-town businesses sometimes relaxed their security. He slipped inside and listened.

Nothing. A morgue. Stepped outside. Listened. Quiet.

"Guy. You heard it too, right? Sounded like a girl from somewhere in the building."

"Yep. All locked up here in front though."

"It's all quiet out back. The back door is unlocked." Mark slipped back inside. "Going to have a look inside." Shuffle footsteps upstairs. "Guy. Hearing footsteps upstairs. We need to check it out."

"On my way."

Mark checked the entrance hall. Door to the left. Pushed it open, his hand stretched out in front of him, holding his gun and flashlight. The light beam led the way. Every foot of the room illuminated. Nobody there. Old quilts on the floor. Trash across the room. He picked up the quilts and sniffed. Mold and whiskey. Whiskey bottle under the trash.

Homesteader. Squatter.

Maybe gone.

Phil?

Back in the hallway. Door to the right. Door facing him.

Guy entered the building behind Mark.

Mark motioned with his flashlight that Guy needed to take the door on the right. Mark pushed the door facing him open. A room the same size as the whiskey room. Already named it. Brick wall. Wood stacked beside the wall. Old table and chairs.

Every inch.

Nobody there.

Through the next door. Another room that must face the street, upstairs. Brick walls. Stacks of boxes. Their probable future inventory made it difficult to search. Open to the right, where he met Guy pushing through a door. He shook his head.

More boxes and furniture.

Through an opening to the right.

Mark led to the next room, shining his light on what would be toward the street and lost his footing. What was all over the floor?

If it hadn't been for Guy catching him from behind, his flashlight in his hand, he'd have gone down on boxes and piles of broken dishes.

He stepped around the mess, illuminating the broken vintage dishes—all in pieces. "Dang." Oops. Voices would carry in this quiet building. He looked up at Guy and nodded thanks.

Guy leaned down. His flashlight illuminated what looked like bright red blood against the mostly white dishes.

There was so much Mark could say right now. That was

blood. It was fresh blood. They needed to have it analyzed. But needed to search out the building, find the screamer.

They edged around the boxes and dinnerware on the floor and tip-toed up the steps. If the scream had come from this store, they might bump into the woman.

Or ghost.

Or Phil.

Guy tapped on a light switch and shook his head. Yeah.

This was like finding a needle in … a … worse than a haystack. He and Guy had worked together for so long, they didn't have to point or nod. One man covered while the other opened doors or cupboards, all the while checking their perimeter. Then they might reverse places.

Main room—check.

Mark backed into the middle room, but bumped against something very substantial. He turned. A huge, painted pillar—a row of them—divided the two rooms. Amazing. Not wood. Had to be cast iron.

Guy's wide eyes—even in the dim light—alluded to his surprise.

Mark nodded.

Nobody here. Nothing. But he knew he had heard footsteps above when he was downstairs in the basement. He nodded his head toward the ceiling.

Guy nodded.

Mark led the way. Stairway to upstairs, the grand Opera House, itself, was in the back of the store, through another old door. You could never depend on an old door to open quietly.

This one didn't either. A faint growl, perfect for when they had Monster Bashes for Halloween. He opened it as slowly as he could. He swore that he'd oil every damn door in Osceola tomorrow. It still growled.

Up the stairs, one step at a time—they all creaked and

groaned, but Mark knew where he was going, from his investigation a while back.

They spread out, each taking a different side of the immense room. Opera House alright. Guy took the steps up to the balcony —still under renovations. Mark continued across the floor to the front of the building. His flashlight reflected yellow eyes from Halloween paintings on panels and he gasped.

"You okay?" Guy used his radio.

"Yeah. I found the possible reason for the scream."

They had employed him as security during the owner's yearly Halloween Monster House event. The guy was creative in setting up panels and creating monsters with art and music.

The monster, he remembered.

Crash!

That came from upstairs.

"Guy?" Mark yelled. Too late, he remembered to be quiet.

Mark ran as fast as the dark would allow and stopped short. HIs flashlight revealed Guy's leg hanging through the wooden boards in the ceiling.

Bang! A door slammed downstairs.

A muffled voice yelled from above. "Go! Go! I'm okay."

Mark tripped as he switched gears and ran to the stairway, jumping down two or three steps at a time, until he reached the street level.

The door swung wide.

He ran out to the sidewalk, faced right, then left.

Gone.

CHAPTER 15

Phil tried to calm his breathing after running across the street from the antique store. He leaned over, his hands on his knees. Too many days and nights in the basement had taken its toll. Too many years of hard drinking and playing were probably the real culprit.

He knew those deputies had heard that door slam. Heard him scream. They were sure to run out and catch him immediately. But he'd had time to run across the street to the courthouse.

Bam! The door slammed against the antique store building and swung almost closed again. One cop burst out the door and ran onto the sidewalk.

Damn! Phil jumped behind some bushes against the court-house building and ducked. Ow. Ow. Ow. Those smelly old quilts had been better than rocks and it was chilly out, but the run might have warmed him. Glad to be out of that basement. Smelled dirt, or was that his own body odor? Or the pee? His pants were wet, all the way down that leg.

The cops split—one ran one way, to Phil's left, down the sidewalk in front of the bank. The other jumped into the street by the squad car, to Phil's right—still parked in front of the antique store—searching under and around it. He limped to the back end of the car.

Phil held his breath. They were making noise so they probably couldn't hear him gasping for breath. It was like watching a movie. Action. But the criminal they were chasing was him.

The street was fairly dark. Only the uniform of the black cop was visible, bending and running.

They'd find him.

What difference did anything make? He was on his way to prison.

The cop by the car shone his flashlight toward the wall of the courthouse where Phil hid. Not good. Don't move. Don't breathe. The other one ran past the front of the courthouse. No way his flashlight didn't pick up Phil's shoes or shirt. Something.

A car drove down the street, stopping right in front of the black cop.

Heh. The car jerked forward, then stopped, and the driver opened his window. "Hey! Whatchu up to tonight?" Pretty drunk.

"Move along. Police business. Move away."

Phil took his chance and ran around the building.

"Stop! Police! Halt!"

Phil raced across the street, ducked, and crouched between the cars and trucks parked alongside the old lumber yard. No. He needed to change course. Not going there. Those cops would look there first. He ran in front of the building, around to the right side, and slammed into a round roof building. Nowhere to go, but between the buildings. Slowed him down, as he stumbled along the channel between. His shoes pounded against the metal buildings. He was toast. They'd hear him for sure.

The cops were on the other side, opening and closing doors on the old cars and trucks parked there. Created time for Phil to get away.

Good call, Daynton. He didn't always make the right choice.

Behind the building, darkness stopped him. Hit him like a brick wall. It was as solid as when the pickup he had been driving rammed into Katty's car weeks ago. He struggled to find his way until he heard the cops hit what had to be the water tower. He tripped over an embankment behind the water tower, fell and cracked his knees on a pipe or something. Not now. He stretched his legs and started again, only to trip into an old tractor or piece of equipment.

Breathing. Was that his own or the cop's?

He limped down the hill toward the implement dealership.

This was familiar. He used to bribe an employee with booze to let Lex and him park the old Buick behind their building, under some trees. Almost like home. Almost.

Phil slipped in among the trees behind a house and stopped. Hard to quietly calm his breathing. His chest wanted to burst. Ears were ringing.

There they were—headed to the convenience store.

Phil's lucky break. He headed up the street, under cover of trees and bushes and cars. Cops were running one way—he'd run the other way—to Katty's trailer.

Phil could feel the world finally turning his way. He'd get to the trailer, deal with Katty however he had to, and do what he'd tried to do for months—get his daughter. The faster he ran, the more he sensed his purpose was coming to completion. It would finally work out. He'd finally have Bea all to himself. This was the moment.

Energy kicked in the last few blocks. Lights were on in the trailer. A dog barked. No. If the owners had tied the dog up, Phil would be ok. Barking was closer. Claws clicked on concrete. Another dog barked, rattling a kennel. Street lights gave an advantage. Barking grew louder. The first dog engaged with the one in the dog kennel.

Phil could have been in the middle of that.

He kept on running from tree to tree, pausing to hide at each one. The light was brighter.

Almost there.

Mission almost accomplished.

A car engine gunned up the hill behind him.

The deputy.

Damn!

No!

Phil collapsed next to a mailbox almost hidden within overgrown trees. He pounded the ground.

Damn the dogs!

Damn the cops!

He headed back down the street the way he'd come, only on the opposite side of the street. Get away while the cop is busy. He looked back. The cop had knocked on the door and Katty was talking to him.

Run! While the coast is ...

Another cop car drove up the street.

Dogs barked again.

Hide.

All of this running, this hiding—all hardly prolonged his freedom. He knew he'd end up in prison this time. The odds were not in his favor.

He slowed by the implement dealership. No traffic.

Still had his gun. He crossed the highway to the park. This wouldn't end well—for him or anyone trying to capture him—for anyone who tried to get in his way. His chest wanted to burst as he tried to catch his breath, but anger swelled even stronger.

Whatever it would take to get his daughter.

CHAPTER 16

Katty yawned and stretched. Day off. She knew what she *should* do today. Clean. Scrub. Dust. Pick up the dirty clothes lying all around and take them to the laundromat. She hated going there. It was always clean. The lady who managed it was nice. But every time Katty went there, she had to wait for machines—both washers and driers.

And it seemed every time the manager left—either to go home, do errands, or go in the back room to do maintenance and clean—guys would come in with their laundry basket all packed with laundry and swap drugs. They literally dropped the basket to the floor, dug through the clothes, and held up their package, never getting caught. They'd glance over at Katty, like she was part of the deal, or like we'll keep your secrets if you don't blab about ours.

Did she have a sign on her back that said "Stupid" or "Sucker?"

She should tell Mark. Super nice of him to come over last night. Phil might have been close by or long gone. She shivered. Even though somebody like Phil was all she deserved, she needed to know she and Bea were safe and free of running. Just the thought of Phil on the loose and headed her way brought tears to her eyes. Mark cared. She could see it in his green eyes, but she was worthless. Not someone who deserved a man like Mark.

Even if she never had anyone, just get Bea raised and she could die.

She blinked. Why did she let herself go to those thoughts? It never ended well. She always wanted booze. It was still early in the morning. But when had that stopped her?

Think about the day.

Yeah. Laundry.

Someday she'd have her own washer and dryer. Washer, at least. She could hang her clothes out on the line. A neighbor even used her clothesline in the winter. Katty had watched her, more than once, knock ice off her underwear and sheets.

Even now, that visual made Katty chuckle.

Time to get up. The day almost felt normal. Katty stopped. Normal? What was that like? She'd watched the nurses at Hillcrest live out their drama. Or at least live out their life: kids, husbands, jobs, boyfriends. Those nurses did everything for some residents—even wiped their butts.

Katty almost gagged. No way she would ever do that for anyone except Bea when she was a baby. Oh, now she could if Bea had an accident. But nobody else. She wouldn't do that for even Clarence. Not Mrs. T. Never Harold.

But those nurses did it every day. For every person there.

Even then, Katty had overheard squabbles between the nurses—one side or the other—both sides, sometimes. "I'll for work for you Tuesday, if you take my tomorrow." Then, "You never pick up my day. I end up just taking your hours. No!"

Humph! Both mad, they would cross their arms over their chests and walk away in a huff.

Was that their normal?

Katty never had to fill in for anyone. She could come and go from Hillcrest as she pleased. She could sleep in if she wanted. Of course, most of those mornings, she was hungover, so technically, she'd been late for work and not just free.

Free, like today.

There were only a few boxes left to dig through. She'd thrown a ton away with Clarence's permission. Filed a bunch he wanted to keep. Organized every paper, each notebook. She was pretty good at organization.

She glanced at her bedroom.

Well … she was good at it with papers and filing.

So, back to her normal.

Drag out of bed. Feed Bea. Search for a bottle behind the veggie canned goods. Drink.

Dang. That all needed to change. She rolled onto her back and listed on her fingers. Cook better. Read to Bea more. Save some money.

Yeah.

She sat up. Felt pretty good. Didn't feel woozy or dizzy. Stomach might even take some Cheerios with Bea. Maybe.

She walked down the hall to the bathroom, and when she finished, she shivered. Was it getting colder outside? It was almost time to start up her furnace soon. She always put it off as long as possible. She hated paying those heating bills.

Looking into the mirror wasn't too hard today, either. Hair was still in a bun and messy, but wasn't that the style? Even in fashion magazines. It was rare that Katty let herself look into the eyes reflected there in the mirror. Those eyes told too many secrets, and she didn't want to face those. Ever. But today. Those eyes weren't accusing. They weren't angry. They appeared hopeful.

Yeah. Back to the list.

Breakfast. Maybe she'd see if they had any eggs. Scrambled eggs sounded good. Convince Bea. Spaghetti had worked last night. Even if it was canned. It was a meal, which was more than most nights. Scrambled eggs and … did they have any bread for toast? That sounded good.

Probably not.

In the kitchen, Bea was up watching Daryl & Dumpty. Of course she was up. She had an internal device that chirped when her favorite TV show was on. Katty stood and watched for a minute, but the images she had painted on the walls began to float toward her. That tree waved at her. A branch moved to the music from the TV. Eyes blinked.

Ooo. Her stomach started doing flip-flops.

No. Not today. Ignore it.

"Bea, you want cereal for breakfast?"

No answer.

Grrr.

Try again. "Bea, do you want chocolate for breakfast?"

"What?" Bea's head popped up, and she turned. "Yes. Chocolate for breakfast sounds good, Mommy."

Heh. "Oh, did I say chocolate? I meant Cheerios. Sorry. Do you want cereal for breakfast?" Katty checked the refrigerator. "We have milk." No eggs. She had been hallucinating. Dreaming. Why didn't she ever buy eggs? Right. Bea wouldn't eat them: not scrambled, not fried, not hard-boiled. Well, she herself wouldn't eat them that way either. Gross.

"Mommy. You tricked me."

"I know. I'm sorry."

The paintings on the walls kept distracting her. Did the tree leaves and limbs seemed to blow in a breeze? What was happening to her? She felt better before, when she first woke up, but now not so much.

She needed to go buy more paint and paint over the entire wall—all of them. Hide those babies and trees and eyes. These eyes accused. So different from her own eyes in the mirror earlier. Her own eyes had always been accusing before. But not earlier. Why were the babies accusing now?

Help.

She was going crazy. That's right. She was crazy.

"Hey Bea, let's eat and go buy more paint. Okay?" Katty poured cereal into Bea's favorite bowl. Spoon ready. Her own bowl held less cereal, but why take chances on wasting it if she threw it up? Flushing good food down the toilet was not a good habit. Of course, buying more shooters was not a good habit either.

Bea slid into her chair and patted her cereal, checking for the right amount. "More paint?"

Katty shook her head. This kid. Had to be enough cereal in her bowl. It had to fill to that green line. "Yes, more paint." Gonna paint over that mess on the walls. She poured the milk in Bea's first, then a little in her bowl. A little at a time. "So eat up and get dressed. Okay?"

Katty scooped a small bite into her mouth.

Bea dove in. Munch, munch, crunch. She slurped the milk. Some dripped onto the table. She wiped her mouth with the back of her hand. Another bite.

Katty belched. Breathe.

"It's good, Mommy. Try yours."

Katty stood and took her bowl with her to the sink. "Yeah. I'm almost done." She faked a spoonful to her mouth but blew out a breath. Another fake bite—same thing. She rinsed the bowl and spoon, then loaded them into the dishwasher.

"You're fast, Mommy." Bea dropped her spoon to the table and slurped her milk.

"Well, I started before you did." Deep breath. "You're like a baby kitty drinking milk from her bowl."

"Meow." Bea licked her spoon. "Meow."

Katty laughed in spite of herself. Felt good to laugh. "Let's get dressed and go get paint." Get that wall painted over before supper so the tree and babies, the eyes, could no longer haunt her.

"Are we going to paint your room now, Mommy?" Bea headed to the hallway, to her room.

Katty followed her and popped Bea's bottom. "Maybe. Maybe we'll paint the car."

Bea turned. "We can?"

Oh no.

As usual, Katty said too much. "Well, we'll see. First the house. Then our car."

Fat chance.

CHAPTER 17

Katty breathed in.

No TV. No music. No screaming or crying. The peace, the quiet, was almost tangible. Oh, to eat it, or drink it in. Buy it at the grocery store. Bea had her favorite cereal. Katty would buy seventeen boxes of Peace and Quiet. All for herself.

She sat at the kitchen table with paper and a pen, drawing lines. Just lines. Enjoying the mystery of watching lines appear on her paper. Yes, her hand held the pen and moved it along on the paper, but it was magical how lines and figures seemed to appear. Strange, but satisfying. She remembered when she discovered that, before Mom broke all of her pencils and crayons. Just doodling and separating herself and her hand from the lines as they appeared. Magical then. Magical now.

She sat back and a sigh released from deep within her.

Bea sat at the table with her. That kid was always putting strange colors together in her drawings and they always worked. Colors like orange and pink. Purple and brown. The peacock Bea was coloring was beautiful. She had drawn it first and the colors she was using on it blended. They shouldn't have.

Katty almost instantly asked herself, why not? Why

shouldn't those colors all go together beautifully? Why couldn't she or Bea, or anyone else, be able to create beautiful color combinations that might cause someone to pause and enjoy. Enjoy them like Katty was now. She almost forgot to draw her own lines. Watching Bea was so satisfying. Mesmerizing.

Thinking about colors reminded her of the cans of paint they'd bought earlier. All stacked up against the wall. Bea had picked orange and blue. Katty had chosen black, brown, and green.

Katty glanced up at the walls. She could barely let herself look for very long, before the images of the tree began to float and wave and she either had to shut her eyes or leave. She'd been drinking so long that the booze must have messed up her brain cells.

That was it.

She willed herself to go back to the good feelings she had just experienced. Go to Bea's beautiful pictures of the peacock and her strange color combinations. She glanced out the window —Mrs. Nosy still had two plants hanging from the deck posts— strange combination of hot pink and purple.

God did that. God made those.

Bea's colors.

God's colors.

Katty sighed.

God created with every color. Wait. He *created* every color, probably.

She walked to the window. The plants swung in a light breeze. The pots turned and twisted as the wind blew. Swinging. Back and forth. Back and forth.

"Mommy?"

Katty couldn't answer. The swinging plants held her in their power. Back and forth. Back and forth.

"Mommy?"

Katty shook her head and closed her eyes.

She opened them again—or so she thought. A storm must be moving in. Instead of seeing the swinging plants, all Katty could see was fog between the trailers. Deep, dense fog. White air. She could barely see Mrs. Nosy's trailer. The doors and windows looked the same—she couldn't tell which was which—even though she knew. The plants still moved—swirling and beckoning—almost taunting her. Nothing else was visible. No trees or flowers or bushes.

Even the inside of the window in her own trailer was foggy. The window jam was barely visible. What was happening? Did she have a window open? Or worse, was one broken? Fall chill was in the air. She must have left one open, or God forbid, had she broken one on a drunken binge?

She barely turned into the trailer, toward the table where Bea was sitting.

But Bea wasn't there anymore.

Mom was.

Gasp.

Katty shuddered and backed away.

Mom waved her finger at Katty, beckoning her to come near.

No. Never!

She bumped into the window and shuddered. Chills traveled up her arms. Her whole body felt like Mom had trapped it into a grocery store cooler. Or in a morgue walk-in. Tremors shook her. The entire room had become a freezer. Frost crackled in the air, from the cabinets, the ceiling light.

The only time she'd been this cold was when Mom had shut her outside during a blizzard because she had accidentally slammed her finger in the car door. They had been to where they got free cheese and other foods. Lots to unload. Katty had caught a bag handle on the inside car door handle. When she saw it was caught, she had already pushed the car door closed, but reached in to free the bag. She would have been in so much trouble if she'd ruined the cheese.

Katty could still feel her finger throbbing, even now.

Mom had grabbed the bags, run inside, and locked the door. Katty pounded on the door, crying. Her finger bled against the unpainted wood. Snow swirled around her. Mom screamed from inside. "Stop your crying or I won't let you in!"

Finally, a neighbor had run out in her boots and coat to see what was going on. Shamed Mom into letting Katty in.

That cold invaded every cell of her body, even now. Never to warm up. She couldn't stand to be cold.

"Katty." Mom yelled her name from the table—crayons rolling off to the floor and papers flying—commanding her. "Come here, you little brat." She started to get up off the chair. "Katty."

"No." Katty stumbled against the wall, right in front of the tree she'd painted there. "Stay away." Leaves and branches reached out from behind her, slithering through her hair and winding around her body, clinging to her T-shirt..

"Mommy?"

No! Not the babies, too.

"Mommy!"

Fog began to clear. Katty blinked. Kitchen walls. No more frost.

Bea stood where Mom had sat.

Bea clapped her hands in front of Katty's face. She jumped up and down, waving her hands. "Mommy! Where'd you go? Please come back. You're scaring me." Tears ran down Bea's cheeks. Her face was flushed. "Why won't you answer me? Why'd you tell me to stay away?"

Katty collapsed on the sofa. How long had she been in that awful place?

Visuals of Mom morphed over Bea.

Awful, awful.

Bea wasn't Mom, or vice versa.

Bea was pure, sweet, innocent. Ornery but innocent.

Mom was evil. Every pore of her body oozed out evil, and she directed most of it at Katty.

Bea stepped toward Katty, clearly unsure. Uncertain if this was Good Mommy, or Bad Mommy.

"Oh God, help." Katty could feel the evil dissipate. "Bea." She held out her hands to Bea.

Bea was still unsure, but took a step closer. "Why'd you yell stay away?"

Katty slumped. How could she tell Bea what she'd just seen? What could she say to her? This was totally different from her drunken dreams or nightmares. It was too real. She glanced at the wall—the tree. How on earth had the tree come alive?

"Bea, I… it was like a dream … a scary dream." Katty covered her mouth with her hands. "My mom, I saw her."

Bea looked behind her. "Is she still here?"

Katty shook her head. "No. No. Thank God." That was so strange. The evil had been real. Her mom had been real. The cold had been real. She rubbed her arms. But as soon as the evil disappeared, she felt better, but she felt … God. Blinking back tears again, she held out her hands to Bea.

Bea slowly stepped into Katty's arms.

The warmth. The purity of this child—her child—even though Bea had been conceived in … by her and Phil.

God, help.

But somehow, yes, God. This little girl, this child, was pure —in spite of her parents.

A deep sigh grew within Katty and forced its way out.

Bea sighed at the same time.

Katty chuckled and felt Bea giggle against her chest.

"We breathed at the same time." Bea drew back and looked into Katty's eyes. "Mommy. You're back?"

A sense of peace and strength dropped in where the fear and evil had been. A visual of Mrs. T popped into Katty's mind. Was she praying? Mrs. T always prayed.

Katty nodded. "Yes, Bea." She closed her eyes for a second, then opened them. Bea's wide eyes still on hers. "I'm back." She tapped Bea's nose. "I think Mrs. T is praying for us."

Bea nodded. "She prays all the time for us. She teaches me, too, Mommy. Like this." She backed away and folded her hands. "She says I don't have to close my eyes. I keep them open to see the angels."

"The what?" Katty grinned. "The angels?"

But Bea was serious, nodding. "Yes. I can see them."

No words. This kid. Seeing angels.

CHAPTER 18

Bea's tummy growled. Ice cream at Hillcrest hadn't lasted very long. She had begged for more and even gotten her way. Bea had learned that when Mommy was working, it was easy to get what she wanted. And she always wanted ice cream.

Bea was starving.

That was okay. She had a plan.

She had her own little system. Every time she had cereal, she rinsed the bowl, and put it in her own special spot behind the cereal boxes. That way, she didn't have to bother Mommy.

Spoons were easy—just lick them off and put them back in the drawer.

She knelt and opened the lower cupboard door, pulled out the Cheerios box, and reached for the cereal bowl. Art supplies and toys and paper litter piled high on the table. She pushed some aside, set her bowl down, and poured her cereal.

"Mommy?" Bea munched on a piece that fell on the table. "You want some?"

No answer. Guess not.

Bea tamped down the Cheerios in her bowl with the back of her spoon, making the surface flat. Back to the box. She needed just a little more—until it filled to the green line on the bowl. The line must have been painted there to stop little kids from wasting too much cereal. Mommy always worried about wasting food.

Bea dug into the box and fished out another handful. Just right. "Mommy, I need the milk." She patted the cereal again—perfectly flat.

No answer, again.

"Mommy?"

Mommy sucked in a deep breath and leaned forward. "Please? Say please, Bea." She slowly dragged to her feet, stumbled to the kitchen, and opened the refrigerator. "Mind your manners."

"Please? Please, can I have the milk?" Bea straightened in her chair and folded her hands into a church. "And this is the steeple—"

"Here, Bea." Mommy stumbled, but caught herself just before she fell into the refrigerator. "Heresh the milk for your cereal." She grabbed the gallon of milk and steadied herself before walking to the table. "And don't use too mush. We can't go to the store until tomorrow… ran out of… money."

Bea wiggled her fingers. Lots of people in this church.

Mommy started to walk to the table with the milk, but stopped.

Bea looked up. Mommy's face looked funny. "Mommy?"

Mommy belched. Loud. She wiped her mouth with the back of her hand, standing as still as Bea was right now. She sucked in a breath, then blew it out so slow that Bea couldn't tell when she took another breath.

"Mommy."

Mommy shook her point finger at Bea, hard. "Not now, Bea!" Her voice sounded different. It was loud and sputtery. Words were funny.

"Don't you feel good, Mommy?"

Mommy burped again, holding the back of one hand over her mouth, her finger pointed in Bea's face. The milk jug dangled from the other hand.

Bea blinked. She hadn't seen Mommy do that since—

Mommy took a step toward the table, the milk still in her hand, her face all puffy like the pet frog Bea had captured during the summer. Every time the frog's face had puffed up like that, it had croaked.

Mommy swallowed hard and took another step. And another. She was just about to the table when her eyes got big, and she burped, but this time, stuff came out of her mouth. She dropped the milk, the plastic jug cracked when it hit the floor, and milk chugged out everywhere.

Bea screamed. "Mommy! The milk!"

Only Mommy didn't hear.

Mommy rushed to the kitchen sink and puked in it. Coughed and sputtered.

The milk ran across the floor to the cupboards. Just like videos on TV of the ocean and how it seemed to race to the sandy beach. The milk flowed under Bea's chair and then under the table—just like the ocean. Bea clapped her hands over her mouth and raised her feet to her chair. "Mommy, the milk is …"

As soon as Mommy raised her head, her feet slipped on the milk, and she fell. She crawled on her knees through the mess to where Bea sat huddled on her chair, picked up the empty plastic jug and swung it at Bea.

Only she missed.

Bea stood on her chair and jumped to the next chair and the next.

Mommy slipped on the floor again and rolled onto her back, all the time pointing at Bea. "You little bi…! You are in so much trouble!"

She sat up. Mommy seemed to wake up, like she had been

asleep, dreaming. She blinked as she looked at the floor, then at Bea.

Bea sat huddled on the chair, watching. Her body was shaking—all tingly. She didn't remember being this scared in a long time. She glanced toward the windows, then quickly back to Mommy. Where was Clarence?

This Mommy was Bad Mommy. Why was she back?

Mommy belched again, her hand at her mouth.

Bea remembered.

She silently slipped from chair to chair, down the hallway to Mommy's room and down under the rocker, her thumb in her mouth.

Jerahmael watched as Bea hopped from chair to chair, and as she ran down the hall. His job was to stay with her, watch over her, protect her, minister to her from Father's heart.

If he had been human, he would have picked her up and taken her to Clarence.

But he wasn't human. He was an angel, and even though angels see everything and know the kingdom intimately, they cannot interfere with Earthly situations. Especially when Father dictates that the angels are to draw back. In those instances, they know Father has a plan for the human to rise, turn to Him. Draw strength from the Lord and fight the battle.

If the human chose to.

If humans only knew, the war had been fought and won already.

Before Jerahmael even got to the bedroom, he knew where Bea would be.

Under that old rocker, where she had spent countless hours hiding, crying, finally falling asleep—exhausted.

And there she was.

She hadn't taken the time to drape the chair with the quilt as she might have in the past, but she pushed pillows underneath and around so she was invisible.

He leaned over to look into her face.

Pillows didn't hide things from angels.

She was trembling, her thumb in her mouth, eyes wide and wild.

This tiny, tiny being whom he'd had the job of keeping track of ever since she'd been born.

Born to Katty on that day over four years ago.

Both humans had been all alone at the time of the birth.

This child had come into Earth's atmosphere to a druggie mama who had been beaten, traumatized and scarred. But to a mamma who believed that something in this child was worth keeping, holding onto and giving birth to alone.

That she was worth saving.

She had swaddled the baby in towels—sweaty and in pain herself.

All alone.

Just the two of them.

Jerahmael sat right beside Bea, right beside her little hiding place and watched, his hand on the child's back.

Bad Mommy *was* back.

The mommy who had fought so hard to hide this baby from the murdering hands of her earthly father was now putting fear into Bea's heart … again.

CHAPTER 19

"Jesus loves me ..." Bea leaned back to inspect her drawing. Songs from time with Mrs. T always made her feel better.

"Mr. Angel, sing with me." She cocked her head up. He was so tall, she had to lean back to look into his eyes. "Please?"

She knew the please word would make him feel good. "Jesus loves me."

He slowly smiled. She could tell he wanted to sing. He had before, when she had been hiding under the rocker. She'd been crying because Bad Mommy was back. He had sung a song to her. So soft. He'd called it a lull-lull, a lullaby.

He smiled at her now.

She bounced her head with the words. "Jesus loves me, this I know. Sing."

Her angel cocked his head back and forth along with her singing. Smiling. He kept looking at the door.

"It's just a car driving on the street." She swung her legs. "For the Bible tells me so." She giggled. "Mrs. T tells me so, too."

Angel straightened.

Bea watched him. She glanced down the hall toward the

bedrooms. Mommy was reading her Bible, so Bea needed to keep coloring and not bother her.

Quiet.

"Does Mommy know you're my angel?" She picked up her paper and studied it. "Does she have an angel?"

She looked at him. He never answered her questions. Mommy always told her to answer. Especially when she was mad. She'd yell, "Answer me!"

Guess angels didn't have to answer questions.

She reached for the red color. The heart had to be red. Or pink. She fiddled with the pink crayon, then chose the red one, and colored in the heart.

She leaned back again.

Perfect. She hummed the tune, kicking her feet to the beat.

Well, she'd missed a line there. Where was that black pen Clarence had given her? It was like a skinny marker. A few little flowers would cover the missed line.

There.

She tapped the black pen on the table as she traced the flowers with her finger.

A deep breath escaped out of her mouth. It had come from deep in her tummy. She knew it—she was sure. Didn't know how. She just knew it made her feel better.

She glanced at the floor, under the table, at the kitchen cupboards. Most of the milk mess was cleaned up. A long drip was still running down the cupboard door where the big pots were.

Another deep breath. Angel smiled. He held up his sword, looking toward the door.

She looked at the door, then at him. No milk dripped down the door. Maybe when she finished this drawing, she'd go over and wipe up that drip on the cupboard door.

For Mommy.

She glanced down the hall again. It made Mommy feel better when she read her Bible. That's what Mrs. T always said, too.

"It'll make you feel good, Bea." Bea could hear Mrs. T's soft voice even now.

Bea needed a Bible. Her own Bible.

Knock. knock.

Bea's head bounced up from her coloring.

Pound. Pound.

A man's voice shook her. "We're here, little Katty. We're here."

Angel had his stick out.

She looked at him and back to the door.

She ran to the window and peeked out. Mommy got mad whenever she let somebody into the trailer without asking her or telling her who it was. A pickup and a car were beside Mommy's car.

This guy sounded big and loud.

And scary.

The doorknob wiggled.

Bea blinked. Sword—Mrs. T called it a sword. Angel had his sword out and pointed at the door.

Bea was sure it was locked. Mommy had done that just before going to her bedroom to read her Bible. Bea remembered because Mommy had said it as she pointed at the doorknob.

The knob wiggled again.

Bea tip-toed closer to hear.

Click.

The knob turned, and the door opened.

Three big, big men stood outside the door on the deck, grinning. "Looky here. We got a live one." He reached for Bea.

Spit caught in her throat as she sucked in air. Her insides scwiggled and trembled. Her feet wouldn't move.

He stepped inside the door.

"Eee!" She ducked and ran.

"Yep. She's a live one, alright. Cute too."

He clomped inside the living room. His big boots made the floor sound funny. Bea had climbed under the trailer once. A side panel had fallen off.

It was all musty and empty under there. And scary.

"Mommy?"

The big man laughed. "Yeah. Call for Mommy, little girl. Go get your mommy."

His voice was big and loud, but there was something else.

Even when he still stood way over by the doorway, he was too close.

———

"Mommy, Mommy!" Bea burst into the bedroom, tripped on the runner of the rocking chair and fell at Katty's feet.

"Bea!" Katty picked her up and felt her head. She hoped Bea's head didn't hurt as bad as her own. Why was she doing this to herself again? Why was she drinking? She cuddled Bea on her lap and started to rock her back and forth, but stopped. "You okay?" She swallowed it down. "You hurt yourself?"

"Mommy." Bea shoved Katty's hand away. "There are bad guys at the door."

"Bad guys." Katty stood, steadied herself against the bed, tipping over the pile of folded laundry. "What bad guys?"

A voice boomed from the hall. "Hey, my Katty girl!" A man appeared in the bedroom doorway.

Kathy froze. "Wh-what are you doing in here? Get out!" She shivered. Took a step toward him, then stopped, tried to slow her breathing. "You have no right to be in here." She shoved Bea behind her and took another step toward the man, steadying herself at the dresser.

"You don't remember me, do ya?" He chuckled seductively, almost a growl. He winked, raised his bushy eyebrows, and held out his hands toward her. "It's Daniel, your old buddy. Par-tay." He swayed his hips from side to side. "We used to get sloshed together … and," he reached for her arm, his eyes on Bea, "other stuff. We heard you was back in the game … like … in the game." He pretended to hold a bottle to his lips.

She sidestepped his reach. "H-how would you … what do you mean, back in the game?" Stop stuttering. "I'm not—"

Daniel stepped aside to let another guy peek into the bedroom.

Shit! The cashier from the convenience store. The one who sold her two $0.99 cent shooters for twenty bucks, but at the same time, saved her life. She'd needed a drink so badly.

Gag. She'd only had hot flashes once—after she'd had Bea— but her face felt like a fire burned inside. She backed away, bumping Bea back at the same time. How many steps would it take to get past him and through the doorway?

He moved to where she was planning to step, and another man appeared behind them.

"Mommy?" Bea pulled on Katty's T-shirt.

Katty could feel Bea's little fingers trembling against her leg. God help.

The men had them blocked in. Trapped.

The old Katty kicked in. "Well, yeah, I remember you." She swiveled her hips. Yeah. Why wouldn't she? This is all she'd ever be. "Why wouldn't I remember someone as … memorable as you are … big man of God?"

What? Where had that come from?

He burst out laughing, beer belly bouncing up and down. "Man of Go …" He gasped and roared out again. Slapped his leg. "Hell, not quite." He stopped. "Looks like you been doing alright for yourself." He pointed behind him at the trailer. "A few upgrades, I see." He held out his hand, eyebrows bouncing up and down again. "You got some money?"

Katty squirmed. Took a step to the side, shoving Bea along

behind her. "Uh. This old thing? Same old trailer. Same old furniture."

He edged her off. "Naw. Somethin's different. You upgraded some things. You got yourself a sugar daddy?" He stared at her. "You look better than you used to, too. You working out?"

She felt for her phone. No phone. On the charger.

"Mommy?" Bea pinched Katty's leg. "Mommy, I gotta go."

"Oh. We keeping you from something?" He pulled his hands from his jeans pockets and held out a cigarette - homemade.

"Uh. No, I uh, … she has to pee." Something rose in her from somewhere because Katty stepped into the man and pushed him aside. "I gotta take her to the bathroom."

And get the phone off the charger.

He backed into the wall with his hands up. "Wow. No. No, you gotta be the momma and take care of your kiddo. Don't let me stop you."

Too easy. Something was up.

Katty skidded into the hallway. She burst into the bathroom, pushed Bea in front of her, and slammed the door behind them. Locked it.

"Mommy? Mommy, who are they?" Bea stood in front of the toilet and started to take her shorts down.

"What are you doing?" Katty unplugged the phone and dialed 911.

"I told you. I have to pee."

Come on, phone. Ring. "I thought …" She held her phone to her ear. "Yes. Hello? Yes. Some men broke into my home. Osceola, Nebraska. My daughter is with me. Please. Please send someone." She gave the address.

Bea finished and hopped off the toilet. "Mommy, why are they here? What do they want?"

"I don't know Bea." Katty leaned down to hug Bea. "Good timing to potty. We are staying in here until help comes."

Footsteps clomped to the door, and someone knocked. "Hey,

little woman. We will wait in the living room and have a great time. We brought your stuff." He pounded even harder.

"My stuff? I didn't order any stuff. I don't want any stuff. Just go away." She paused. "We have company coming anyway, so you gotta leave."

"Oh, little Katty. We remember the good times." He rubbed his hand along the door. "You never were a good liar."

Just that sound made her want to puke, gave her shivers.

"We can wait. We can hang out as long as it takes. You're our kind and we need to stick together."

Katty hesitated. Right. He didn't have a place to live. He'd been kicked out. Didn't pay his rent or his old lady booted him out.

Right.

So, she was the next free meal.

Bea jumped.

The door shook every time the man pounded on it.

"Mommy, he's breaking our door." Bea pointed to the top hinge where the door hooked onto the wall. "It's cracking." A screw popped out of the hinge. "Mommy!" She shrieked.

Something broke inside her. "Mommy, hold me. Mommy! Up me!"

She couldn't stop shaking. Inside, her tummy shook. Deep sobs broke out of her mouth. "Mommy, help! They're gonna get us! Jesus! Mommy!"

"Bea!" Mommy talked into her phone. "Yes. Come right away. Three men broke into my house!"

The men stomped past the door down the hall, their deep voices laughing.

Bea's crayons and paper. Her pictures! "Mommy my pictures! They'll take my pictures."

"Yes! Hurry! They've pounded our bathroom door in!" Mommy pushed her phone into her pocket and sat on the floor, her back against the door. She pulled Bea to her, holding her on her lap. It always felt safe when Mommy did that. Even when she'd been drinking. Sitting on her lap, all snuggled, Mommy's arms around her felt like the best place in the world. Even better than at Clarence's having ice cream.

In Mommy's lap or not, she couldn't stop crying.

Stomping.

Loud voices from outside.

Mommy held her tighter.

"Mommy?" Bea hiccuped. She didn't know why she whispered.

"Shh." Mommy covered Bea's head with her own. Whatever was going on outside, Mommy would take care of her.

No matter what.

CHAPTER 20

Mark shrugged his shoulders. "Sure. I'll go." He clicked off his computer. Took one last sip of coffee and stood.

Chantelle grinned. "Well, she's your girlfriend, right? Good excuse to see her."

He squinted and grinned. "Right. My girlfriend." It'd been a really long time since anyone had teased him about having a girlfriend. It'd been even longer since he'd really had one.

Kinda stopped him.

Was she? They hadn't even had a date. He'd given her a ticket, once, after the convenience store incident. He'd been dispatched to her trailer several times, after a neighbor had called in a complaint.

He grabbed his jacket. Dating must be different these days.

"Be careful." She nodded—almost to reinforce her words.

Odd. "I will." He started to the exit but turned to face her. "Thanks."

In the squad car, he slammed his door just before Guy rapped on his window. He opened it.

Guy leaned in. "I'll meet you there."

"Really? It's okay." Why were they sending two deputies?

"Sheriff seems to think you might need back-up. He heard Katty's call. He's in his office, so if we need him, he's ready. But he definitely said he wants me to go, too. Just a hunch he got when Katty called in. " He glanced at the building. "Chantelle has a bad feeling, too."

"Okay. Get in?" Mark started to move his hat from the passenger seat.

Guy shook his head. "I'll drive myself." He started to walk away, but turned. "Just a hunch from what Sheriff and Chantelle said."

Strange. Mark checked his memory. They all were aware that Mark had been to Katty's trailer many times to investigate complaints against her—both for *her* safety *and* Bea's. He never had any trouble—not once. Interesting. What had Chantelle and Sheriff heard?

Buzz.

Mom.

Always.

Always when he was busy or ready to go on shift. He started to silence the call and ignore it. But, what if … what if this was more than Mom being … Mom?

He tapped his phone. "Hi, Mom."

"Hi, son. Won't keep you, but something told me to call. You get it." Click.

She hung up?

Super weird. The air seemed charged—ready to ignite his entire world. His skin had goosebumps.

Guy backed out, waited for Mark to back out, and followed.

Mark hit his radio. "Hey Guy. Thanks for sticking around for this run." He turned right at the corner and barely stopped at the stop sign. Turned right again.

Guy was right behind him.

"Oh, sure. No problem. We have nothing going on right now at home, so … here I am."

Silence. Even from behind Mark, in the other car, Guy was grinning from ear to ear. "So … I see we're going to your girl-friend's place, right?"

They drove close together—in formation—almost with precision. Mark shook his head. "Dork. Really? Does everybody think she's my girlfriend? Do you all talk about this in the break room or the bathroom or over the radios, when I'm not around?"

Guy's laugh boomed over the radio. "Yup. We do." Another chuckle. "In all those places."

Mark had been no angel. In fact, when his uncle took him in and made him take responsibility for his own messes, he demanded that he get a job and keep it. He even wrote rules on a kitchen blackboard: make the bed—every day. He took him to the bank to open an account and taught him to keep track of it and reconcile it. Another rule always on that blackboard he tried to ignore—brush teeth—until Mark decided the girls liked him better when he didn't have nasty breath.

Until then, he'd tried everything: booze, drugs, cigarettes, patches, injections, worse. *He* should be dead.

But now, he wanted a life with a family. He wanted what his uncle had always talked about—what his uncle had before his wife died. Wife. Kids. Football with his son and daughter. Feed a baby that nasty soft stuff in little jars. Coach softball teams.

At the trailer court, there was an unknown pickup bearing out-of-county plates and a car with 41 plates parked in Katty's driveway, beside Katty's Taurus.

"Company. She has company all right." Guy called it in. "Chantelle, we're gonna need backup. We're stopped at the residence and reporting a 1972 Olds Pickup, 25 county plates and I think a 1989 Buick LaSabre, 41 county plates, parked out front. Condition of both vehicles is paint scrapes and dents and dings. Discolored. We are parking and exiting our vehicles." He eased his car back between some trees, at the entrance of the trailer court, almost hidden.

Huh. Good plan—if there was only one car parked in Katty's driveway. But there were two.

Just as Mark raised his hand to knock, the door burst open from inside. A massive man stood in the doorway, with two more standing behind him.

God. Pray, Mom. Where were Katty and Bea?

Where was Guy?

"Hey. Mr Deputy, Sir." A worn leather vest over a dirty sleeveless T-shirt revealed thick hairy arms—the outline of either a gun or a bottle tucked in the jeans waistband. Eyes, in a thick bearded face, appeared puffy, red-rimmed, bloodshot. The man saluted, pushed his way past Mark—stretching to more than a full head taller, making it clear who had the rights here and who could ultimately defend those rights. He paused next to Mark, obviously for effect. "S'cuse us Deputy. We were just leaving."

Right. Where were Katty and Bea?

The two other men lined up behind. No visible guns. Not as big or bulky as the first guy.

All three surrounded Mark on the deck.

Breathe.

Cigarette smoke almost choked Mark. Stench of body odor heat and whiskey closed in. There was something else, but Mark couldn't identify what. He was surrounded.

Where the hell was Guy?

"The department received a call from this residence." Mark pulled up as tall as possible and still he only came to the hairy guy's armpit. Barely. "Said there was a break-in."

Hand on his gun.

Hairy guy matched his movement—hand on his waistband.

Guy. Now's the time. Make your big black body known.

Hairy guy stepped down to the driveway, and one other followed. The third man stood beside Mark in a sort of challenge —shoulder-to-shoulder, Mark still facing the door. The man slowly, deliberately, stepped down one step. Only one.

Through the open door inside the trailer, Katty and Bea burst around the corner from the hallway. Katty's eyes were wide open. She looked like she wanted to kill, like a woman been wronged. "They broke in!" Tears ran down her cheeks as she pointed. Chin jutted out. "I was in the bedroom and they walked in. Just appeared in my bedroom. I had that front door locked!"

Hairy Man grinned and slowly stepped toward the trailer. "Oh, Officer, we go way back, her and me. Even her little girl." The guy didn't waste a move—every movement intentional.

Mark glanced at him, still on the top step. "If you're so close, what's her little girl's name?"

"Uh, well. I-It's something like Sting or Birdy. Something like that. But we go way back." The man turned to Katty. "Why, I remember when that beautiful baby was born."

Katty visibly shuddered.

For a second, Mark caught himself staring at her. These were her people? These were guys she knew? Why had she reacted by shuddering? From back—

"Yeah, we were good friends back then." The man took another step toward them.

Good set-up. If only Guy would show.

Bea backed away behind Katty.

Mark cleared his throat. "We got a call from this residence. Who was that?"

Katty stomped farther into the kitchen, dragging Bea with her. "That was me. O-Officer. Daniel … and … they broke into my house. They are trespassing. They need to leave and never come back."

Daniel pointed at Katty. "We're just good friends. We used to date and party." He flickered his eyebrows up and down. "We know the little girl's dad." He glanced at Katty. "In fact, I was the honored one who told her real dad that he, in fact, had a little daughter."

Katty's mouth dropped open, her fists clinched. She took a step toward the man. "You? You did that? Bastard!"

"Okay, gentlemen, if the lady wants you to leave, we will escort you out." Mark stepped closer to the man on the steps. The air sparked with tension. Dang, these guys seemed to think they had a right to be here. They had put down roots. They seemed to have something on Katty.

"We?"

Awkward.

Stand-off.

More than awkward—downright dangerous. Where was their backup, after all?

Guy. Now!

Daniel moved quick for his size. Gun in hand—aimed at Bea. Cocked.

A tangible silence landed, like air sucked out of a burning building.

This couldn't be happening.

Breathe. So many thoughts. Mom, pray. God help. Protect Bea. Protect Katty. Kill Daniel.

Another gun clicked from somewhere.

All froze.

"Put your guns down!" Mrs. Nosy, at the neighboring trailer, aimed her shotgun at Daniel.

Guy was on Daniel before the others could move. Just the break they needed. He was big, and he was fast. The man still on the steps jerked his hands straight up—surrender. The other one glanced at Mrs. Nosy and obviously entertained the thought. He took off. The other one took courage, lowered his arms, and ran, too.

Mark drew his tazer. "Halt!" One slammed to the dirt— surrendered, again. The other kept on running. Mark ran to restrain the one on the ground. Cuffed. He dragged him to a stand and started to drag him to the patrol car.

Even though Daniel had been disarmed and cuffed, he shoved his shoulder into Guy's chest. Guy was big, but Daniel had a hundred pounds or more on him. Guy stumbled back, but held on. "You're coming in—"

"Not on your life. You are not taking me in." Daniel kicked Guy in the gut—hard.

Guy doubled over, but he never let go of the handcuffs.

Daniel started to kick him again.

Light flashed.

Blam! Dust and leaves kicked up at Daniel's feet, and he jumped. Pellets scattered the ground, the deck, and against the metal trailer.

Bea screamed.

Mark clicked his chest radio, his cuffed suspect pulled away. "Back up! We need back up!" Would she shoot him if *he* moved? He yanked the man down to the ground

Daniel edged around Guy, putting him in the line of fire.

Mrs. Nosy must be stronger than she appeared. The gun had kicked her back, but she still stood. She kept it trained on the two men. She might get *herself* killed.

God help.

Guy dragged Daniel across the gravel driveway.

Daniel yelled. "We'll be back, Katty, girl. Little girl. Maybe we can Barbie-Q sometime." He head butted Guy in the abdomen and he broke free.

The man in Mark's custody wrestled away and followed Daniel.

Mark took off after him, stopped and aimed his tazer. "Stop or I'll shoot!"

The other surrendered on the ground. Good thing. Fetal position with his arms over his head.

Chase the man? Protect Katty and Bea? Mark shot his tazer at Daniel.

Daniel faltered but kept on running. Damn tazer! He drew his gun.

Guy had landed hard on the gravel, but pushed up and ran after them.

Mark raised his gun, but Guy was in the line of fire.

Daniel, hands cuffed in back, and the other man ran toward their vehicles.

Until Sheriff appeared.

Two more deputies slipped out from behind the dumpster across the street, guns raised. They tripped Daniel—laid him flat. For a big man, he was agile. He pushed off the ground and took off again.

Daniel reached the pickup, ignoring them all.

Guy caught up to him and tackled him—his face to the ground—stretched his legs out, and sat on him. The other man landed flat against the pickup, his head bounced off the bumper. The deputies cuffed him. No need for cuffs. He was limp.

"Katty!" Daniel yelled into the gravel. "Tell em! We're old buddies, we—" The rest of his words sputtered into the driveway.

Guy hooked his arms through Daniel's elbows. "Enough. You are going in …" Guy yanked Daniel up and pushed him toward the squad car, yelling the rest of his rights directly in his ear.

Sheriff and the other deputies drove their vehicles close to the trailer and loaded all three trespassers into the squad cars, driving away.

"Katty!" Daniel's voice could still be heard yelling for her.

Mark glanced at Katty.

She slowly sank to her knees onto the deck, her face white, silently weeping.

Bea crawled onto her lap, trembling.

Mark wanted to rush to them and embrace them. Protect them. He wanted that more than anything in this moment.

Guy stepped up behind him. "Uh … I'll leave you … I'll go to the car and report in … to Chantelle." Guy climbed into the car and glanced up at Mark.

Mark barely nodded, still rooted to the ground. He slowly broke free, walked to Katty and Bea, and knelt down in front of them. "You ok?"

Bea raised her head. There were no tears, but she was crying. No sound. Terrified. Shaking. Sobbing. Hiccuping. She stared beyond him.

"They're going to jail, Little One." Mark wanted to pick her up.

Before now, he wanted kids—someday—just like almost every man. That someday was usually far off, after they'd partied and gotten to know a few women first. Get to know themselves first. Have fun first.

But this Little One. This Bea. She tugged on his heart like no one had ever done.

A kid.

He'd loved a girl or two. He'd dreamt of family, especially after Uncle Ted had taken him in and shared his stories.

He wanted that.

He saw himself playing with Bea. Tossing a ball back and forth—Bea in a baseball team uniform. He could ride bikes with her, change the tire with her. Even play dolls with her.

How could that ever happen if Katty didn't love *him*? Want *him*?

Love him?

Did he love *her*?

Almost in response, Katty lifted her head and, just like Bea, looked beyond him, outside. "Are they … are they gone?"

He nodded.

Even with her make-up smeared across her face, even with her eyes red-rimmed and wet … she was beautiful.

Bea watched the bad men get pushed into the cars, the big fat guy still yelling for Mommy. The other cop, the one who looked like Lisha, sat in his car.

Hiccup.

She wiped her cheeks, but the wet slid across her face. Ick. She leaned into Mommy's sleeve. She knew Mommy would be mad, but she did it anyway. Wiped her snot on Mommy's jacket sleeve.

Mommy didn't yell. Didn't slap her. Mommy didn't even say those bad words.

Not this time.

Depdy Scott knelt on the deck. His eyes looked scared. His eyes looked like Lisha's did sometimes when she helped Mrs. T at Clarence's house. Only Depdy's eyes were green. Lisha's were brown-brown. Black brown.

It still felt scary—even with the bad guys 'rested. The men had handcuffs on. She and Mommy were safe—they couldn't take her or Mommy anymore, like they said they would. They didn't get to stay in Mommy's and her house anymore, like they said. They wanted to have a party. She was sure she didn't like their kind of party.

Depdy was here. He always made her feel safe.

Depdy loved her. She could tell. His eyes told her. Some people's eyes yelled bad things. Some people's eyes laughed and twinkled like tiny stars. Mrs. T's eyes said she loved Jesus *and* Bea. Bea could sometimes tell when people had Jesus in their hearts, and Mrs. T did. She had Jesus and the angels and Bea in her heart. And Clarence. When Mrs. T looked at Clarence, her eyes said she loved him. A lot.

Depdy's eyes said it now to Bea—he loved her. Sometimes even when he looked at Mommy, his eyes said he loved Mommy, too.

Mommy's eyes. Mommy's eyes didn't talk very much. A couple of times, Mommy's eyes told Bea that she loved her. Lots of times, Mommy's eyes told Bea that she was in trouble—a bad girl. That's when Bad Mommy's eyes talked. Loud.

Bea sat straighter.

Angel.

Her angel. His eyes said he loved Jesus, Papa in heaven, Depdy, Mommy.

And Bea.

Angel's eyes looked wet.

Mommy's face was wet, too.

When Angel leaned over them, his huge wings like a tent over them—Depdy, too—a big breath pushed out of Bea. She blinked. Not scared.

The cop cars drove away, throwing gravel onto the deck.

Angel leaned over them all again, bouncing the rocks off his pants and his wings. Depdy saw it, too.

He didn't look at Angel, he just saw the rocks bounce away. Bea looked up at Angel. He just smiled. Mr. Depdy couldn't see Angel, either. Just like Mommy.

She knew the big bad guys left—she'd seen them ride away in those police officer cars—but what if they came back?

What if they got loose, like on TV?

Katty swallowed.

She watched the deputies as they pushed Daniel and the other guy's head down, helping them into the back seat of the squad card. One was out cold and was being loaded into an ambulance. They slammed the door once they were inside. Scattered rocks as they drove out of the trailer court.

Strobe lights on the squad cars flashed. Almost made her sick to watch. The radio from the squad car squawked and sputtered as they drove away.

The Black deputy stood behind Mark—Deputy Scott—leaned over and said something to him.

Deputy Scott nodded.

He tried to smile, but something held him back. Maybe he was scared for them, for what could have happened. Maybe he was mad at her for letting those men inside her trailer.

How could she read his mind?

He pulled a pen out of his chest pocket and a small notebook from another pocket.

Bea struggled to get down.

Katty knew she wanted to run to him, but she held her back. She knew he wasn't happy. Like all this was her fault.

He had always been very attentive and kind—even seemed kind of interested in her.

But right now there was no interest except to get his story.

"Are you two okay?" He clicked his pen open.

Katty sighed and nodded. "Just scared, huh Bea."

She didn't understand it, but she wanted to weep. If it hadn't been for Bea, Katty might have let herself get lured back into that gang, that lifestyle. Back into the drugs and booze. They had brought her stuff, or they said they had. It might still be in the trailer. Maybe she'd go find it and use some. With the way she felt, a numb-out would feel so good. She was a failure. Why all this now? Things had been going better.

Well, except for a few days there when she went to work at Clarence's.

Maybe that was what was wrong. She was lonely for Clarence and Lisha and Carol. The whole place.

Big stuff had happened. Clarence had adopted them—legally. He was a lawyer and knew how all that worked.

What if Clarence decided he wanted someone who knew

more about the legal system than she did? She'd never find a job with such freedom with Bea.

"Did you know those guys?" Deputy Scott poised his pen over the paper.

Katty blinked. Did she ever. She'd done drugs with them. Partied with them. Had sex with them.

"Yeah. I used to. Well, one …" A tremendous sigh burst out in an audible sob. She hadn't realized how much they had scared her. She might as well spill all. "We used to do drugs and drink together." That was all she was going to say. Not going to add about the sex.

She choked. Lunch was going to come up. She swallowed it down. Just the thought of … with … with those guys made her want to run for the bathroom.

"Mommy?" Bea patted her shoulder. "You okay Mommy?" She jumped down. "You want to sit down?"

"Yes, Bea. Thanks." She sat on the deck chair.

Breathe.

Deputy Scott sat across from her at the little table and placed his notebook on the tabletop. "Can you tell me their names?"

"Uh, Daniel is all I remember for the one with the beard." She glanced at where the squad car had parked. "And the one from the convenience store."

He was looking at her. She knew it.

She was so stupid.

Whatever made her think he might someday …

Not going to look at him.

He had to know she'd been at the convenience store at the same time he had been.

"Better?" Deputy looked concerned.

"Better? With them gone? Yeah. Yes." Katty blinked. Why was she so weepy? Whatever it was, she was truly glad those men left.

"Can you tell me what happened?" He poised his pen over the paper.

Bea perked up. "They banged on the door." The little reporter. "Loud. They busted in. I was coloring and making pictures. You want one?"

Katty blinked again and shook her head.

He raised his eyebrows and tried to keep a straight face. "You mean as evidence? Sure, I'll take one. It might help with my investigation."

"Mommy, can I go inside?" Bea looked from Katty's face to Deputy Scott's. "Can I get a picture for him ... his bestigation?"

She glanced up at him and raised her eyebrows.

"Sure. Go ahead."

Bea hopped down and ran inside, slamming the door open against the stove behind it.

Katty jumped.

"You okay?"

Katty nodded. "Just ashamed."

"Of what?"

"That my past has come back to haunt me." She shook her head just slightly and looked away.

Tears slipped down her cheeks.

What on earth had she been thinking—that she could go out with this cute cop? She didn't deserve him.

She didn't deserve anyone better than Phil.

Or those monsters that had just gotten hauled off.

Breathe, Mark.

"C-can you come inside?" Katty's eyes pleaded with him. Her voice shook. "They said ... they might have left some drugs inside." She glanced behind her into the trailer, then back at Mark, tucking her hair behind her ears. "They ... he used to be my supplier." She visibly swallowed, looked down at her feet.

Nervous. Katty was nervous.

More trouble?

"Sure." He waved at Guy outside, just to let him know he was going in. Before he could step inside, Bea rushed into him. He caught her before they collided and knelt down to her level.

"Here it is, Mr. Depdy Mark." She swallowed and held out a painting.

"Is this the one I need?" Her big brown eyes mesmerized him. "For my …." Just to hear her say it again.

"Your 'bestigation? Yes."

So grown up. More than mature. He stood and glanced at Katty. "Is it okay if I take this to the department? I'll hang it on the wall with our other evi—"

Bea broke in. "Ebidance?" A deep, ragged breath escaped her. "For your wall." She nodded and wiped her eyes.

"Sure." Katty swept her hand, then stopped, seemed lost for a second. When her eyes landed on an enormous stack of papers, she relaxed—a little. "We have more."

He stood and stepped away from Bea. Always so aware. Had to be careful and professional. "Thank you, Bea." He bowed. Shouldn't have. Did it anyway. To Katty, "Um, where do you think they might have put it … the drugs … or whatever?" He straightened.

She looked at the kitchen counters, the table and shook her head. "I-I don't know. They just said they brought the stuff." She blinked and shrugged. Pushed her hands up. "Honest. I didn't order anything. It's been a long time." She looked at Bea. "Years. Since … I—"

Mark drew in a breath. "I believe you, Katty." He pointed at Bea. "You're saying since Bea, here, was born, right?"

Katty's chin crumpled and quivered. She slowly nodded. "You believe me."

Mark nodded. "I believe you."

Something changed in her eyes just then. Something … she glanced at Bea, then back at him. More trust? More … she relaxed … just a little? "There's other stuff, sometimes." She seemed to carry the world on her shoulders at that moment. "I … drink."

So aware of Bea watching them—her gaze bounced from his face to her mommy's, and back to his, again.

He knew Katty knew. She knew he knew. Crazy. Honest. Open trust.

Katty flinched. "Come in. Sorry. We … come in." Katty shoved a chair up to the table. "It's a mess." She threw up her hands.

"It's okay, Katty." It was a mess. He'd seen worse. "Well, let's have a look, huh Bea?" He held out his other hand. "I really like your painting. Thank you."

He stepped all the way into the trailer. Bea pulled him to the table. "I don't see any—"

Something caught his eye. The paneled walls of the living area burst with beautiful … paintings?

He turned. Faced the walls. Just stood there—staring. Blinking. His mouth hung open. Every wall, every board, every color. Clouds of clouds? An amazing tree. He wanted to climb it. Leaves floated all over.

He almost forgot Katty and Bea were there.

Bea stepped close. Closer. She leaned against his leg. "Mommy did it. Mommy painted it." She pointed to the tree. "She painted that. And the babies."

And the babies? All over. On clouds. Floating.

He blinked.

Babies looked back at him.

Katty was an incredible artist. He could almost walk into the scenes. Sit under that tree. He used to climb trees, sit under them with Mom and eat lunch.

But those eyes. Each baby's eyes bored into his—seeking …
imploring … pleading with him.

What?

They became real, almost. He swallowed. Katty was talking
to him, but he couldn't disengage. He couldn't stop. He couldn't
hear her words … until Bea touched his leg.

"Mr. Depdy, Sir?"

Sigh. "Bea, I see where you get your artistic talent."

Bea yanked on his jacket.

"Wha-what?" He stepped away from the wall. "Katty, I'm
sorry. What did you say just now?" He turned to her, but she had
left the room. "Katty?" To Bea. "Where'd your mommy go?"

Bea pointed to the hallway.

"I—could you go get her? Tell her I-I need to …."

Bea scurried down the hall. "Mommy?" She called again.
"Mom! Depdy wants to talk to you."

Mark turned to the walls again and shook his head. Amazing.
Beautiful.

"I know. It's crazy."

Mark spun around to face her.

"I bought more paint to cover it over." She looked at Bea and
twisted her hands, her fingers clasped.

Mark turned. "No. It's." He looked over his shoulder at the
closest wall. "Don't paint over it." Back to her. "It's a master-
piece. It's real. The tree. The clouds." He shook his head. "The
babies. Their eyes." He swallowed. "Please don't paint it
over."

Katty's eyes again. Something shifted in them, in her.
Softened.

What awful things had been said to her, done to her?

"Mommy. No. Don't paint it." Bea pushed out her chest. "Or
Mr. Depdy Mark will arrest you!" She peeked up at him. "Right
Mr. Depdy Mark?"

He laughed out loud. "Yes. Bea. We arrest people for illegally painting over … beautiful artistic treasures. That's … that's vandalism."

Bea just stared at him for a second, then nodded. "See Mommy? That's … bandle-ism." She wrinkled her nose. "Is that what you said?"

Even Katty laughed. She picked up Bea and hugged her. They rubbed noses like kitties.

Mark looked away. His face felt hot. "Well, I guess I better get going." He waved Bea's painting at her and headed for the door.

"Mark." Katty blinked. "Deputy. Thank you."

Mark nodded. "Call anytime." He reached out and touched Bea's cheek. Overstepping. Again. Up to Katty's eyes. Nodded.

He turned to go and waved the painting again. "Thanks Bea." One last look at the walls. Then, back at Katty.

Leave. Now.

Mark clomped down the deck steps to the squad car. He let his eyes flit everywhere, except at Guy. Not looking. He'd be in for a drilling for sure. He opened the door and slid onto the seat.

Silence.

Mark stole a look at the trailer house.

He shook his head. Tough to interview her for the police report.

Evidently, those lunkheads were from Katty's past—they'd done drugs and alcohol together … probably other things.

He shook those possibilities aside as Guy backed the car onto the street.

Katty was ashamed—he could feel it when they were talking —especially when he closed his notepad.

It felt as though she didn't want him to leave. She needed someone to talk to, badly. But then, she wanted him to leave at the same time. She might be ashamed.

Those paintings. If he hadn't seen them for himself, he would not have believed how beautiful they were. How beautiful Katty was. Bea, too.

Too bad his own mom was so religious and opinionated. She had never liked Katty, nor Bea.

He loved his mom, but sometimes she didn't see past her nose, and sometimes that nose was stuck-up.

There.

He'd said it—well, thought it.

Katty needed a friend, but he wasn't sure it was him.

CHAPTER 21

The next morning at the department, Mark pinned Bea's painting on the Suspect Wall. He stepped back. The beautiful rainbow and unicorn painting definitely didn't quite match the suspect photos and crime scene research already hung there. Some papers posted there might scare people, but Bea's added a certain purity they all needed at the department. As he turned to his desk, he caught Chantelle smiling at him. She didn't say a word.

Back to work. Reports. He'd rather look at Bea's painting, any day.

"Hey Deputy." Daniel sauntered past where Mark sat. "Missed you last night. We had a part-tay."

Mark glanced up and shook his head. Even with Daniel's hands cuffed behind his back, he still exuded a cocky attitude.

Guy shoved Daniel on past to the cells. "That's enough talk. Keep on moving." Check-in on Daniel—done. Now it was up to the courts. Assaulting an officer. Resisting arrest—several times. Mark guessed he'd spend some time in prison.

Between Phil and those old druggie buddies making an appearance, Katty and Bea's life had been hell. But with the help of Guy, they'd put those boys behind bars for the time being. He should call Katty and tell her they were in jail. Or … let Chantelle call her. That seemed the right way to do it. He didn't want to scare her and appear too … forward.

Because. Truth be known? He really liked her and wanted a chance to get to know her.

He was super uncomfortable doing that because he had a past too. His wasn't any better or worse than hers. Or was it?

Chantelle walked outside on break. She liked to get fresh air, but mostly she liked to do laps around the station. Said it helped her breathe out the toxic air from inside and breathe in the fresh air when she was outside. She always came back in happy.

He should try it.

Place was quiet right now. Chantelle outside. Guy and prisoners in the back cell block.

Unusual.

The radio always blared, and somebody always walked through the office.

As he looked into his monitor, no one behind him reflected in it.

Sheriff was at a city meeting across the street at the courthouse.

He completed his reports from the night before, clicked enter, and checked the window again. Chantelle just passed it. She would walk at least another lap or two.

He clicked on the archive file—the file where every case and report ever done was stored—ever since computers were first installed in the department. Employees had taken records still stored in hard copy files in a back, unused office and scanned them into the archive file on the system.

There. The file opened, and he scrolled down.

Why was he doing this?

Mark held his breath and listened, quieting his body at every cell level. Whatever he had heard must have been the wind outside or Guy setting up Daniel and his cohorts.

Katty's old file had to be in those archives. At least, that's what he guessed.

He scrolled through to the Rs. He was in the correct file, but … maybe she didn't have a record.

No. Here. Katelyn Randolph. Had to be her.

Actual name was Katelyn? Katty? Katelyn?

He glanced around the room. Breathed through his mouth, slowing every breath.

Ring!

He jumped and almost knocked his coffee mug off the desk. Caught it just in time.

Chantelle had the phone with her so she answered it, but she'd for sure be back inside, lickety-split.

He clicked on Katty's file.

The knot in the pit of his stomach just got bigger.

Armed robbery?

Robbing booze from the drugstore?

Hard to visualize her holding up a store. With a gun.

Or was she threatened?

Shoplifting … again for booze. Shooters.

Several crimes had gotten pinned on her … maybe by … Mr. Phil Daynton. Sounded like something he'd do. Theft for surgical instruments? Robbed the emergency room at the hospital?

Huh.

Reports of assault by Daynton. That didn't surprise him, either. But what did surprise Mark was how Katty had survived all that. Three calls reporting assault, then nothing. Reports of victim taken to the hospital for extensive blood loss. One report detailed her injuries, brutal wounds inflicted by—

Oh God help.

What she had been through. Yeah, she had done some stuff, but nobody deserved that.

He counted. One. Two. Three. Four. Maybe five trips to the ER—either drug overdose or domestic surgery.

Exact words in the file.

Domestic surgery.

There was more. He skimmed the file. Both Katty and Daynton had been hauled into the department. Both had been drunk. Daynton blacked out. Katty had apparently taken that as an open door and blurted out that Phil had done … the surgery. He came to when she yelled it out. She insisted it was abuse. The report stated that she became violent when Daynton denied any surgery or abuse. She had kept yelling, "Bad Phil. Bad Daddy."

Whew.

Slowly, he leaned back in his chair and stared at the crack between two concrete blocks on the wall.

How could she even be normal? How could she even walk?

Mark had drank some in his day. Okay, he wasn't that old now, and it had been more than some, but he had cut back … a lot since working this job. In his day—sounded like he was eighty years old—Mom always teased him that he had made her life miserable.

Partly true. Mark was sure he had made her life hell from time to time. Because of his alcoholic dad, and other things, he'd made some bad choices.

He glanced back at the file still open on his monitor.

Squeak.

Chantelle must have opened the outside door.

He wiped his eyes. Better close it down. She might head this way—or to the restroom.

"Yes." She opened the inner door and checked the radio. Nodded at Mark.

He smiled.

She sat in her chair and made some notes beside her computer.

He slowly slid his computer screen, angled away from her.

Rearranged his desk chair so he could prop his feet up on the desk. She'd never know why.

"Thanks! You too." She nodded into the phone. "Sure. Anytime. Bye." Turning, she shook her head, her curls bobbing, laughing. "You gonna move in? Making yourself comfy?"

He grinned. "Sure. Maybe." He reached for his coffee, but couldn't reach it. His feet slid off the edge of the desk and knocked his coffee mug over. "Damn!"

He stood. Drenched again. At least this time, it wasn't soda.

She rushed over with paper towels, but stopped herself and handed them to him. "Guess you can wipe your own self up."

He blotted at his pants and his desk.

"Hey. Whatchu into there?" She leaned over his computer.

Oops.

He quickly sat and opened another file. "I was doing a background check on those intruders we brought in. Just doing research."

"Oh. Right." She walked to her station and sat. "And their files are under Katelyn Randolph?" She grinned.

He wiped his eyes.

"It's okay. I've done that, too."

Ring!

"Polk County Sheriff's Department. This is Chantelle. How may I help you today?" She stuck out her tongue and picked up a pen as she listened to the caller. "Sure."

Mark reopened Katty's file and skimmed it again.

His gut lurched for what they had done to her.

The file just covered her time with Phil.

What had she gone through as a child?

Katty tapped the paper with her crayon. She had been sitting at the kitchen table for half an hour.

Bea was happily drawing and coloring, swinging her feet back and forth.

Katty glanced around at the room. Kitty drawings lined up along the door frame, going into the hallway. Doggy pictures lined the soffit above the kitchen cabinets. Bea had taped rainbows everywhere: on the blinds, on the window glass, hanging from the side of the table they didn't eat at. She had even taped drawings to the TV. When they watched cartoons, they taped them on the side of the TV. All colors. All kinds of subjects.

They lived in a regular art gallery.

Back to Bea.

Bea appeared to be lost in her drawings. The whole time they were sitting at the table, she seemed totally unaware of Katty's presence. Bea picked up a crayon, colored with it, held it against another one—evidently to see if they blended. She wasn't mean or disrespectful—she just wasn't in the same world as Katty was.

That made sense.

Pain, wounds, and little bottles filled with booze made up Katty's world.

Bea escaped to another world. Like another realm. Where did she go? She relaxed. Her breathing slowed, her body moved with the pencil or crayon, swayed to some inner music that only Bea could hear.

Even as Katty watched her, her own body relaxed and slowed down.

She'd give anything to hear Bea's music and escape into Bea's world of peace.

Katty tapped the paper again and checked her own drawing. Lines. Doodles, really. Some were recognizable subjects. Some were abstract. She hadn't had a lesson but found when she doodled without thinking or planning—letting the pen or pencil just flow; the picture became magical. Took on a whole new meaning. A life of its own.

She used to love to draw trees, color the leaves in beautiful greens and oranges. Vibrant colors. Blues. Full of life. Mom never would have saved those pictures, like she saved Bea's. Never would have taped them up to enjoy. Her mom probably burned them all.

As the pen followed the curves and lines, her mind strayed back to Clarence and Mrs. Hat—Mrs. T … their wedding.

Their faces.

Their love for each other. Even though they were what—eighty years old—they looked like young lovers ready to take on a lifetime of marriage and commitment.

"I do."

When they had kissed.

Katty's eyes misted over. She blinked and turned away from Bea. Not letting her see. She'd be all over her. Little girl could read her mommy's every expression.

Even with Phil, Katty had never experienced that sweetness.

Especially with Phil.

That man was evil.

With all Katty had done and gone through, would she ever have that … that kind of love?

Last night when Daniel and his buddies broke in, proved it. She'd never have true love.

She was too … too used. Too used up. Absolutely no virginity left. Her heart … crushed. Her body ruined. Trauma ruled every cell of her being—physically, emotionally, spiritually.

If she could just make it through Bea's graduation, her life might count for something. Raise this little girl to be someone other than Katty had become. Maybe someone like Mrs. T, or Carol, or Lisha. They all had been through rough times, but seemed so strong and settled.

Maybe Bea would have a chance at genuine love.

Then maybe Katty could start over.

Or.

When Katty had been little, she envisioned herself marrying a gorgeous man—she in a beautiful white wedding dress and him in a white tux. In her imagination, as they looked into each other's eyes, his would have been all for her—full of love as he gazed down at her. Maybe some orneriness—but never evil. She had always seen his eyes as blue—not sure why. But full of kindness and love.

Dreamy day.

Beautiful.

Beautiful dream. Beautiful dress.

But that was just what it was—a dream.

Not reality.

Not for her.

Reality? There was no knight in shining armor.

Katty blinked.

Sigh.

Where had she gone?

Yawning, she looked at her own drawing and sucked in a breath.

Trees.

All over the paper.

Trees on top of each other.

Old trees.

Dried up and tangled trees.

Dead trees.

"There, Mommy." Bea held up her picture.

Rainbows. A unicorn—her usual. No surprise there.

Katty chuckled as she nodded at the twenty or more drawings taped on the walls again. Probably about half of Bea's drawings had unicorns in them.

Bea's new drawing seemed no different at first. All around the edge of the paper were kids—little tiny babies, each with a different hair color and all dressed differently—from just diapers to full outfits. So cute.

Katty held it up.

Really cute. The rainbow colors were beautiful. Every color in the rainbow. Even black. Blue. Yellow. Greens—lots of greens. Reds. Oranges. Every color and several hues of each color.

Glad she had bought the large box of crayons.

Such a talented little girl.

Bea already had the tape out on the table and as Katty stood, she reached for it. She glanced at the drawing again.

All those babies.

All those babies.

Her legs crumpled beneath her and she shuddered, the picture floated down onto the floor. She sat down hard on the chair.

"Mommy?" Bea ran around the table and picked up her picture. She snuggled onto Katty's lap and looked into her eyes. "Mommy? What happened? Don't you like my picture? Where did you go?"

Despite herself, Katty smiled.

Exactly the question she always asked Bea when she got hurt, or cried, or laughed—anything.

She'd ask Bea, "Where did you go?" Mainly to distract her from the pain or whatever she was going through at the time, but today, she heard it directed back at her.

How could she tell Bea where she had gone?

How could she tell her the truth?

CHAPTER 22

Phil held his breath and froze. A man and a woman walked on the roadway in the park and were just a park bench away. Even though it was dark, if he moved behind a tree, they'd see movement. If he even breathed, they'd hear him.

The woman giggled. They were holding hands. The man leaned into the woman and spoke into her ear. She giggled again.

Really.

Take it home, fella.

The man sat on the nearby park bench and pulled the woman onto his lap. He nuzzled into her neck.

Were they gonna make it an all-nighter? He left that moldy basement for this? The basement had become stifling and the store owner had left, but the demon hadn't.

Damn.

That demon.

Maybe it only lived in the basement and was still there. Maybe, while Phil was in the park, the demon had stayed behind in the building.

But he knew better. He had a working knowledge of demonic infestation. The demon was around here at the park with him.

Somewhere.

Had to be.

Christians talked about guardian angels.

Well, he figured he probably had guardian demons—a whole host of them.

Just like that guy in the Bible. People in his dad's cult used to laugh when they talked about Legion in the Bible. They all wanted to be like him, like it was a contest for who could have the most demons living inside of them.

Visuals still haunted him of older members who had begun to physically resemble demons. Huge long noses. Eyes that bugged out. Bumpy, scabby skin.

Then there were the women who, to the normal person, appeared flawless. But in reality, demons had overshadowed their physical bodies, presenting a terrifying demeanor. The individual could actually choose which version that they could project: flawless beauty, or hideous demon.

How long had he stood there? Replaying his life with demons.

The man laid the woman down on the bench. Smoochy, smoochy. Get a room. Get a room at your house and not in the park.

Call 911. Hanky-panky in the wholesome park tonight.

Phil flitted his eyes. He was close to a tree. He was close to the old slide. Maybe if he shuffled sideways a little at a time, one step at a time.

Step. He measured with his eyes. Too dark to tell.

Another step. Not much closer.

The man came up for air, just as Phil took another step.

The man jumped. The woman fell off the bench and screamed. "What are you doing?"

"I saw something." He pointed right at Phil. "I saw something move." He jumped up from the bench.

She scrambled to her feet and looked where he pointed.

Right at Phil.

She screamed. "Eyes! Those are eyes."

Damn. Just enough light from the streetlights.

Phil flickered his eyes open and shut. Eyebrows up and down.

The man screamed and took off running out of the park.

The woman pointed at Phil, then at the man. "Wait!"

Phil lunged at her and yelled, "Scram!"

"You!" She stepped closer. "You're that man … the one who caused the accident that day." She pointed behind her at the convenience store. "You rammed that poor lady and almost killed her little girl!"

That was enough to light the powder keg in Phil. He drew his gun and stepped closer to her. Shooting her would only make his future worse, and he didn't want to kidnap anyone but Bea.

But she was no chicken. She appeared fearless. Much more than that wimpy man.

Phil summoned every evil presence he had ever known existed and roared. It literally blew her hair back and made her blink.

She shuddered, her eyes popped wide, and she stepped back. "You. You are evil. You are—"

"I am. I am evil. I am he." He roared again and jumped at her. "Go away!" He'd wake the entire neighborhood if he had to. "Go find your wimp of a man and leave me!" The last words literally blew her back against a tree. Whoa. He didn't know he had that in him.

The woman shook herself, eased around the tree, stumbled on a root or something at the foot of the tree, and ran.

"Finally! Run. Your life depends on it."

He lifted his gun and cocked it. Oh, how he wanted to shoot her—to vent all his frustrations out right now—frustrations from his childhood, his dad, his life. He aimed the gun. She just barely made it under the bridge. He was an excellent shot, but reason and common sense took over. He raised the gun to the sky but shook his head.

Not this time.

He blew out one breath after another. The main purpose, his whole reason for coming back to this damn town, was to nab his daughter.

He lowered his gun and stowed it, as the woman ran under a street light past the bridge. She knew who he was. Maybe had been at the accident. She remembered his face, even in the dark.

The woman didn't know how lucky she was.

He should have shot her.

Mark made sure the squad car was ready for his shift—did his nightly squad check. He'd slept hard after last night—clear into the afternoon. Didn't even remember dreaming. Ached when he woke up, but he needed to get going. Needed to move. Never enough time—even as a single guy.

He finished up and scanned his windshield and dash, making sure he had forgotten nothing. He needed to check in with Mrs. Nosy after last night. Where had she gotten that gun? Where did she store it? How did that blast not blow out her hearing? Maybe she was already deaf.

He stirred as something else morphed over his dash, over the windshield. Another car dash. Another vehicle layered over the squad car dash. What the? What was happening?

Then he realized.

That accident.

It still haunted him, still unnerved him.

He had hardly gotten that Lex character restrained—under control and in handcuffs—when Katty's neighbor lady, Mrs. Nosy again, the one who had reported her for child abuse, ran out with keys to her white Chevy. "Take my car!" That lady knew everything going on in her little trailer park neighborhood.

Highly unusual for him to borrow a citizen's car, but he had been in a pickle—no vehicle. His prisoner would wake up soon, and his squad car appeared to be out of commission.

If it had not been so serious, he might have laughed his head off at the picture Mrs. Nosy had made. Little old lady in an out-of-date dress, apron covering it with a mix of colors and patterns, her hair in rollers, one falling loosely at her shoulder. Keys dangled from her hand. Must have taken time to apply lipstick because there was more under her nose than on her lips.

He grabbed the keys—didn't even thank her—and dragged his prisoner to the car. Lex had come to and flailed his arms at Mark, but one more bash to his head with the gun and Lex appeared to be subdued long enough for Mark to get him locked up in jail for the moment. Chantelle, the dispatcher, could deal with him. The only person not intimidated by *her* was her little boy. She didn't abuse him, but she made sure that he and the deputies did what she told them to do.

That dash, Mrs. Nosy's car dash, slowly disappeared.

Mark put emotion aside and finished his check-in, making mental notes. He'd just had his cruiser serviced and tires rotated, and that place downtown always did a thorough job, so he knew everything was A-okay. But he got out and completed a walk around anyway, kicking the tires and checking the car body.

Hard not to skip that and just jump in the car and shove off to find Phil. But on days like today, it was even more important to follow protocol. Extra important.

One morning—the morning of November 1st—the day after Halloween, someone had keyed the whole car. Not only the usual spots by the car door handles, but on the hood and trunk, and especially through the words Sheriff Deputy along both sides of the car. They'd done some exceptional artwork, taken extra time to carve that deep. The damage had been expensive—he guessed—to the department and the county.

Today, everything checked out okay and as he turned over the engine, he breathed a silent thanks for no bombs. Thankful for supernatural protection. He probably watched too many movies where the bomb blew, activated by the car's ignition.

Silly, but it happened.

Sometimes his mom drove him mad, but he also knew she prayed for him and the entire department every day, and he felt it.

Very thankful for her and her little Bible Study group.

Radio on and time to check in with Chantelle. "You're good, Mark. Everything checks. Have a good run."

Comforting to know that she and others were on the other end of that radio—just in case.

As he shifted into reverse and backed away from the curb, goosebumps rose on his arms. Strange. He wasn't cold. Shivers ran up and down his arms, from the steering wheel through the palms of his hands, to his shoulders.

Was there a short in the car? He'd just had it serviced and everything checked out.

Strange.

Mark held a sort of faith, maybe because of his mom. But things had happened while on the job and off that couldn't be explained any other way, except through divine intervention.

When a man should have died in an accident but walked away, there was no explanation for it except the Lord.

Mark shook his head even now.

He shifted back into park. Just to be safe. His mind ran a thousand different directions, checking every possible automotive cause for the shivers he felt. Almost an electrical charge.

Back to the accident.

Helping to save little Bea and Katty was the most recent example. Bea should be dead, but that old guy—Clarence—had somehow crawled into that car without being stopped. He unbuckled her car seat and pulled her out before it blew up.

No. The words from the police report stated that Clarence had *ripped* the straps. With his "old, burn-scarred hands." Exactly the words on the report. Super miraculous and divinely orchestrated.

Even Chantelle had said that the angels had been busy that day, and Mark guessed she was right.

Now. Where was the bad guy? Mr. Phil Daynton.

Mark always started his shift with a drive around the square. Usually in the evenings, not much was going on in this little town. Stores were mostly closed, nothing going on after hours. Except for carloads of high school kids, like the other night.

The new pickup trucks parked at the car lots along the square reflected street lights on their shiny new bodies.

One summer, he had thought he was crazy because he saw shadows darting in between and under the trucks parked there. It hadn't looked like kids vandalizing or stealing, but he drove past again and stopped, got out and stood watching the lot. He hadn't felt threatened until the shadows shifted and moved right toward him. Five baby kitties ran toward him, saw him, and darted under the nearest truck.

Cracked him up.

When he walked beside the trucks, more cats chased each other around the truck tires. Maybe thirty cats played among them.

A real Kitty Kingdom.

Mark shook his head at the memory. Some memories were like that—fun and even joyful.

Others—not so much.

Turned the corner.

Sometimes the visuals he had seen on the job ate at him until they morphed over the actual physical world, tainting anything real.

He didn't know how to deal with those things, so he stuffed them inside, under the surface, just like he guessed every other cop did.

Probably not the right way to handle it.

A man walked his dog beside the new trucks. Shop the trucks and walk the dog. Pretty efficient if you asked Mark.

Were the countless kitties in danger, or was the dog?

The man waved.

Mark did, too.

Trucks parked outside the American Legion, on both sides of the entire block. Usually, this time of year, they'd be celebrating end of harvest. Guess he'd celebrate too, after a long growing season.

Tonight, he figured they all would assess the day. The new ordinance. The outcome of a new court decision.

They always got it wrong.

Stop sign.

Left turn.

Former bank, now the city offices.

Crap! Needed to pay his water bill. The little house he rented required little as far as upkeep or didn't cost him too much in utilities. He had lived in a trailer when he first moved to Osceola after cop school, and that had been expensive to heat and cool. Drafty little dump to live in. Trailers could be nice, but that one was dreadful.

The house he lived in now was nothing fancy, but it was home. He guessed he wouldn't be there forever. Helped to lower his bills, as it was better insulated than the trailer, he guessed, and was cheaper rent, which had surprised him when he first looked at it. Little two bedroom place. Didn't need the second bedroom, but it was nice to have for his fishing pole collection and his books—he loved to read—everything from sci-fi with Gordon Dickson's stuff, to the Bible, to local authors he'd discovered. He might be labeled "widely read." He even read romance. Not smutty stuff, just guy meets girl and they live happily ever after.

Some guys might call him gay, but he just wanted to be happy and when life was crappy—either from some tragedy on his job or just life—he'd open a romance novel.

Just one of his deep, dark secrets.

The west side of the square was badly lit and quiet at this time of night.

Mark slowed.

He turned in his seat. Nobody in the antique store window tonight. How had Daynton … have gotten away? Where had he gone and how had he escaped from the scene of the accident even, with no one seeing him? He'd trailed blood on the concrete for a block, but then it disappeared.

Tonight, no cars or trucks parked along the curb and no people milled about. No stores were open. Sometimes the Opera House might host an event like a wedding or Halloween haunting, but nothing was going on right now.

Bet any little kid—boy or girl—could give him ideas on where to hide, from the back alleys, between buildings, behind dumpsters.

Mark used to play in back alleys himself.

He shook his head.

Back then, it didn't seem unsafe, just exciting. Mom had always worked, so when he got home from school, he'd grab a snack and meet a buddy behind some old stores. Cops and robbers had never been acted out so good. The small town he grew up in always had someone who declared it their civic duty to watch over the latchkey kids. Only, they didn't call them latchkey kids back then.

The Opera House building was amazing. The owner had called, wanting the department to inspect what they thought might be a break-in, but it had turned out to be a false alarm. Mark had been upstairs and throughout the building. It was ancient and a just-as-ancient window glass had shifted to where wind was blowing through, making animal or even human sounds. Juveniles might have wanted to break in and party upstairs in the old Opera House. He might have wanted to party there back in the day.

Mark was sure it was Phil hiding in that building last week. Or had it only been days ago?

But that day when … last year, when the owner had called him in, he had explored every inch of the place, partly to satisfy the freaked-out owner, but also to satisfy his own curiosity. Glad he'd done that, because chasing Phil around that old building might have been dangerous. Thank God Guy was okay after falling through floorboards.

He loved old buildings and his job as a county cop enabled him to explore—always with the knowledge of the dispatcher— but always lured by an adventure bug.

Right now, lights were on in the upstairs apartment. That would be a wonderful building to live in. He'd have to put a bug in the owner's ear for when it might vacate.

The new bank corner. Magnificent building. Great staff. People would classify it as the new bank for at least twenty years. Maybe thirty.

But across the street on the corner was an eyesore he'd love to buy someday. He slowed and shined his light into the old pharmacy building. Nothing to see, but he envisioned a gallery or little cafe in there with his own apartment upstairs. He'd heard it was cool up there, but had never asked for the opportunity to explore it.

Trash blew across the street and into the sewer.

He shook his head. People needed to keep their stuff up. To maintain their properties.

Even pick up trash.

Mark turned left: the little pocket park, thrift store, community center, insurance, drugstore, and coffee shop—newly reno-vated. Really cute.

A cup of coffee would taste so good right now. And they served excellent coffee. They were only open during the day unless someone rented the space out for a party or some such celebration.

Back at the department.

Not much going on downtown.

The radio sputtered. "Hey Mark, I saw you drive by just now. Just an FYI. There have been reports of someone hiding in the park. Even screams."

"What? Screams?" Mark sat up straight.

"I know. Who called in had their TV on loud, though. So … it's not super cold out yet, but it's dark and the people living right next to the park … uh, North of it, also spotted something or someone, running from tree to tree. She called in and said it looked funny—like a cartoon character making a getaway. With Mr. Daynton still loose, it might be good to keep an eye open. Got it? Pardner?"

Mark smiled at her wordisms. Mixing cultures or countries or social play on words was her claim to fame. "Headed that direction. Thanks Chantelle."

"My pleasure to send you into the dark unknown, to suffer at the hands of the public."

Mark laughed.

He could hear her smile over the radio.

Grinning, she was.

Sure. She could laugh. She wasn't in the line of duty.

Well, she was. He'd heard of dispatchers being threatened by suspects and criminals. And Chantelle was a single woman who worked full-time and had full-time care of her elderly parents. Plus her son. Everyone had hard stuff in their lives.

He guessed he would care for his own mom someday.

But right now, Mom was in charge of her own life … and tried to run his life, too.

He slowly turned onto the park roadway and flipped his lights off. Easy enough to see without them, with the moon so bright. And a couple streetlights. He swore phases of the moon had a lot to do with the crimes committed. He'd read that somewhere. People seemed to go crazy during that full moon, and this definitely felt like it was the howl-at-the-moon time of the month.

He didn't know if he believed all that, but there it was—a full moon peeking through the trees.

He shifted into park. There. Must be a dog or cat. Squirrel maybe. Something definitely moved right there. From the playground equipment to the old slide.

That was creepy because Phil himself had tied little Bea up and taped her to the top of the slide. Then he'd started a fire in the dry grass and weeds at the bottom. Mark could still hear in his memory what Phil had yelled back at them as he ran away. It had echoed in the park that day, and it echoed in his mind right now. "No seed of mine will live on this Earth!"

That man was crazy.

The same shivers that had traveled up his arms when he begun his shift took the same track up his arms again.

He shuddered.

What *was* that?

He saw something run, or stumble from the slide to the little digger thing—a shovel digger for little kids to dig in the sand.

Whoever it was, stumbled and fell in the sand.

He held his breath and exited his car without a sound. The park was so quiet that the snap from his holster almost echoed. He was like a highly trained animal, eyes alert and fixed on the person in the sand.

Muscles tensed, and his heart pounded. Breathing came

faster. Too many nights of sitting in the driver's seat, "easy-does-it evenings" and … too many donuts. He was outta shape.

Training hadn't slipped, though. He settled himself—his trainer had called it, finding his center. But most times, he prayed. God could be his Center.

He slowed his breathing.

Even his steps on grass and leaves were silent.

He slowly slipped his gun out of the holster and pointed it at the body.

It didn't move. Like they might be dead. Or injured.

Might need backup.

Emergency unit, maybe.

Gun pointed.

Closer.

Closer still.

A branch.

A huge damn branch.

Just a branch.

He had gotten pumped up to shoot a branch.

Gun lowered.

Straightened upright.

Breathe.

How would he report this to Chantelle?

Damn. That cop was good.

Saved by a branch.

Phil hardly breathed. Tried to tuck in every loose part of him, as he crouched into the shadows of the picnic table, not ten feet from the cop.

Why in hell was that dork roaming around the park with his gun drawn?

Oh yeah. The woman had screamed. So had the man. And Phil had roared—twice.

Damn.

The deputy needed to leave.

Phil's muscles cramped—the ball of his foot especially wanted to curl up. He tried to wiggle his toes, only it made his foot spasm.

Why did he need to become a living part of the picnic table?

Why didn't he just leave this dump town?

He had a car.

Had some money.

He had a gun.

Why did he stick around?

Well, he had needed to heal from his injury so he could drive.

But he was better now.

He could drive and wasn't dizzy. His nose had been healing until the demon showed up. And, by how it felt, it was gonna heal crooked. Oh well. Women liked men who were rough looking, tough looking.

From where he squatted, he could see the old slide that he'd taped his kid to—when last spring? He almost shook his head just now. That had been the action of a purely irrational man. Kill her so no one could have her—including him?

Insane.

But if he really took time to admit it, Bea was the reason he stayed around now. Maybe this time, he'd be successful in nabbing her for himself. Even if he had to kill Katty. Katty was used up anyway. No man in his right mind would want her now.

The cop relaxed, evidently convinced that what he had thought he'd seen was just the branch.

Come on. Get going, Mr. Deputy, Sir.

The cop turned, holstered his gun and tapped his fingers on the kids' steam shovel.

If he knelt to play with the thing, Phil might bust out laughing. He could feel it welling up, even now.

But the man walked to the squad car and got in. He took the time to radio in, then pulled away.

Damn.

Knees. Ow. Feet. Ow. Just a minute longer.

Stay.

Phil stayed still until the car pulled out of the park and onto the street. Good thing he'd broken the outside light on the building when he entered the area. It wasn't easy to throw a rock through the wire cage protecting the bulb.

His elbow popped as he slowly stretched out one arm and then the other. They did not make human bodies his age to tuck up under a picnic table for an hour or longer. Sitting Indian style had seemed a good idea when he first hid under the table. But now, his back hurt from bending over his legs. And his legs hurt from … bending.

He tried to push his butt along under the length of the table to freedom, only it didn't happen as easily as his mind thought it should. What had ever happened to mind over matter? Wasn't his brain supposed to be command general over his body?

Was he getting old?

Stretching his legs, he limped back and forth between picnic tables. The lights were off in nearby houses, so he took time to work out the cramp in his foot.

Back and forth.

Phil blew out a breath, loudly—because he could. The cop's squad car taillights were red as it stopped at the highway, driving away.

The air outside was better than that old store basement. He breathed deeply. He needed to find a temporary place to live. A place without mold and dirty old quilts for a bed.

Without rats.

And demons.

Sometimes, he had lived what most people—even his dad—called the good life. Nice apartment. Cushy furniture that would impress any woman. Fully stocked liquor cabinet. A huge contrast to where he and Katty had lived together.

That was definitely called squalor. Drugs. Booze. Sex. Trash all over the little house they'd occupied together.

That house was party central. People stayed there for days and days. A few visuals stomped through his brain. Almost made him sick. He never could comprehend how that worked. Certain memories that drew him, like a little kid on candy, made him want to vomit.

Whew.

He needed to find a place of his own.

Since he'd left Katty, he'd been lured into a collaboration with the Warden and his ring of crime stars—Phil's own word for the brutal people who had helped take over the prison. The corrupted structure they had built within those walls had to have been a pillar of Satan's kingdom. They had promoted Phil to a whole new level from what he'd left behind with Katty. Time with her had been small potatoes—Warden had led him to a whole new world. And now that bastard was in prison himself.

Phil shook his head. Bonnie and Clyde had gotten caught. Their rainbow of fame and fortune didn't end with the pot of gold they might have dreamt of. Many bullets had shot their grand illusion down—the number stands at 150—so many that the undertaker found it difficult to embalm them.

The report he'd written in school about the famous couple had fascinated him, but nauseated his teacher, earning him a D.

Now. Where to hide out? Lex was nowhere. Probably in jail. Phil usually could depend on him for hideout ideas.

He sat on the top of the picnic table, his feet propped on the bench.

He kind of knew the surroundings of the nursing home, because he and Lex and staked it out once.

If Phil remembered correctly, that girl's house was near here. A big two-story with a garage and a shed out back.

He perked up.

And an old camper.

What was her name? Noell? Noell … Noell … something about a woodworker, woodpecker. A carpenter?

That was it.

Noell Carpenter.

Oh yeah. He remembered the inside of the house, too. It had been so packed with junk that he could barely walk up the stairs. They loaded every step with magazines, books, cookbooks, boxes. Only enough space on each step for a foot. He had been breaking and entering and in a hurry, but he remembered going back down to the bottom landing and starting with the correct foot, or he'd have to cross feet at a certain step.

He shook his head. The baggage and clutter in that house rivaled his personal baggage. He should write a book, a book about a house, a house of rooms. One room could represent his true self—his worries, his fears, but thoughts that shocked even him.

The bathroom. Ick.

Yeah.

There had been no physical clutter in Noell's upstairs bathroom, but he knew secrets could hide anywhere.

Just like his life. Plenty of outward attributes of his sexploits —pursuing women no matter where, no matter what age—with the way he dressed and where he hung out.

But secret thoughts that played around the corners in his room, his mind—that bathroom of his book, would more than likely get him a check-in at a mental asylum or worse, his own personal cage in his dad's coven.

The one time Dad had shown Phil the row of dog crates, only one had been vacant. Almost naked humans occupied the rest.

He'd never forget the wild eyes and gurgles, the growls as he walked in.

Goosebumps up and down his back weren't entirely his own body's response.

All his dad had to say to him was, "Be good or crate."

Just like a dog.

He blinked.

Even now, he gasped at that memory.

Maybe he wouldn't write that book. Because he'd have to describe his dad's room in that house. His own was bad enough.

Back to Noell's house.

He'd driven past it several times, then broken into it that one day. Found out some stuff at the courthouse.

Didn't even make sense why he had done that.

What did he have on this Noell?

Phil just needed a place to hide, a place to hangout until he had a fix on what the next step was.

Prison was looming, hanging over his head, no doubt. He'd realized that some time ago. Needed to be extra careful wherever he holed up. Whoever he talked to. Whoever saw him.

Especially now. That woman. She had recognized him—in the dark.

He wasn't sure how many people might have seen him after the accident. Cops should have noted his whereabouts, but a little girl was in danger. That old pickup had exploded. Fire erupted.

Busting through the windshield and waking up on the pickup hood was Phil's only claim to fame.

He should be dead.

Years ago, he might have been all cocky. Like damn. He might live forever. Nothing had killed him yet—beatings from his dad had come close.

He *should* be dead.

Phil chuckled, but shivered at the same time. The novel he

could write would have interesting weapons as part of the torture instruments.

He always tried not to let the visuals of his past overrule what he needed to be thinking about, but they always came to life—hammers, baseball bats, knives—all your basic abuse weapons.

Yep. It would make a horrifying book.

He might write it in prison.

If he didn't die first.

Mark blew out a breath. What a busy night.

A visit to the city park should have been fun. But someone or something had been lurking there. A little humbling to confess it had been a branch. What ever was lurking could have been a squirrel settling in for the night. Or a bird.

If it had *only* been Phil. The click of the handcuffs around that evil bastard's wrists would be the best sound in the world right now. Most satisfying. Maybe then Phil would be tried in a court of law, locked up in prison, and Katty and Bea would be safe and free from fear.

Probably dreaming.

Back to the park, again. It wasn't even Halloween.

Yet.

Reports of screaming. Evidently, whoever had called it in, like Chantelle said, was hearing a scream from the TV.

He should have stayed at the park and taken a nap. The screams would have made sure he didn't sleep *all* night.

Desperate, tired cops needed desperate naps.

Now where?

Clarence was a detective, if Mark remembered right. Or was it Harold? The department should turn those two loose on the case.

He did a mental check. The department had hired a forensics agency to study the blood and DNA at the old Opera House. Mark knew in his gut that Phil had been there. The blood would be his—DNA from those whiskey bottles would be his, too. They should get the report back soon.

Tomorrow, maybe he'd check in with Mrs. Nosy and make sure she was okay.

The druggie friends had gotten locked up—even the cashier from the convenience store. Three more people off the streets. Three more jailed to keep Katty and Bea safe.

Huh. Hadn't planned on it, but here was Katty's trailer. He was on her street.

He shook his head.

Probably just habit.

CHAPTER 23

Katty opened the trailer door. "We're going to Hillcrest this morning so I can finish organizing those boxes." She shook her head and whispered. "I hope for the last time." There had to be other things a paralegal could be doing.

Bea hopped along beside her, their hands clasped. "Will Mrs. T be there?" She bounced out the open door and took the deck stairs one hop at a time.

"Mrs. T? Is she okay with you calling her that … instead of Mrs. Timmelsen? Or Mrs. Timm?" Katty had to admit, Mrs. T was cute and … easy. Even she had trouble calling her Mrs. Timmelsen, since the wedding.

"She told me to." Bea glanced up at Katty with a hesitant expression on her face. "I couldn't say … Mrs. Timm … Mrs. Timm." Bea shook her head. "I couldn't say her big name. So she told me to call her Mrs. T."

Katty cocked her head. "Huh. That's okay if *she* said you can call her that. And she is always there, Goof. She lives there. Remember when we got to live there before Clarence came back?"

Bea waited beside the car until Katty unlocked the doors. She grinned and nodded. "Ice cream. Every day."

Katty laughed and opened the door for Bea. Something about this conversation with her daughter seemed so normal. No booze. No thoughts of shooters … well, just now, but.

Stress levels low.

Oh, God. Please let this happen again.

There was no shame. No guilt. No deception.

Just a regular conversation.

"Is she our grandma now?" Bea climbed into her car seat and buckled one buckle.

Until Katty tapped her hands. "My job." She buckled the last two straps. "Well, kind of. Because Clarence is legally our, your, our … he is my dad and your grandpa. Or my grandpa and your great-grandpa." She shut the car door and opened the driver's door. "I think."

Discovering adoption papers in one of those boxes when men had kidnapped Clarence to prison was a sweet but shocking memory.

Maybe today would be just as revealing. Seemed the old boxes had just enough information in them for her to have to stay alert, but not enough to be exciting. The day she had discovered the adoption papers for her and Bea, and even Noell had been an exciting day. Probably the most exciting day of her whole life.

Not every box had held that kind of revelation, unfortunately.

Most had a trail of business transactions from when Clarence had been in prison for the first time. Sixty years represented lots of transactions, both personal for him and for other inmates he had helped. There had been an entire stack of boxes from Clarence's dad, Dawes Timmelsen.

Reminder: gather the information on all the properties Clarence's dad had purchased into one file, or one document on the computer. There were lots of them—all purchased while Clarence had been in prison—as a sort of revenge against the judge who had sentenced Clarence. Evidently, the judge had proclaimed himself as king over Osceola, but Dawes had proved him otherwise. He owned over half of Osceola, that wasn't privately owned.

Clarence's own decision to become a lawyer had proven to be healthy, both personally and financially.

"Ready?" Katty backed out of the driveway, waved at Mrs. Nosy, and drove out of the trailer park. Another reminder: find out Mrs. Nosy's real name—somehow.

"Humpty Dumpty sat on a wall." Bea kicked the back of Katty's seat, her feet moving up and down.

"Humpty Dumpty had a great fall." Katty grinned and sang along. She didn't even mind Bea kicking her seat.

"All the king's horses," sang Bea.

Something moved beside Bea in the back seat.

Naw.

"And all the king's men," Katty stopped at the highway.

"Couldn't put Humpty Dumpty together again." Bea finished the song.

Two little kids.

She checked the traffic.

No traffic.

Two little kids moved back and forth with Bea.

Katty blinked.

Seeing things.

Again.

Could she be put back together again?

Jasper smiled and tapped the seat in front of him, to the beat of Humpty Dumpty.

Interesting song.

The guy, Humpty, sat on a wall, fell down and broke. Nobody could fix him, apparently.

Huh.

Humans had some strange things.

Strange songs.

Strange all the way around.

But they didn't have the perspective that he, as an angel, had.

He could see both worlds—the physical world that humans lived in and also what they called the invisible world.

Little Bea's angel flew along behind them.

Jerahmael.

Grinning.

Grinning from ear to ear.

And singing. "Humpty Dumpty had a great fall," right along with Bea. He knew all the words to those little kid songs. Hilarious. Tender hearted angel. Jerahmael loved that little girl.

He had, himself, been with Katelyn since her own mother had birthed her into the Earth realm. He'd seen everything: Katelyn's brutal mother, her father. The few things that had comforted her and how her mother had ripped them away.

He shook his head.

Took a special angel to hover and guard children. Stuff they saw. Things they had to do.

And Jasper guessed all angels were super special because of what their job entailed.

He nodded along with the song.

The only problem was that three demons followed along fairly close behind the car, too.

Behind them.

And he knew they had a plan—a plan for destruction of these two wonderful humans.

"Mommy?" Bea turned back around in her car seat.

"Humpty Dumpty had a great … what, Bea?" Mommy glanced back at her in the mirror.

"Mommy. There are three scary angels behind us."

"Angels? Scary angels?" Mommy smiled into the mirror. "Angels aren't scary, are they?" She tapped the steering wheel, still humming the song. Moved her head back and forth in time.

That angel beside Bea in the car was huge and smiled down at Bea. Bea smiled back.

She'd seen him before, with Mommy.

Sometimes.

He was nice, but not always around.

But those other angels, behind her own, were scary.

Her angel waved and kept on singing. Or his lips moved anyway, and he bounced to some beat.

She watched him, then turned around to watch Mommy.

Same beat.

Maybe same song, only she could hear Mommy singing. "All the kind's horses, and all the king's men."

She couldn't hear her angel.

Back to him.

He waved again.

Mommy singing.

His bouncing.

Same song.

The three angels behind her angel weren't singing.

They weren't smiling, either.

They had icky eyes—yellow eyes.

They had claws instead of fingers. She could see them. They flew like angels.

Definitely scary.

She leaned closer to Mommy's angel.

Her own angel flew closer.

Mommy couldn't see them. The scary angels, or their own angels.

Mommy couldn't see them.

Like the Mommy and Daddy in Polar Express.

They couldn't hear the bell anymore.

Mrs. T could see angels, though.

She could still see.

Mommy couldn't see.

Bea held out her hand, where Mommy couldn't see.

A huge hand covered hers.

———

Katty followed Bea to the entrance door of Hillcrest.

Bea skipped ahead—to the door—she pushed hard on the auto-open button. The door finally opened. Bea looked back at Katty and grinned. Proud of herself. It didn't always happen. If Katty was slower than usual, someone would give the door a push from inside. Bea still won.

Katty grinned, despite a hangover. It was always easy to open one more little bottle—just one more. But the next morning, the next day, there was never the freedom to stay in bed—especially with a four-year-old. Her stomach churned—she never knew if its contents would come up or stay down. The little bottle inside her jacket pocket comforted her. Somehow, she'd make it through this day.

They had spent so much time at Hillcrest, even staying overnight for a time, when Clarence had been kidnapped. She and Bea had needed asylum when Phil and Lex were chasing them, and this had been the best place to be.

Ice Cream and all. Some days felt like they lived in a movie —Phil chasing them, Lex, too, former druggie friends breaking in, being adopted by a rich lawyer—well, he was rich and Clarence was a lawyer. But he was their lifeline.

Bea stopped by the ice cream machine and raised her eyebrows.

Little Bea was so pretty.

Katty doubted Bea got her looks from her own bloodline.

Because she was so pretty.

Now that Katty knew they were related to Noell as cousins, beauty was definitely in the bloodline, just not through her own veins.

Hard to admit Phil was Bea's dad. Bea's looks betrayed that fact—she looked so much like him. It hurt Katty to think Bea would have to deal with him as her real dad someday for sure— she *was* Phil's daughter.

Katty wished to God that Phil would die.

Just go away somehow. Never, ever be in their lives. Never, ever influence them—especially Bea.

"Mommy?" She raised her eyebrows again. "Do you want some ice cream? I'll get it for you."

Kathy laughed despite herself. Little sneak. Bea knew if she pulled a cone from the dispenser for Katty that Bea would get one too. Smart little girl.

She'd get what she wanted in life.

"Bea. Let's get one. Both of us. Treat first. Work later." Katty watched to make sure Bea didn't make a mess. Her mind was always going a million miles a minute: when was the next drink, from where, who would find out, would she ever be able to beat it?

But this one moment, she felt the quiet.

The peace, again.

She licked her cone at the same time Bea licked hers. They smiled, with their eyes, at each other.

Sweet, sweet moment.

These turned up more times than not when they came to the nursing home.

Interesting to connect that.

"Should we get one for Clarence and Mrs. T, too?"

Bea gave her such an innocent look that Katty laughed straight up from her toes.

"Oh, you stinker. You have a plan, don't you? Mrs. T can't eat ice cream, so you could probably have hers because Clarence would eat his. You could eat hers and yours." Katty shook her head. "No. If Mr. Clarence wants ice cream, we'll come back down and get him one. Or he can get one himself. He's in better shape than I am, and he's … how much older than me?" She stopped to figure it out. "He's eighty and I'm twenty-five, so … he's fifty-five years older than I am. Wow."

"And don't you forget it either, beautiful daughter and granddaughter of mine!" Clarence held out his arms and Bea ran to him, her ice cream cone frosting his cheek. "Well, I wanted some ice cream, but it's usually better when it's in my mouth and not on my cheek."

Bea giggled. "Sorry, Clarence. I din mean to."

Katty grabbed at the napkin dispenser and wiped his cheek.

"Thank you, Katty." He held out his arm.

She walked straight into his hug and breathed in his after-shave. Even when he'd been in prison, she bet he had been classy enough to use cologne. Well, it probably wasn't allowed. But he was one amazing man, even after a second stint in prison. "How are you, my father? Married man?"

She felt him nod against her, his rough beard against her forehead.

In this man's arms, she would never have to fear again. She'd never drink again. Never be afraid again. She was free from everything that had ever haunted and pained her.

"You okay, Katty?" He withdrew from her for a minute, his eyes searching hers. "You're shaking. Trembling. Are you getting sick?"

"No. Yes. No, I'm fine. Just tired. But I'm okay." She swallowed. "It's good to see you, Clarence. I've missed you so much." She hesitated. "I mean, I know you and Mrs. T needed honeymoon time and I know … I've seen you … since. It just seems like a long time since—"

"Well, I've missed you, too." He scooped up Bea, ice cream and all, and hugged Katty as they walked. "I was telling Mrs. T just now that we needed to invite you both over again, and here you are."

"How is she doing?" Katty licked her cone and wiped her mouth with the napkin. "Is she doing better now that you're back from prison and married?"

"She is! She's an amazing woman of mine … and God's." He shook his head.

They stepped into a rhythm as they walked down the hall on the way to Clarence's rooms. They stopped by Harold's so Bea could hop down and give him an ice cream kiss, too. He chuckled so hard that his American flag pin righted itself.

"Ha!" Clarence laughed out loud. "Look at your flag, Harold. Bea has that American flag magic."

Katty breathed. It was definitely the right thing to do. Get some work done. But this was so worth the time. She'd strayed from where Clarence had helped her get. She needed him. Harold. Lisha and Carol. Mrs. T.

She had to get back there.

Get sober.

She sighed.

Clarence turned to her as Bea ran into his office. "What is going on, Kat? You seem very down—heavy right now. Almost dark." He turned full on, face-to-face, his hands on both her shoulders. "What's going on?" He hesitated. "It's that break-in by those men, isn't it?"

Katty blinked. "How d'you know?"

"I walk to the Sheriff's Department almost every day." He nodded. "We work together on some cases." He lowered his voice. "It was on their report. Part of what they do."

Something in Katty froze. Her legs crumbled.

"Katty!" He caught her and eased her to the floor, still in the hallway.

"I can't breathe." Her heart pounded in her chest. "I can't …"

Clarence ran into his office and pounded his call light.

Lisha peeked around the corner at the nurses' station and gasped. "Carol! Come! Now!" She punched her radio for help and lumbered toward them.

Carol ran after her as she flopped her stethoscope over her head and around her neck.

Medical training kicked in immediately for both women.

Lisha checked Katty's pulse as Carol placed the stethoscope on her chest. "What she do? What happened, Clarence?"

"I … I don't know. She just collapsed."

"I'm … I can't breathe. Something's on my …" Her hand hovered over her chest.

Lisha moved so Katty could focus on her face. "Look at my pin, Katty."

"You-your pin." She squeezed her eyes shut, then opened them again. "Your pin. You …"

Lisha's pin was a round yellow happy face.

Katty glanced up at Lisha's beautiful brown face.

Her eyes.

Those eyes.

Lisha tapped the pin. "Look here."

Katty glanced at the pin, but back to Lisha's eyes.

Everything inside of Lisha—her own past, her pain, but her strength—poured out through those dark brown eyes. Stuff in Lisha's life—the scar, her tough-girl attitude—all spoke of deep wounds, but of deep empathy and love.

She saw.

Lisha saw.

Everything.

She saw Katty's struggles and pain.

As Katty kept her eyes on Lisha's, her breathing slowed. She could take a breath. A tear rolled down her face into her hair.

Clarence wiped it.

Those faces: Clarence's, Lisha's and Carol's.

All so concerned.

All loving her.

"Where's Bea?" Katty lifted her head. "Bea?"

Bea sat against the big emergency hall doors. Her eyes wide and scared. Ice cream cone empty. Ice cream blob beside her on the floor.

Lisha pushed Katty back down. "Don't move yet, Hun."

Clarence scooted to Bea, pulled her to his chest, and rocked her. "She's okay. She just had a … a moment. But she's okay, Bea."

"Bad Mommy was back last night."

"Bea!" Katty dropped her head back down to the floor. No. They would all know she was a … she was a drunk.

Clarence straightened and looked over at Katty.

Bea crawled out of his arms to Katty. "Mommy?"

Katty sucked in a deep breath and lifted her head again. She patted Bea's arm. "I'm okay. It's okay."

Bea's face.

Her expression. Her eyes—big and brown. Not happy. Scared.

Terrified.

"I have to sit up."

Lisha and Carol supported her.

"Go slow." Carol smiled. "You're coming out of it."

"What was that?" Katty tried to stand.

Lisha on one side, Carol on the other.

Supported.

She caught the glance between the two nurses.

"Maybe a panic attack." Lisha nodded. "But you go get checked out."

That would never work. The alcohol level in her blood right now?

Katty started to walk to Clarence's office.

She faltered.

"Let's go sit down." Clarence walked her to a chair, his arm around her shoulders.

A fresh glass of water appeared on the desk beside her.

Lisha.

"Thanks." Katty wanted to weep.

Being cared for.

Loved.

Carol patted her shoulder. "Lisha's right. Go get checked out." She glanced at Clarence and left the room.

Lisha hesitated for a second, then followed Carol.

Thoughts of going to a doctor right now almost pushed Katty into another panic attack.

Clarence slid his chair close to hers. Face-to-face. "What's going on, Katty?"

Mrs. T sat in the next room on the bed, Bea in her arms.

Bea peeked from under Mrs. T's arm. Her eyes were wide. She'd been crying.

Oh God.

A tear slipped down Katty's cheek. "It's hard right now."

Clarence caught the tear and wiped her cheek.

Another slipped, and she gulped. She couldn't break down right here. Well, she guessed she just had in the hall.

He wiped her other cheek.

Deep breath.

Bea snuggled into Mrs. T.

Katty plunged in. "Old drug friends," she shook her head, "not really friends, but guys I used to—"

"Do drugs and stuff with?"

She nodded. "They broke in the other day. Made me feel so—"

"Vulnerable? They made you feel—"

"Naked. They made me feel exposed." She blinked. "They know stuff about me." How could she ever tell him about the actual stuff—that stuff?

Over his shoulder floated three tiny babies—all giggly and bouncy. And a little boy, right behind the babies. The boy could see her.

She definitely was going crazy.

Her own private horror movie.

Babies.

Floating.

Little boys?

Bea giggled from the other room.

Bea saw them?

Mrs. T, too?

What?

"Stuff I'd never want Bea to know about me. Things I've done." She studied his wall of framed credits, certificates, and photos—her own framed certificate. "And ... Phil." She bit her lower lip. "I know he's her father." She bit both lips between her teeth and shook her head. "He's still around. I can feel him. I feel his evil."

Clarence scooted closer, and slowly surrounded Katty with his long arms and just held her. Didn't say a word.

She could feel him breathing in and out, hear his breath in her ear.

Oh God, she was going to fall apart right here. Again.

He knew.

She was sure of it.

He knew she was drinking again.

She had never been able to hide it from anyone, much less from him. He had found her in the park before and prevented her from beating Bea. He had known then, and he knew now.

He didn't say a word.

But that was enough to convict her.

Was it enough to stop her from buying those stupid little bottles and drinking?

Conviction was totally different from actually changing.

To change, you had to never buy the stuff. To never lift that little bottle to your lips. Never go out and get numb, so that things somehow looked brighter.

Or happier.

Or different.

For a night, an hour.

For a moment.

CHAPTER 24

Phil stretched and yawned.

Sunlight pierced just right—through tree branches—right into his eyes.

He sat up and bonked his head.

Hard.

"Ow. Damn."

Giggle.

He jumped and hit his head again.

"Damn!"

Where was he? What was that laughter? He rubbed his eyes. Bright pops of red, blue, and green almost blinded him. Slides. Steps.

Damn.

The playground.

He'd crawled up onto the playground equipment and hidden partly inside the plastic bowl. That thing had been intended for little kids to lie in and watch the world, not for a full size man to sleep in.

And now, when he woke up, he'd slid into it part way and the sound of his head banging against the plastic jarred him. Echoed along the bars and pipes.

He shivered. Not the time of year to be camping out in the park, in the equipment. Seemed like a good idea last night after the cop left.

At least it hit on the back of his head and not his face, not his nose. He gently touched it. Still tender. Still squishy. No blood on his fingers, though.

He must be tired, because he'd planned to go to Hillcrest and sneak in—hide in there and maybe have a snack from the kitchen.

Giggle.

What was that?

Bam!

Hit his head again.

More giggles.

He rubbed his eyes.

A little girl stood just in front of him.

She was maybe four—three or four. Her hand covered her mouth. She had curly reddish hair and a dimple in one cheek.

Cute.

She giggled again.

She turned to look behind her and another girl appeared, just a little taller.

He carefully slid out of the plastic bowl. "Why do you kids like playing on these things? They're dangerous."

Several other kids peeked at him from on the ground below.

Two others stood a few steps away from them, holding hands.

"What is this? A class field trip?"

The little girl closest to him laughed and hopped down the steps to the ground. The others followed. They all turned to watch him.

"Shoo. Go back to your mommy. Your parents."

There weren't any cars or trucks in the park, so the kids had to live nearby. Usually people parked along the park road or at the picnic building.

"Go. Go on."

His old bones wouldn't let him jump down like the kids had. Muscles hurt and his legs were stiff and sore. He guessed sleeping in playground equipment wasn't the best thing for anybody.

He used to do it all the time, usually in a drunken stupor, or drugged up so he didn't know where he was at, or how to get home.

Nasty taste in his mouth. He hadn't even been drinking. His Buick supply had run out already. Only a few snacks left. And one bottle of water. If that. If no one had broken into the car and done what he himself would do.

His stomach growled.

It forced him to think about finding new digs.

Until …

Those kids were still in the park.

"Go a-way!" He pushed at them with his hands, only they didn't leave. They just stood there and stared at him.

Creepy. Made him nervous. Why didn't they leave? Why didn't their parents come and get them, or at least yell for them to come home?

Many creatures had harassed and heckled him—

But never in this way.

It was almost like they were … waiting for … him.

"What do you want?" He stepped toward them.

They scattered a little, but crowded back in, holding hands.

Some still giggled.

This was feeling like a Star Trek episode, where strange creatures appeared and turned into monsters. Very normal appearing characters morphed into terrifying aliens. Kinda reminded him of his childhood. During the day, Dad and his cult member friends had jobs and lived what appeared to be a normal life. But just get them into darkness—anywhere—in the forest somewhere, or in some run-down building, and they all changed into beings that people made horror books and movies about.

That'd make a good book—normal looking kids, dressed nicely, then boom! Naw. That book had been written. He had lived that book.

He wasn't afraid of kids.

He just didn't like them.

Reminded him of *his* kid years—the pain, the terror. Never knowing his dad's response to a seemingly innocent act. Riding bikes made his dad crazy, for some reason. So crazy that he'd gone into a rage one day and broken Phil's bike, dismantled every piece, until it was a pile of parts.

When his dad had left, he hadn't even picked the parts up. He's just driven over the pile, squealing out of the driveway, cussing the entire time.

Phil had spent the better part of the day trying to put it back together.

No. No kids.

He wanted no kids from his loins to live.

Except Bea.

He stepped toward the group.

They didn't move. They stayed put.

Close up, they appeared real.

The little girl he'd seen first smiled just now.

Sweetly.

He almost wished they appeared evil, because he couldn't handle their sweetness.

Goodness.

Sweetness.

Kindness.

Terrified him.

Where was his demon when he needed him?

Bea walked to Clarence, moved his hand from his knee and climbed onto his lap.

"Hey, my little Bea." He let her turn her side against his chest. He wrapped his arms completely around her tiny body, his head rested on hers. "I thought you forgot all about me."

Bea smiled faintly, but closed her eyes and breathed him in. Soap. And something else. His smell. His heart beating against her ear. His warmth.

"Is Mommy okay?" She swallowed. "Will she be okay?"

Clarence lifted his head and looked into the bedroom. Katty was resting on his bed.

Bea followed his gaze, then back to him.

He took a breath—she felt it through his chest.

"It's hard, Little One." He combed her hair behind one ear. "It's hard." Another breath. "She did it before—quit drinking. She can do it again." He nodded. "I love you, Bea." He kissed the top of her head.

His love felt like … Fruit Loops? Too crunchy. Ice cream? Cold.

She shivered.

"You cold?" He snuggled her tighter. "Mrs. T is at therapy. I'm second best now, I know."

She giggled and nestled her head even closer into him, her eyes closed.

He continued chatting with Harold, while Bea breathed and relaxed into her own little world. She opened her eyes and watched the birds at the feeder outside the window. Several birds stood on the rim and they flicked the seed up and out, munching bites, their tiny beaks opening and closing.

Deep sigh. Bea had noticed lately when she took those deep breaths. It always happened when she was with Mrs. T—when they sang, or prayed. She especially liked to hear Mrs. T pray. She had the first verse down: "My Father."

She still couldn't pray those baby talk prayers.

Or when Mrs. T combed Bea's hair with her fingers and traced her face. She got deep, deep breaths then.

One bird caught her attention—Harold said it was a robin—still around these parts, he said. It was flittering. Poking under its wing with its beak.

Did that hurt?

Then the bird pooped. Ick!

But it still sat there on the post of the feeder. The other birds twittered around it, but it didn't even move. Were those other birds bothering it?

The robin almost closed its eyes.

The other birds flew away, and the robin sat there all alone.

In the sun.

In the warm sun.

Bea snuggled back into Clarence's chest and he rubbed her hand with his thick, burn-scarred fingers. She turned a finger up and touched the scars. He'd told her all about the burns. From fire. When he was a kid.

And fire on the slide.

She remembered that fire.

It could have burned her, too.

She gently cupped her tiny hand around a finger and tucked back into his chest.

The robin was still there, almost asleep. Birdy dreams. In the sun.

Bea blinked.

Sunshine.

So warm.

So like a hug.

Mrs. T was always tucking her in on their bed in the sunshine.

Sunshine was a hug.

She blinked again.

Love was like the sunshine.

"Clarence?"

"What, my Precious."

She giggled and sat up. "Did you know?" She pointed to the robin. Only it had flown away. Didn't matter. The sunshine was still outside. "Did you know that love is like the sunshine?"

He stopped talking to Harold. "What, Bea?"

"Love isn't like Fruit Loops or ice cream." She shook her head. "They're too crunchy, too cold. Love is like the sunshine."

He glanced at Harold.

She knew he wanted to laugh, but he didn't. He smiled.

He was nice.

"How?" He looked outside.

"Sunshine keeps you warm. It makes you grow." She thought of the seeds they had planted in the garden tables at Hillcrest last spring. "It makes food."

That wasn't quite it.

"It hugs you when … it goes through your skin and … fills up your heart. Here." She flattened her hand against his chest. "Just like love does."

Neither man spoke.

Were they holding their breath?

She knew she'd said something almost grown-up by the way they blinked and swallowed. They didn't even smile. Didn't laugh.

It was 'portant.

She tucked back under Clarence's chin, against his chest.

All three looked outside.

Nobody said a word.

Phil checked the street between the park and the nursing home, and the one just up the hill.

Nobody. Nothing.

What time was it? Damn phone. Had to be past eight … or nine in the morning. The park board should install chargers on … the … playground equipment. Or a tree. He glanced behind him. Or the picnic shelter.

Stupid little dump of a town.

Why did people even want to live here?

Well, he had lived in Osceola when he and Katty were together, but that was so he could … hide. He'd already started getting in trouble with the law back then.

Heh. He'd started getting into trouble when he was eight. Or nine. Maybe even younger.

He glanced down at his shirt. Damn. Wrinkled. Dirty. He brushed it off and shined his shoes against the back of his pant legs.

Where to go from here?

That house—Noell's house—was near here.

He rotated in the other direction, took a few steps, and the nursing home was right in front of him.

He and Lex had explored that building a while back. Plenty of places to hunker down. Scare a few night nurses away, and he'd have the entire kitchen to himself.

And … was that Katty's car parked in front?

Maybe he'd change his plans.

Noell's or nursing home?

He pointed. This way? Or that way?

Katty's car cinched the decision.

Hillcrest.

Would have been so much easier if he'd snuck into the nursing home last night under the cover of darkness. But he might not have made it inside. They had some kind of locked door policy at night.

Better to walk like he had a purpose and a plan. Like he belonged. Like he had his dear gramps to go see and share life with. Share stories and reminisce with.

That was it.

Find someone who appeared out of it, or at least confused. And pretend Phil was their long-lost grandson or nephew.

Snuggle up to someone, let him or her see the gun—didn't take a rocket scientist to recognize a gun and danger—and he'd have a place to stay for however long he needed.

Brilliant!

***

Jerum's eyes stuck to the human.

His human.

Phil.

A storm was brewing in Osceola, Nebraska, USA, Earth. A storm always stirred up trouble around his human. Moving into a new season always brought crisis and trouble. Chaos. Confusion.

Phil was already crossing the street. Phil looked behind him, right at him, but didn't appear to see him.

Only pure of heart humans who were seeking Father could see angels, unless Father opened a portal. And lately, more and more humans saw faintly through the veil.

If it was up to him, he'd open a portal and scare the hell out of Phil.

Oh, he had nothing against Phil. Or *for* him. He just did his job as an angel. It didn't matter where a certain human went. Father directed Jerum to follow Phil. Ever since Phil's birth.

Follow him. Stay with him. But don't interfere.

Another angel landed next to him. "Greetings, Jerum."

Jerum nodded back as he followed Phil across the street. "Percaunde. Are you well?" Funny greeting for an angel. Of course, they were well, but when decorum was called for, they all embraced honor and respect.

And they always called for decorum in preparation for battle.

Percaunde nodded and bowed slightly.

Several more angels landed and greeted one another.

Several thousand became visible in the earth realm, only to angels. All in armor. All with swords raised.

Jerum himself raised his sword.

Percaunde reported in. "Michael is ready at Command Center. He will give the signal from there."

Jerum nodded, stepping back. Not in fear, but there was no need, at this time, to stir up the enemy any more than they were.

Speaking of … a group of demons snarled as they circled the human. Another legion of demons seemed to emerge from the dark clouds, sector by sector.

Angels backed away—not because of defeat or fear—but because of the stench and gruesome features. Talons. Scabs. Scars. Braided slimy hair that flipped down to their knees. Eyes with worlds deep inside—movement, layers of evil flitting.

Evil that might make the greatest commander—like King David—tremble and back away.

Scavenger demons hung around the perimeters, picking at angels with their small swords, trying to stir up a fight. Trying to engage and distract. Adolescent, underling demons, who would never captain a sector.

Percuande cocked his head toward the Hillcrest building. "It always amazes me … the most unassuming habitations are the first places the demons choose to inhabit. Satan is all about grandeur and pomp, but his underlings have none of that."

Jerum nodded and watched as a demonic prince flicked an apprentice demon into another realm, his screams fading out of Earth's atmosphere. "Satan will steal, kill and destroy—even his own. He is no respecter of beings—bad or good. He destroys them all."

Phil opened the entrance door to Hillcrest Homes. Just walking past the signage out front gave him chills—that cross and the words "Hillcrest Homes ~ Compassion of Christ." He used to get the heebie-jeebies as a kid, from one church building in particular, as he walked to school. Something about that cross. He had seen into the invisible world from an early age—demons, mostly—but just now, in passing that sign, an icy fear stirred. He had experienced nothing like that since he was a kid.

Until now.

There was a goosebump kind of fear, as a kid in a cult, yeah. Anytime the cult leaders suspected infiltrators and then implemented a cleansing. That goosebump fear.

But this was entirely different.

His heart still pounded as he entered the building. His legs wanted to go limp. Maybe since he'd been out of the cult's influence for so long, he'd lost the edge.

No. This was definitely the enemy's territory he was walking into right now. Here, dead things wandered … or maybe something truly lived—depending on a person's perspective … in Hillcrest Homes.

He hadn't even made it past the entrance reception area yet, so his plan hadn't quite gone as he'd thought. Well … he had no plan, but he hoped the nursing home residents and staff would be easy to con.

He rounded the corner into the hallway and the first person he ran into … the old man … Clarence, his name?

Damn.

Phil scratched his nose as they met. He kept his hand there and slid it through his hair, his head down, in case Clarence turned around for a second look.

Phil's face was an everybody-has-one type of face. Worked well for a criminal.

Clarence stood out—too bad for him—with a tall young man's build but an old man's wrinkles and long, white hair and close shaved beard. Guess he wasn't running from the law anymore, because he had those ageless good looks that Phil would never have.

Clarence just nodded and kept on walking.

Phil stopped and listened.

The entrance door must have opened and now was closing. The sound of the door closing was a loud growl. Bet they didn't have any escapees from the residents, because they'd get caught sneaking out through that door—every time.

Damn.

Clarence. Right off the bat.

Phil started down the main hall, but stopped so fast that he almost fell.

A huge angel stood in his way, right where Clarence had walked.

Phil shuddered. Evil inhabited very cell of his body—because they had forced him to invite it in as a kid. Now? He didn't know who he was without it.

He'd seen angels before—around a dietary employee back at the prison. She had angels all around her and could walk through that prison, demons in almost every inmate there, and never get attacked. He was not sure that she knew it. If she had—

But this … this angel. A different kind of … evil?

The angel was huge. Looked down at Phil from the ceiling and even then appeared to be stooping over just to look down at him.

An eerie light shone out of the angel's eyes, along with a knowing amusement. Long golden hair fell loose around his shoulders. Dark armor protected massive muscles.

Phil couldn't take his eyes off him. "Hey, Dude." He swallowed. "Your weight lifting program is working … real good."

No response.

Just those eyes.

Phil had pulled his lies over girls, women, priests—even a judge once—but … those angel's eyes. Kinda reminded him of his kindergarten teacher—old Mrs. Glorenstein. She was built like a brick and even back then had been ancient. But she'd had some kind of sensory switch that flipped every time he lied to her.

Must be the same with this angel. Not gonna even try.

Back against the wall.

Phil used to be afraid of some demons. Sometimes the really tiny ones manifested into the scariest. Phil had tried playing with one, like a little puppy once, but it had exploded like those soft, cuddly, teddy bear like creatures exploded into a gremlin.

But this angel. "Dude. Wh-what's your … name?"

The being stared at him for an entire minute. Maybe more.

Phil slid along the wall, on down the hallway, when the angel bowed his head, hands clasped in front of him, and huge wings slowly lifted from somewhere in his back—until he filled that whole end of the hallway.

Phil's body shuddered, his legs gave way, and he slid down to the floor.

"Hello, Michael." A tiny old lady pushed a walker between them, past them. "How are you today? Glad you're here because there is a rumbling in the atmosphere's foundation today." She patted Michael's leg as she walked past, pulled her pink sweater closer around her shoulders and walked on down the hall.

Phil couldn't breathe.

Dead quiet. Michael didn't move a cell of his body—except for the corners of his mouth, which barely curved up.

Phil didn't laugh.

He leaned over and crawled away.

Terrifying.

Who was that woman?

Just down the hall, he managed to pull himself to a stand and literally ran into a huge black woman.

He glanced past Michael, toward the way he'd just come in. That girl's house—Noell's house. Even with all the garbage filling every room there. That would've been safer than this place.

"Excuse me." He tried to slip around her, but she was almost as big as the angel.

She grabbed hold of his arm.

Damn, her entire hand encircled his bicep.

"Hello." Deep voice. Her brown eyes might pop out of her head. "And who might you be here to see? Sir?"

"Uh … anybody that's … lonely?" His voice squeaked on the last syllable.

He was gonna die.

"Aw. Really sweet of you." The only reason she let go of his arm was that she had to answer her pager with one hand and hold a glass of juice in her other hand.

He hadn't planned on meeting up with Osceola's own self-appointed citizen policewoman.

Too early in the morning to be that pushy. He hadn't had coffee—for days.

First the angel over all the host of heaven and now Commander-in-Chief of the nursing home.

She held up one finger. "I'll check on this page and be right back." She started to walk away, but then turned to face him … full-on. "Don't go anywhere … I-I'll bring you a cup of coffee."

Phil stopped. Wait. Coffee?

When she waddled to the nurses' station to check out his story, he slipped into the end resident room and closed the door.

"Hi, Grandma."

The old woman in the bed glanced up. "What do you want, Sonny?"

"Aw, Granny. Do I have to always … have a reason for

visiting my favorite grandma?" Phil leaned over and kissed the top of her head.

Whew. Didn't they have showers here?

Her hair was short, curly—kinda old lady style, but tied back with a ribbon or headband of some sort. Her blue eyes twinkled behind huge, round black frames.

Huh.

But the lipstick. Bright red. Not up her nose, just very thick lips. And red.

She didn't push him away when he kissed her, so she must be batty.

The clothes she wore confirmed his suspicions. Her shirt was all paisley with purple and green. Her skirt had horses running all over in browns and blues.

Nylons.

Last time he'd seen nylons had been in some hooker's parlor.

Only Granny's were ... tan.

Just.

Tan.

And her shoes?

Jellies.

She wiggled her toes in them. "Like them? They're new. I ordered them online."

He slowly sank onto the chair next to her bed and knocked the call light to the floor. "You have Wi-Fi here ... Granny?"

"Yep." Pretty pleased with herself. "For anybody who wants it. Or for anybody that can figure it out." She patted her flat chest. "I figured it out."

He couldn't think of anything to say.

Speechless.

She rustled under her sheets—she was just lounging on top of the bedspread—and pulled out a bottle of whiskey. "Want some?"

Phil's eyes popped. "Granny." Don't laugh. Not now. "Do they let you have that here?"

She swung it in front of his face.

He jumped. "Careful. You don't want to hurt yourself. You might break it and then where would you be?" He'd cupped his hand over his nose.

"You'd go buy me another one." She winked. "Sonny."

He'd been with a lot of women in his time. Lots. Big women. Small women. Gorgeous ones and once even a really ugly one— he'd found himself snuggled in her arms one morning.

But never in his life had a woman outsmarted him.

Until now.

Maybe.

"Well, Granny."

She waved it again. "Have a sip. It'll do ya good."

Who was he to turn that down? After a night in the park on the hard plastic of the playground equipment and a week of mornings without coffee, he needed a drink. He'd slept with birds and squirrels and rats ... maybe little kids. Demons, especially.

He shook his head.

She tucked it away. "No?"

"Well, Granny. I don't want to hurt your feelings." He rubbed his head. "I was just thinking about something else." He held out his hand. "Sure I'll take a sip."

What was nursing home protocol for passing whiskey bottles back and forth?

Germs.

She held it out again.

He wiped off the opening just as his eyes landed on her lips.

Damn.

The smell of the whiskey lured him in and won him over. He wiped the opening with his hand again and took a sip. And another. His hands weren't too pure either.

But those lips.

"Whew." Worth it.

"Well. I'd better get … back to work." He stood and waved.

"See you next week?" She lifted the bottle to her lips and chugged—all the while, her eyes never leaving his face.

She didn't even wipe it off.

Damn.

She capped it and slid it under the covers.

Gotta go. The room was suffocating him, just like the antique store basement.

"By the way, You're not my grandson." She patted around on the bed. "Where's my call light?"

He grinned, turned, and pointed to the floor. "Want it? Get down and get it."

Her red lips parted, and her tongue stuck out. "Bastard!"

He opened the door. Heh. Teach her.

Beep, beep, beep, beep.

He turned.

She had the phone to her ear. "Hello? Front desk? There's a strange man in my room and I'm terrified!" She sniffled, then flipped him off.

Shit!

CHAPTER 25

Phyllis Scott opened the oven door and pulled the heavy rack toward her, careful to not let the huge pan of meat loaf slide off. "Mmm. This is going to be good." She'd made too much, but she and Mark both loved meat loaf sandwiches. Besides, he hardly ever had time to visit anymore and share a meal with her.

She glanced behind her. The table looked so pretty, decorated for fall—plastic orange leaves, little turkey candles—which she never lit, cute pilgrims scattered among the leaves as a center-piece. She skipped Halloween—that holiday was for Satan, and she wasn't about to help *him* celebrate.

She lifted the pan onto a trivet on the counter beside the stove, careful not to touch it to her counter, which wouldn't take the heat. Steam rose from the meat in a satisfying swirl.

The timer on her phone chimed.

Noon. Time for Mark to be here.

She slid a metal spatula under the meat and lifted it onto the platter. Those sandwiches were going to be good.

Was she out of ketchup?

She had set the table with her favorite set of dishes for fall. If she had any vices, it was collecting dishes. She never packed them away, except for a set of her mom's dishes that she cherished from her childhood. She used every set at one time or another—whether a true holiday or one she made up. It gave her joy to invite someone over and prepare her best meal and serve it on special dishes.

Besides, it made her lonely day better.—so much happier and satisfying.

Today the dishes were from Mark's past, when he was a little boy and loved the leaves scattered on each plate and at the bottom of each coffee cup.

The leaves matched her centerpiece.

She gripped the potholders around baked potatoes and dropped one onto each plate just as the doorbell rang.

"Come in, Mark."

Dang.

He'd told her not to yell "come in" just in case it wasn't him. It could be someone dangerous.

He was always the cop.

The door opened. Mark shook his finger at her. "Mom. You know what I tell you. There are too many weird people around, just waiting to prey on unsuspecting—"

"People like me." She finished the sentence for him. "I know. I know. I was getting the baked potatoes out of the oven and couldn't come to the door."

He shook his head and kissed her cheek. "When I was a kid, was I like you are now—never listening or obeying?" He raised his eyebrows. "Never mind. I know the answer to that."

Phyllis chuckled as she popped the rolls into the warming basket, making sure that the cloth snuggled each one, and placed them on the table. "It's about time you admitted that."

She kissed him back.

Dang, he was cute. Maybe he was shorter than most men, but … with those green eyes and long, black eyelashes … he was cute.

She was his mom, but she would find him attractive.

Bad girl.

"Can I help with anything?" He sniffed the air. "Smells amazing. My favorite." He chuckled. "You know the way to my heart, for sure."

She blushed. If he knew what she had been thinking.

Oh, she was a sinful woman.

She sneaked another peek.

Still, he was cute. Proud moms could say that.

"I think we can sit and eat. After we pray, of course." She scanned the counters and stove as she sat. Meatloaf. Baked Potatoes. Rolls. "Oh! The green beans." She jumped up, opened the microwave oven, and reached in to retrieve the pan. "It's not even hot! Damn! I forgot to—" She turned slowly and winced. "Sorry. Didn't mean to swear."

Mark visibly swallowed down any comment he might have made, almost choking back laughter. "Mom. I hear it all the time —either from the prisoners and people we arrest or from my fellow deputies. It's not that—"

"Well, I'm your mom and I shouldn't be talking that way. Besides, your father, God rest his soul, would not approve." She tapped the microwave oven buttons, and the oven flashed on. The turntable lit and turned and hummed.

She turned to Mark. "You serve yourself—get your rolls buttered and your potatoes." She fluttered. "There's sour cream and chives there, in front of you."

Beep.

She stirred the beans and pushed the buttons for one more round.

How could she have forgotten the beans?

Beep.

She pulled out the glass bowl and stirred. "Hot. Hot. Hot!" Where was that extra potholder? She grabbed the dishtowel and wrapped the bowl with it. "There. Beans. Done." She held the bowl out to Mark, stuck in a spoon and piled some on his plate, right next to the place he pointed to.

"Mom."

"Oh, sorry."

He caught her before she could pick the pile of beans up and move them over. "It's okay. I'm okay. I can handle it."

They hadn't prayed. "Shit!"

Mark glanced up. He appeared surprised. "Mom. You okay? You rarely cuss like this." He reached his hand for hers. "Let's pray over our food and then we can relax and eat this beautiful meal you just cooked. Okay?"

Breathe. "Yes. Okay."

He bowed his head. "Lord, thank you for this beautiful day. Thank you for this food that smells delicious." He glanced up at her. "Mom. Bow your head." He grinned.

Stinker. He was enjoying being the parent right now.

"And Lord, thank you for Mom, for all she does. Amen." He stopped. "Oh Lord, please bless this food to the health of our bodies. Amen."

"Amen."

He remembered.

He prayed just as she'd taught him to pray.

"Thank you, Mark. Did I get your napkin?" She reached for hers.

He held his up, then put it back on his lap. "Got it." He watched her, his hand ready at his fork.

"Go ahead, son. Don't wait for me."

He picked up his fork and peeked up at her as he cut into his meatloaf. He poked his fork into the meat and slowly brought it to his mouth. "Mmmm." Smelled amazing. She hadn't cooked an entire meal for … awhile.

He opened his mouth around the bite and closed his eyes. "Mm-mm!"

She sighed.

He did all that for her.

He had acted it out over the last few years, knowing she took pleasure in watching him eat the food she had prepared.

Childish of her.

But he did it anyway.

She picked up her fork and did the same.

It *was* good.

"So how've you been, Mom? Busy? Church meetings and stuff?" He divided his potato, cut a chunk of butter, and smeared it on. Next, the sour cream.

Oh, how he loved his sour cream. "I've been fine, Mark. Looking forward to you coming over." She didn't want to whine. "You've been so busy lately, so I was really looking forward to this."

He grimaced. "Yeah, and that's just getting worse. Carl just got transferred. His wife got a job in Omaha and it pays really well. So they're moving. He's going to be at home with the kids. For now."

"Oh, that's nice, dear." Was Mark losing weight? His shirt didn't fit right. The collar was looser, wasn't it?

"So that means more hours for me—which is okay. I'm almost out of debt." He bit into his roll, butter dripping onto his plate.

"That's nice dear." Was he still helping that girl—that addict? Phyllis hoped—with all her heart—not.

He went on talking.

She stirred her food.

He deserved someone like … like … Shelly from high school. She had been so nice. Pretty, too.

Phyllis' bible study ladies had prayed for a life mate for Mark —maybe someone's niece. Or a woman from church.

"So, she has really had a hard life. Her little girl, too. Hard to see the effects on the little girl." Mark reached for more sour cream. "I hope somehow, that I, uh we all at the department, can make a difference in their lives."

Phyllis choked. "What dear? Who?" She dropped her roll onto her plate. It bounced on the table and onto the floor. Butter side down.

"You okay?" He jumped up and rescued her dinner roll and swiped the butter spot off the floor with his napkin. "Don't get up. I'll … I'll wet a paper towel and wipe it up."

He rushed to the sink and ripped off a piece of paper towel, wet it and wiped up the butter. "There. All taken care of." He held up the roll. "Five second rule?" He grinned.

He knew she hated that, but she nodded.

"Sure." She held out her hand. "Did I hear you correctly, son? You … you've been with that girl—what's her name —Kat?"

"Katty." He sat back down. "We're helping her at the department. She is struggling right now, so we're helping her and her little girl."

"What's the little girl's name?"

"Bea. Spelled B-E-A. Bea. Like the busy bees. And she is every bit as busy as bees. She's always drawing or making up songs."

He stopped and looked up. Almost as if he realized something that Phyllis already knew.

She was pretty sure he loved them.

"I'm sure Kat, er, Katty is a good mommy, Mark. But …" *Careful Phyllis Scott. Careful what you say right now.*

"She is a good mommy. She's just had some problems."

He appeared to be thinking hard—his brow furrowed. He shook his head and stared at the centerpiece and blinked. "That's. That's a lot of leaves, there." He still stared.

"But she drinks, Mark."

His eyes popped up to hers. "What?"

"She drinks. And I think it's bad." Oh-oh. Phyllis couldn't stop now for anything. Couldn't get that picture from the other day out of her mind. She'd been at the gas station and gone inside to get some coffee. She hardly ever did that. Buy the gas, go in and pay, nod at the farmers sitting at the tables and back outside to her car. She never, well, hardly ever bought coffee in there.

But she had that day.

Katty had been there with Bea, and Katty had been drunk. Phyllis was sure of it. She couldn't get that picture out of her mind, and that's where she went every time she and Mark talked about Katty. She had been drunk with her little girl and she was buying more whiskey or liquor—whatever was in those little bottles. She was buying more.

Phyllis just couldn't forget what she'd seen.

Or maybe she just couldn't forget Mark's dad.

Mark leaned forward. "Mom. Are you forgetting something?"

"What? Forgetting what?" She couldn't come out of that visual.

"Are you forgetting that I used to be in trouble with the law? That I used to drink and drink hard? That Dad used to drink? He was an alcoholic." His voice was getting louder and his eyes wide. "Are you forgetting that I am an alcoholic?"

Phyllis blinked.

He continued. "And not *was*." He sucked in a deep breath, licked the butter off his lips and opened his mouth. "I *am* an alcoholic."

Mark tapped the steering wheel out in the cruiser after dinner.

It was good to say out loud just now, "I'm an alcoholic."

Good for Mom to hear, but good for him to say it out loud.

Good for the Earth to hear it—the atmosphere, the cosmos, or whatever—the universe to hear it out loud.

Not hiding it any longer.

Besides, the department all knew—well, Guy knew. He'd been sober for a few years now.

Power in speaking truth.

For that reason, he could discern what Katty might be feeling. There was some connection.

Yeah, she was pretty and all.

No.

She was really pretty. It was kind of obvious she'd been around a little—there might be a few wrinkles around the eyes from smoking and booze.

But when she smiled, she lit up the Earth. Her brown eyes twinkled. Even her beautiful teeth sparkled.

What was he doing?

There had only been one other woman he had felt this way about, and she had dumped him long ago.

He shook his head and looked up at the sky through the windshield.

If this was meant to be …

He … he might be in love.

"Stupid. Stupid." Phyllis slammed the platter onto the counter.

Good thing the plate was strong and well-made, because she wanted to whack it a couple more times on the counter.

"Why, oh why, can't I keep my mouth shut?" She picked up Mark's dirty plate and caught herself before she slammed it down, too.

"No matter how I feel about that girl and her child, I have to keep my thoughts to myself." She dumped her unfinished dinner into the sink, swirled water, and flipped on the disposal. The grinding noise was exactly how her emotions were—grinding, growling, chopping. "I'll just drive him to her, if I don't stop."

Grrr.

The water swirled, making a vortex as it drained—mesmerizing, hypnotizing her. She stared at the water.

Memories of her past layered over the visual in the sink: her ex-husband throwing a bottle at her, him coming at her with the meat cleaver, his dark face before he—

Something caught in the disposal and she flipped it off. "Oh, no! What now?"

"Lord, protect my fingers." She sucked in a deep breath.

Cringing, she stuck her hand down inside the disposal and felt around. "What on earth?"

She pulled out her hand, fingers holding a ring.

"What is this?" Even though she knew. But, how? She hadn't even noticed her ring was missing off her finger. The ring had been her mother's and was precious. She turned it over and over. Didn't appear to be scratched or hurt. The tiny stone was still intact.

Whew.

Shaking her head, she turned on the water and rinsed the ring.

It glistened under the water. The tiny stone was a diamond chip—all her dad could afford—according to her mother. The story was, he had sold his favorite horse to buy the ring for her. A horse for her diamond.

Phyllis had never said this to her mother, but it must not have been much of a horse for that tiny chip.

She dried her hands and walked to her bedroom.

She didn't have to think—she knew where it was.

Why had she even kept it, anyway?

Under the tiny pillow in her jewelry box.

There.

She'd had it inspected after Carl died. A whole three carats.

Beside her mother's old ring, her own diamond looked huge.

Well, it was.

Side-by-side, there was no comparison. One diamond was huge, the other a chip.

The rings were opposite—the meanings so different.

One, the tiny one, symbolized a love, pure and deep. The sweetness of those years, of that life built together.

Branches waving in the breeze caught her eye out the window.

She stared.

Must be tired.

The other ring, the enormous diamond, represented no love —just control and authority. Pride. Painful memories.

She could have sold hers for, she guessed, a couple thousand dollars, but she'd always hoped Mark would find the girl of his dreams and that he could give it to her as an engagement ring.

Or something like that.

Only now.

Phyllis had seen it in Mark's face—his eyes.

He loved that woman.

And even more so, he loved that little girl.

CHAPTER 26

Phil stepped around the corner, his back tight against the wall.

"He was down this hall." Nurse Bitch's loud voice echoed. "Crazy day. Katty having a spell. Now some strange guy?"

Phil rushed past an open door.

No. Inhabited by a resident.

Another open door.

Whew. Whoever lived in that room needed to get it over with and die.

Closed door.

Utility closet.

Yes.

Fast.

Phil eased the door shut just in time, then leaned against it, listening.

"He was right here."

"Who *is* he?"

"I don't know, but he looked familiar, for some reason."

The big black woman, Nurse Bitch. He did not want to tangle with *her*.

Their radios buzzed. "Hey Lisha or Carol? This is the front

office. Could you please check on Candice, quick? She seems really upset."

"Sure, but. How would *you* know she's upset?"

"She called down here—direct. Said there was a man in her room and he had terrified her."

Lisha and the other woman laughed. "Girl, she been saying that ever since she came in here. Her family gave us a heads-up that she had a great imagination—especially about men."

"But why would she call the office?"

"She must have lost her call light. Again." Lisha's loud voice boomed. Her laughter bounced off the walls. "She's done this before. We'll check, though."

"Thanks."

The voices traveled on down the hall.

Phil cracked open the door.

Nurse Bitch knocked on Granny's door. "Candice? It's me, Lisha. Coming in to check on you." Lisha pushed the door open and disappeared into the room.

Thanks for the distraction, Granny.

He stuck out his head and scanned the hallway in the other direction.

A little boy leaned against the wall, a couple rooms away, toward the nurses' station. He waved at Phil.

Shit!

"Okay, Candice. We got your call light fixed."

Phil closed the door just in time.

No mistaking those voices as the nurses walked past the door again.

"Hey Son. You don't go in there. That's the utility closet—mops and junk. That's for the housekeeping people."

Phil froze.

That kid.

Must have tried to open the door.

What the hell?

"You waiting for someone, Son?"

Quiet.

"Well, why don't you come down to the nurses' station with us. You can wait there. We'll find your people."

Nice.

Nice Nurse Bitch.

Michael nodded at the other angel, Uriel. "I had a run-in with the human, Phil." He thought again. "Well, not a run-in. He was definitely a little shattered."

"You let him see you?" Uriel raised his eyebrows, a half-smirk on his lips.

"It was good for him." Michael adjusted his belt. "He needs to see the other side of things. I gave him a fresh perspective."

Uriel chuckled. "And did it … did it help him see a different side of things?"

Michael nodded as Mrs. T walked, walker-style, into the room, patted Katty on the shoulder, as she walked past the desk.

Katty looked up. Just as soon as she realized who patted her, her entire face relaxed, eyes softened, and she leaned into Mrs. T, like a kitten leaned into its mamma cat. Almost purred.

"Are you better, my Katty?" Mrs. T had claimed her, just as Clarence had.

Katty blinked. Blinked again and nodded—busied herself with the papers in front of her.

Mrs. T could soften the hardest heart, smooth away any fears. She fairly twinkled. That was the only way to describe her. Sparkles and twinkles.

Michael bowed low.

Uriel followed suit.

Mrs. T giggled. "Oh, quit fussing over me, Michael."

"What, my Dear?" Clarence met her, kissed her on the cheek.

"Hi Michael. What's with the—" He glanced at Michael and then at his wife. Clarence visibly swallowed. "What's with the sword, Michael?"

Michael held it up, glanced at Uriel, then Mrs. T. "This old thing?"

Uriel sputtered and turned his back. Even with his back turned, he was clearly wiping his eyes. Laughing and wiping his eyes.

Clarence's office was now Command Central, a gathering place for the angels and creatures serving the Father under him in the upcoming battle.

But Clarence didn't know it.

Somehow, Clarence had been able to see Michael ever since he'd moved back to Osceola from prison. But he couldn't see the other angels.

Not yet.

Mrs. T could see everyone and everything.

An amazing warrior.

Michael chuckled.

Clarence stepped closer.

Oh, no. Curiosity of Clarence might get them in trouble.

Uriel turned and blew on the papers in front of Katty on the desk. Papers scattered everywhere—on the floor, into boxes already sorted, onto the desk chair.

Katty jumped as the papers magically floated around her.

"Wha?" Clarence jumped and grasped at the papers. He only caught one. "The window isn't even open. What …?" He shook the paper in front of Michael. "You did this, right? What else am I not seeing?"

"Um." Michael blinked and smiled at Mrs. T and Uriel. "Uh … if I told you, I'd have to immobilize you!"

Clarence wrinkled his forehead. "What?"

Mrs. T bit her lips and pushed her walker into their bedroom. "I'll be in the bathroom Dear Husband."

"Oh, Mrs. T." Katty gathered the papers from the floor around the desk.

"Yes, Dear?" Mrs. T turned.

"What'd you do with Bea?" She picked another off the desk. "You sign her up for therapy?"

"She's coming. I needed to visit the little girl's room." She took a step toward the bedroom. "She dropped her books, and I told her to pick them up and hurry along."

Clarence watched her totter into the other room. "Did I say something wrong, Michael? I'm just a newlywed." He scanned Michael up and down. "You. You're ancient. Got any marriage tips?"

Michael prayed for self-control. Busting out in laughter would not be easy to explain. "Um. Nope. I'm just an angel."

"Katty. What did I say wrong?"

She smiled, probably still wafting in the fragrance of Mrs. T's love. Definitely stronger.

Uriel coughed and pretended to clean his weapon, although he had already wiped it several times.

Michael shook his head. For such a time as this. The Host of Heaven was sparing and clashing, ready for battle. And Clarence was asking for marital advice from an angel.

Priceless.

He watched Mrs. T settle into her chair in the bedroom, fold her hands to pray. Michael found himself mesmerized—watching her, settled by the sight, no matter the coming battle.

Clarence calmed down. They all did when Mrs. T prayed. A quiet fell over them as they watched her.

One eye open.

The world had no clue.

Angels and humans.

Learning.

Bea could see them all, too. Only, she had already started to think it was a game of sorts. Mrs. T was just beginning to teach her the truth—that the angels and other creatures were there to protect and guard her. Bring her messages from Eternal's heart.

Maybe if Mrs. T lived long enough, Bea would believe, too.

Uriel unfurled his wings and flew off, headed for Katty and Bea's trailer house. He was to join the others already positioned there, for when the humans returned home.

Positioning for the attack that always came, ever since Lucifer had been kicked out of heaven.

Michael shook his head. Back to business. Strange to be strategizing against the angel who had once so powerfully led worship of the Father.

The first foray between him and Lucifer back then had been heartbreaking. They had lived together, worshipped together, created and worked together for the Kingdom. Heartbreaking to fight against someone who had been his brother. Michael and Lucifer, he still had a hard time calling him Satan, had stepped around each other, eyeing each other, swords ready.

They had circled face-to-face.

Eye-to-eye.

Only those were not Lucifer's eyes.

Michael remembered Lucifer's eyes. Full of Light. Of Joy. Markers of his Maker. Sparking with readiness to worship the One, the Only Creator—Father. Eyes that glinted with mischief, knowing who he was as part of the Kingdom—to worship the Lord—to create that readiness, that atmosphere of worship and praise.

But all that had changed.

That day, Michael had refused to fight Lucifer. He even laid his sword down, the heavy weapon releasing a sigh as the heavenly metal slid against the rocks. Lucifer's eyes, always reflecting eternal love and deep joy, had morphed to madness and darkness.

Michael had broken away and run from him. Not in terror,

but in shock. He'd never seen a transformation as startling as Lucifer's.

The darkness had seemed to boil from within him. A thread, a root that tangled deep within the body—the body of an angel—who was now called Satan.

One thread that grew into many.

Changing him.

Nothing had ever happened like this before—all across time.

The transformation was startling, but fascinating.

As Lucifer had stood before him in all his beauty and colors, stones glistening, and wings gloriously unfurled, he begun to morph, to change.

Within his eyes, first. Those beautiful bright pools of light had turned black—-circle by circle until the whole eye appeared dark.

So odd looking, still surrounded by the otherwise beauty.

Then his chest had bulged out, as the threads entangled, wrapping from within, like fingers lacing through from the heart, exposing what had been growing inside for some time.

Father had known from the beginning.

A black hole opened up in Satan's chest as his shoulders, then arms, then legs sucked into the hole. He became a ball, turning in on itself, and body parts opened where the others had been.

Different body parts.

Black.

Dark.

Filthy.

Scales.

With a stench that was indescribable.

Nothing in Michael's existence had prepared him for this.

Nothing he had experienced compared.

He had no reference for what he saw or smelled or felt.

He felt pain.

And love.

How could an angel, who had served so willingly and beautifully in the Father's throne room, turn into what now stood before him?

The total absence of Light.

Michael slowly picked up his weapon again.

An emotion had flickered across Satan's face.

Regret?

Now, back in Clarence's office, Michael tapped his leg.

The memory was encapsulated in time.

It *was* yesterday.

It was *today*.

It was *now*.

Time on Earth and no time structure in heaven.

Even now, Michael transcended time and saw a younger Katty enter the convenience store.

Back when Phil had first met her.

And now, in a convenience store today.

Katty entered the store—the same store—much older looking. She appeared very distraught and disheveled. And terrified.

Needing that fix, Michael guessed.

Now in Earth real time, she sat before him at Clarence's desk, reading papers, digging through Clarence's boxes. She kept patting her pocket, where Michael knew there was just one sip left.

He met eyes with Mrs. T.

No one saw her nod but him.

Katty had been through hell and back, and it wasn't over yet.

She had a long way to go, in human time.

His heart broke for her, but there were sounds of battle and he had to command the hosts of heaven.

Nodding to Mrs. T and the Guardians lining the office and bedroom, he unfurled his wings and lifted off.

Phil peeked out of the utility room door and breathed.

With all the buckets and damp mops stored there—the faucet dripping into the tiled mop sink and the cleansers behind him—he could suffocate.

He sucked in fresh air from the hallway, but realized where *that* air was coming from.

Gag.

His throat tickled.

Not coughing now.

He swallowed.

Hard.

Better. The cough subsided.

Achoo!

Damn!

He didn't get the door shut in time.

About four "bless-you's" filtered through the door. Hopefully, they all thought the sneeze was from a resident.

He cracked the door open again.

"Hey, Daddy."

The boy.

"Shoo! Go away!" Phil shoved the boy.

"Mister, I—"

Phil grabbed the kid's shirt and dragged him into the closet with him. "What the hell do you want?"

The boy immediately became distracted by all the cleansers, mops, buckets, and equipment stored in the small room.

Phil shook his head. What the hell? He just wanted Bea and now he gets this damn kid? What on earth was he gonna do with him?

"Daddy, look." The boy pointed to a shelf filled with tubs of bubble gum. "Can I have some of that?"

"What? Kid, I'm not your dad." Phil was in no mood. He didn't want to kidnap a boy, too.

The boy pointed again.

Bubble gum. In a utility closet?

"Sure kid. Knock yourself out."

Back at the door.

Bea! Bea just walked past with books in her hands. Where was she going? Was the old man's room down this hall?

Oops.

Some nurse headed his direction from the nurses' station, reading something on her phone.

"Hey Dad. I can't get this open."

Just as Phil softly closed the door, the lid popped off the bubble gum tub, creating a hailstorm of wrapped pieces of gum flying all over the room, pelting Phil and the boy.

Outside the door. "Hi little Bea. Are you reading books today with Mrs. T?"

Phil froze. He leaned against the door, listening.

He could hear Bea's tiny voice, but he couldn't understand what she was saying.

He barely opened the door, suspecting they were right outside.

"I am." Bea answered.

"What's your book about?"

Phil strained against the door, but couldn't hear, because the boy was unwrapping the candy and popping it into his mouth. Even a dog couldn't chew that loud.

"Bye, Bea." The nurse must have walked on down the hall.

Where was Bea?

Something dropped onto the floor.

Books.

"C'mere." Bea's little voice.

A book slid into Phil's line of sight. And another. Right outside the door.

Bea grunted as she tried to gather them up. Dropped another one.

Phil reached his hand under the door and caught hold of a couple, sliding them under the door into the closet.

"Cool. Books." The boy leaned over Phil. Smelled like a bubble gum factory.

Bea peeked around the edge of the door, her eyes wide. She apparently recognized Phil, for she appeared ready to bolt.

"Hi." The boy waved at her.

"Shut-up kid." Phil grabbed to cover Bea's mouth, only missed, and punched her instead.

She fell.

He caught her in time, slid the books in with his foot, and pulled her into the room. Laid her down behind him and shut the door.

The last visual Phil saw before he closed the door was an old woman sitting in a wheelchair across the hall.

Her mouth was wide open, and she was babbling.

And pointing.

The prize was delivered right into his hands.

CHAPTER 27

Katty stepped back and surveyed her progress. "You know, Clarence, if we could find a place to store some of these boxes—the ones we don't need right now—it would help."

Clarence glanced up at Katty, then scanned along the wall. "Wow. You're almost done." He nodded. "Yes." He hesitated a minute. "Bet I could find out from Sheriff if something … like a storage unit, is available. He monitors them—he owns them!"

Katty hesitated. *Stop reacting every time someone says sheriff or cop.* "Yeah. That way this would look more like an actual office … instead of a—"

"Nursing home room?" He chuckled.

Harold pushed up from his chair. "What don't you like about nursing home rooms? What's wrong with them?"

Katty relaxed and giggled. "Nothing. Nothing at all. He meant a … storage room, right?"

"Well, gotta go." Harold pushed his walker out in front of him. "And … I gotta go."

Katty jerked her head up. "What?"

Clarence shook his head and grinned.

"What do you mean, what?! This *is* a nursing home." Harold

took a step. "We talk about the weather, our grandkids, and our bowels." Another step. "And, not in that order."

Katty broke in. "Well, I hope everything—"

"Comes out okay." Clarence broke in.

"Ha-ha." Harold gave Katty an air kiss as he passed her, step-by-step. He peeked into the bedroom. "Tell Little One bye for me." He tapped her on the shoulder. "And take care of yourself. Okay?"

"Okay. I'll try." Katty swallowed. She could barely contain the emotion. When Harold talked right to her like that, she always wanted to cry. Especially today. He loved her almost as much as Clarence did.

Clarence glanced at the clock. "Bea should be here."

"I think I hear her now." Katty grinned.

Her tiny voice was so sweet and … pure.

Most days.

"Mommy?"

That voice was pure, but it wasn't Bea.

Mrs. T joined them in the office, perched on her wheelchair, walking with her legs.

Clarence stood and kissed her on the forehead.

She giggled. Still the girlish heart. Still … so pure.

Katty blinked. She stared at the sweet scene before her. That would never be her.

Quick.

Head down.

Pen in hand.

Write in the notebook.

Anything.

Scribble.

Anything.

Only when she opened her eyes and checked the notebook, nonsensical scribbles covered the page. Every line filled with nonsense. Like when Bea tried to write words—she just filled the page.

Nothing in her life made sense, anyway.

Nothing.

It was all nonsense.

"Where's Bea?" Mrs. T scooted from the wheelchair to Harold's chair.

"She's not back yet." Clarence peeked out the door, down the hall, in both directions. Back into the room. "I thought she followed you. She had her books with her and was going to read while you—"

"Wait." Katty came to. "What?"

"Bea's not back." Clarence checked the bedroom and the bathroom there. "Not in here, either."

Katty jumped up. "She's always here." She checked the office bathroom, shaking her head.

"Mommy?"

"Bea?" Katty stepped to the office door. "I just heard her. Bea?"

Shooter was still in that pocket. It bounced against her body.

God, she needed it now.

"I-I'll go down to therapy and see if she's there." Katty nodded. "She followed you part way though, right Mrs. T?"

Mrs. T nodded. "I told her to hurry." She wrinkled her forehead. "She was right behind me ... but I had to get back to the bathroom."

"I'm sure she's visiting someone." Katty headed out the door. "She took several books. Probably dropped them."

Katty sucked in a breath, only it stuck in her throat.

An elephant sat on her chest.

A herd of elephants.

The hallway stretched five times longer than usual.

Even with her jacket on, she shivered—but sweat trickled

down her back. She could never tell if it was withdrawals or a fever.

The shooter beckoned even louder.

Just a sip might help calm her nerves.

Keep her steady.

Bea had to be around somewhere.

Bea opened her eyes. Smelly room. Like her towel, when Mommy needed to wash it. She wiped her face.

Ow. Her mouth hurt.

The memory slammed into her.

He'd hit her. Phil. That man had hit her.

She wiped her mouth. It hurt. There.

He was sitting on the floor by the door, peeking out.

She scooted away from him, as far away as she could get, into a corner. Her books. One-by-one, she slid them closer and gathered them to her chest.

That was him. That was her dad. But he was bad. Badder than Bad Mommy. He had tried to kill her on the slide.

She had to hide.

Buckets and mops. Shelves.

A piece of bubble gum slid across the floor to her.

She just stared at it. Then around it.

Another piece.

Her eyes followed to where it had slid from, up to a little boy's face. Grinning at her.

She glanced at Phil, but he was still looking out the door. Slowly, she picked up the gum and looked back at the boy.

He grinned again. "Go on. Eat it. It's good."

Phil jumped and turned around. "There's my girl. My Bea."

Bea scooted a bucket in front of her, between them.

"I'm *not* your girl." She wiped her eyes. "I'm Mommy's girl.

And Clarence's and Mrs. T's girl." She sucked in a deep breath. "Harold's girl." Louder. "Michael's girl."

"Shush." Phil glanced over his shoulder at the closed door. "Who's Michael?"

Bea's lower lip puckered. Her eyes darted around the room.

"Ha. Smarty." He saw where her eyes went. "No way out, except through me. And this door."

The boy leaned forward and tapped her on the arm. "It's okay. He's your dad."

Phil shook his head. "What? How did you know that? What's your name, kid?"

"I don't have a name." The boy leaned closer to Bea. "He's *your* dad," he tapped his own chest, "and he's my dad, too."

Bea studied the boy's face, then glanced at Phil.

Phil looked like Daryl did in her books, Daryl and Dumpty. When Daryl got scared, his face got all white and his eyes got big.

"What did you just say?" Phil shook his head.

Bea pulled the bucket closer. It wasn't big enough to hide behind. Back to the boy. "He's your dad?"

"Yup." He nodded.

Boy was nice.

She sniffed the bubble gum.

Glanced back at Phil and scooted even farther into the corner. She pulled another bucket in front of her, her books close.

Phil shook his head. "No way." Again, he shook his head. "He's not my kid. I only have one kid and that's you." He pointed right at her.

"No!" Bea blinked and stuck her chin out. "If you were my daddy, a good daddy ...." She struggled to stand up, books sliding off her lap. "If you were a real daddy, you'd be 'tecting me, not hurting me." She pointed at the boy. "Us. If you were a good daddy, you wouldn't hit me and keep me in here—you wouldn't try to kill us."

Boy nodded.

Bea nodded.

Phil reached inside his shirt and pulled out a gun.

Bea grabbed at anything close—the boy. She'd only seen guns on TV … and Depdy's gun. But she knew they hurt.

Boy gathered up more bubble gum into a pile.

A huge foot stepped between her and Phil.

Bea jumped. Her angel. She knew that foot. He was too big to fit in this little room. His foot was all she could see. She stood, dropping the bubble gum and books. "My angel is here. You are in trouble."

Phil waved the gun and crawled close to her. "I don't see no angel."

Bea's eyes popped right out of her sockets. She pointed at his foot. "He's here." She gulped and wiped her eyes.

Her angel raised his sword.

"He has a sword."

Just when her angel raised his sword, three other angels landed, armor shining, swords raised.

"Greetings, Comrades." It was getting crowded.

"Whew. What's that smell?" The boy shook his head.

Bea shook her head and pinched her nose. "What is that?"

Her angels surrounded her and the boy, as a big scary monster stepped close. Its eyes were yellow, not blue or green. Or even the color of hers—brown. Icky, icky eyes. He had a sword, or what looked like one, in his hand. Long fingernails. Hairy ears and arms.

Her mouth quivered. Her tummy felt like she was going to puke.

Her angel leaned down and looked in her eyes. He shook his head. "That's not an angel, Little One."

Bea watched *his* eyes. Her angel's eyes always talked love and warm insides.

Those yellow eyes were mean. "What's that word?"

The boy dropped his bubble gum. "Evil." He picked it back up and built a stack of gum pieces. "The word is evil."

Her angel nodded.

This wasn't gonna be good.

Growl.

What was that? Was there a doggy with them, too?

Bea gasped.

That wasn't a doggy.

The growl came from that big monster sitting just on the other side of Phil, growling at her. His bad angel.

She dropped her books again and jumped to the boy.

Those yellow eyes.

That wasn't skin. It was slimy, shiny, oily—like when the old car used to drip oil on the ground.

But his eyes.

Looked right at her.

She snuggled closer to the boy and pointed. "Do … do you see that?"

He put his arm around her and pulled her close.

Nodded.

He was looking right at it.

He didn't look afraid.

He looked mad.

He reached for her hand.

Phil pulled the door shut and turned, the gun pointed at them.

"I don't know who you are kid, but you both better get ready." He nodded his head toward the door. "We are getting out of this stinky closet and making a getaway."

The demon moved closer.

CHAPTER 28

"It's okay, Mrs. Bernadine." Lisha pushed her hand at her. "Calm down. We're looking for that little girl. You know her … little Bea?"

Mrs. Bernadine continued to babble and point. Tears streamed down her face.

Carol walked up behind Lisha. "What's got her so agitated?"

"I don't know. She's been doing that since—"

"Eeee!"

Lisha clapped her hands to her mouth. "Someone screamed!"

Carol twirled around in the hallway. "Close by."

Boom!

"Gunshot!" Lisha froze. "I know that sound."

Mrs. Bernadine babbled even louder and pointed right at the nurses.

"She's … she's pointing at us." Lisha turned.

Carol nodded toward the utility closet. "There, Mrs. B?"

Mrs. Bernadine started bouncing in her chair. "Babble, babble." Her head nodded up and down.

"She's pointing there." Carol backed against Lisha, arm out, pushing her back, trying to shield them.

"Doris! Anyone there at the office." Lisha spoke into her pager. "Call Sheriff. We have gunshot. Someone's in the utility closet. East wing!" She hesitated. "Little Bea's missing."

Carol wheeled Mrs. Bernadine away from the door. "It's okay, Mrs. Bernadine. She called the sheriff." Carol took her pulse. "Calm down. Breathe."

Lisha checked the hall.

Katty.

"Stay in there, Carol." Lisha lumbered down the hall toward Katty and waved her away. "Girl. Git back. We heard …" She pushed Katty back. "We got a call into the sheriff."

Katty's eyes bugged out. "For what?" Her mouth popped open. "The sheriff? For Bea? Bea's missing. We can't find her. She's not in our rooms."

Clarence hugged Katty from behind. "We'll find her, Katty."

His eyes met Lisha's. He got it. Smart old man, for sure.

And Mrs. T, right behind him, standing in the doorway with her walker.

Eyes closed.

Lips moving.

"Hey Mark?"

Mark jumped. He scrambled to hide the romance novel under some newspapers, but didn't make it in time.

"What are you hiding?" Guy slipped in and grabbed the papers.

Too fast.

He pulled out the novel. "What's this? Your … fall reading program?" He flipped through the pages. "Romance?"

Mark grabbed the book from him and threw it in the desk drawer.

"Steamy novel? Right?" Guy slapped him on the back. "Hey.

Get a move on. We got a call from Hillcrest. Someone's missing."

Mark pulled on his cap and beat Guy out the door, into the hall. "Who? A resident?" He shook his head. "That can't be good."

Guy pushed the door open to the sidewalk and held it for Mark. "No." He opened the driver's door. "Get in."

Mark shook his head and followed Guy. Seat belt on.

Guy checked in.

Mark activated the siren and lights. "So, who's missing?"

Guy swerved around a car hauler unloading at the dealership. Barely slowed for the stop sign, turned right onto the street, and zoomed past the grocery store.

Mark checked the highway. "Clear, right."

Guy kept on pushing across the highway and up the hill to the nursing home.

Mark radioed in. "Chantelle, send back-up to Hillcrest."

Guy stopped at the front entrance.

"Who's missing?"

Guy unbuckled his seat belt and glanced at Mark. "Bea."

Michael opened the realm.

Angels and demons layered over the nursing home hallway and rooms. Interesting viewpoint with both realms visible.

There.

The utility closet.

Phil and two, no, three kids. Another child had arrived. Bea had company and Michael knew she could see them.

Interesting thing—Phil could see them, too.

Michael guessed Phil would classify that as a curse. Poor man didn't know a blessing when it was right in front of him.

Mrs. T sat in the office chair Harold had vacated earlier. She pulled her sweater around her. "Michael, we have reinforcements."

Michael nodded.

The more she spoke, the taller she grew, until she appeared to be almost as tall as Michael. She didn't have wings, but she had risen to pillar height, commanding the room. She continued to pray to the Father.

Strength visibly streamed from their Source, on shafts of Light, to each angel and creature of the Kingdom of God. The shafts created a matrix or grid that connected them, keeping them on one plan: a plan to rescue Bea, but also draw Phil to the Father.

A tough job, with his background, for anyone but the Lord.

Michael glanced at Mrs. T.

Still praying.

Tongues of fire enveloped her.

She had stayed pure from day one.

Never given up, even through hardship and pain.

Michael fanned the flame.

From her, fire ignited every stream of Light across the whole grid, exploded strength and might to each angel—Michael and Mrs. T, included.

CHAPTER 29

Katty gulped as she followed Lisha. "What?"

Lisha pushed Katty against the wall in the hallway. "We don't know for sure, but … well, she might be in the utility closet up yonder." Lisha scrunched up her face and pointed.

Katty jumped. "Let's get her out."

Lisha held her back. "Not so fast."

"I've got to get Bea out of there. She might make a mess." Katty jerked away from Lisha. "She might get hurt." Visions of Bea possibly finding her tiny booze bottles always terrified her. What Bea might do with cleanser bottles—

Lisha caught her and held on. "Baby. There's something else goin' on, but we haven't figured it out yet." Lisha hugged Katty to her. "Somethins' not—"

Carol stepped from Mrs. Bernadine's room and pointed to the closet. "We think she's in there. She screamed."

"Screamed?" Katty pushed at Lisha. Air. Air. Something was pushing against her chest.

"No. Yes." Lisha swallowed, still holding onto her. "Yes."

"You sure Bea's in that closet?" Katty grabbed Lisha's arm. "Did you see her go in?"

Lisha pushed Katty back to where Clarence stood outside his office door. "Keep her here, Clarence."

He nodded. "What's going on?"

Katty grasped hold of Lisha's sleeve. "What happened?"

Mrs. Telluride peeked from her doorway across the hall. "There was a gunshot."

"Gunshot!" Katty broke loose, but Clarence caught hold of her arm. "Katty. Let the deputies take care of it. Stay here."

Katty growled. "It's Phil. I know it!" She fought Clarence. "He tried to kill her before!"

She couldn't move. Clarence was stronger than she was. Second time a man kept her from saving her own daughter.

She reached into her pocket.

Didn't care who saw.

Tiny bottle out and open.

Swallowed.

Bea screamed again.

The gun went off.

The boy blinked. "Don't shoot her." He moved in front of Bea.

"Dirtbag." Phil growled. "You little dirtbag." He waved the gun. "I'm not your dad. I'm hers—not yours."

Bea clutched the boy's shirt from behind. "Bad Daddy." She didn't care anymore. "Bad, Bad Daddy." She stepped beside the boy.

Phil grabbed her hair and pulled her in front of him.

"Ow!" She screamed. "Stop it!" She held on to where he had her hair, then stomped on his foot. She couldn't see for the tears streaming down her cheeks. "Stop! Stop! Stop!"

"Little bitch." Phil hoisted her up in front of him.

He pushed the door open, gun pointed out.

CHAPTER 30

Mark slid around the corner at the nurses' station, and he almost choked at the sight before him.

Lisha was shoving a lady into her room.

Carol slammed a door to a resident room.

Clarence struggled to hold on to Katty.

And, just as Guy slid in behind Mark, Phil Daynton pushed the door open from a closet.

Oh dear Lord.

Phil crushed little Bea in front of him. He pointed his gun directly at Mark.

Shit!

"Easy, Pardner." Guy's smooth voice.

"Back off!" Phil shoved his gun against Bea's head.

Cocked it.

Her face.

She stared right at Mark.

Her wet eyes pleaded with him.

Save me!

Guy's voice didn't work on Daynton, because Daynton continued to step toward them.

Katty struggled with Clarence. "Stop him!"

Mark blinked.

Everything in him wanted to rush Phil and rescue Bea.

Phil struggled to hold on to Bea and keep his gun pointed at her.

"Dammit, Bea." He took a chance at losing his grip on her. Bounced her against his leg and circled his arm around her neck. Gun at her head.

Shoved her ahead of him with his body.

Her hands clawed at his arm. Her kicking feet tangled with his legs.

As he edged her towards the deputies, several more people appeared.

Distracted for a second, Phil blinked, but pulled himself together. "Get back! Get back in your rooms."

People seemed to float into the hallway. Huge men stood at every resident door.

Damn, if he had to wrestle even one of them, he'd lose.

Growl.

He knew where that sound came from, and it hadn't left his side since early childhood.

"Put the gun down, Daynton." Big guy. Had to be six-four or six-eight.

"I'll shoot her." He shoved the gun harder against Bea's head.

She bit him.

He bopped her on the head with the gun and she collapsed. "I mean it! If I kill my own daughter, it'll be on you. Put your guns down."

Angels don't get upset.

They don't fear.

But in this moment, even though Michael had peace, he didn't know the outcome.

Only Father knew that.

Concern lined even the other angel's faces.

The humans appeared terrified.

This wasn't good.

Bea hung from Phil's arm.

She was out.

Probably better that way.

Phil appeared to be sweating—clearly agitated.

Mark's eyes never left Bea. He appeared to slow his breathing. In. Out. In. Out.

Guy, too.

Mrs. T stood beside Michael.

She never stopped praying.

"Stop!" Mark would not give up his gun. "Stop!"

Daynton kept on stepping closer. Gun at Bea's head. "I'll shoot her. I will."

God, Help! This visual. Bea still unconscious. Appeared to be a big red bump where he had hit her. Daynton's gun still at her head. Mark knew it was loaded. Daynton had fired off one shot already, at least.

Daynton took another step closer.

Mom, pray.

Katty struggled against Clarence farther down the hall.

God help. God, please.

Lined up in Mark's sight as he stared down the hall were Phil and Bea stepping toward him, and farther down behind them,

Katty fighting Clarence. Lisha and Carol, and another nurse, guarded some doors.

All visible at the same time. All lined up. No way to shoot without hitting someone.

Phil stepped forward, Bea hanging from his arm. He waved his gun back and forth.

Man up, Mark.

God help. Don't let this end badly.

Sweat trickled down his back.

Please don't let someone come out of their room.

Breathe.

"I mean it! Put your guns down." Daynton stepped closer.

Silence.

Mark leaned down and gently slid his gun to the floor.

Guy did the same.

They both stood, hands in the air.

God, if You're there ...

"Oh, no. No. No. No!." Sobbing, Katty twirled around in Clarence's arms, swung him around by the arm.

Still, he held on tight.

She couldn't breathe.

"Bea." Katty screamed her name. "Somebody stop him!" She leaned over and threw up.

Just one sip.

She'd had just one sip.

"Phil, give her back!"

Phil kept on walking toward Mark and Guy.

"Stop him!"

She slipped to her knees, sobbing. "God."

Clarence sat behind her, his legs sprawled on either side of her, hugging her from behind.

"Mark. Please."

Only, he was backing away from his gun.

Guy was too.

"No." She struggled against Clarence.

Old man was stronger than she was.

Every cell in Mark's body rebelled. He'd laid down his gun. Guy, too. Everything in Mark screamed, "Kill the bastard!" But he'd just laid his gun down. What if he shot and got Bea, or Katty, or Mrs. T?

A door opened down the hall, and an old man stepped out.

Distracted, Daynton stepped away, aimed toward the man and fired.

Bea's eyes popped open.

Mark didn't take time to think, but grabbed his gun and fired.

Like slow motion, the last thing that registered with Mark was Bea seeing him aim his gun toward her. Then both she and Daynton flew back, hard.

The sound of gunshot echoed down the hall. Deafening.

The silence that followed was equally loud.

No one moved, until Guy rushed up, retrieved his gun and Daynton's gun—shoving it into his waistband, wrestled him over and handcuffed him.

Daynton yelled out in pain. "Bastard! You can't do this." He continued to kick about.

Guy jumped over Daynton's feet and dragged him to his knees. He searched Daynton—every pocket, patted down his body.

Blood covered Guy's hands and his shirt.

People came to life. Or was it Mark that came around?

Katty screamed. "He shot my baby?"

Clarence still wrestled with her, keeping her from running, keeping her from … seeing.

Keep her there, old man. Don't let her loose. Not until.

Lisha got to Bea first and picked her up. "Oh, Baby."

"Mommy?" Bea struggled in Lisha's arms, then burst into tears.

Lisha wouldn't let her go. She felt each arm and leg. Her head. "She … she's okay." Lisha's big brown eyes were wide, her cheeks shiny wet. "She … she's okay."

Mark slumped to his knees.

Carol called out. "Harold's okay." She pointed to the hole in the wall.

Guy dragged Daynton away. Daynton's left shoulder was bloody. He struggled against Guy, kicking at Mark as they passed. He was more interested in killing Mark than what had happened to his shoulder. "Damn you, cops. Damn you!"

A flurry of movement down the hall captured Mark's attention. Clarence and Katty rushed to where Lisha held Bea—or tried to hold her. She popped out of her arms and ran to Katty.

She ran! She moves. She's okay. Mark let his chin drop to his chest. So not protocol. "Uh, I'll be there, Guy."

Guy looked back over his shoulder, as two deputies rounded the corner. "Take your time, man. I got help."

A hand rested on Mark's shoulder. "Buddy. By the grace of God."

Mark looked up into beautiful brown eyes.

Lisha.

He slowly shook his head. Tried to keep it together. Wasn't working. Tears slipped down his cheeks. He tried to stand, but his legs were jello.

Lisha grabbed his arm and helped him up.

"She … she's really okay?"

Lisha nodded. "Not a scratch on her. Not … anything wrong with that child." She looked behind her as Katty enveloped Bea.

They both slid to the floor, Clarence sitting a few feet away, sobbing.

Bea pointed at Mark. "Mommy, Depdy Mark shot at me, but he missed and hit Phil."

Katty lifted her head and looked straight at Mark. "No Baby Bea. He shot at Phil and got him." Her eyes said more.

Mark slid to the floor again.

Breathe.

CHAPTER 31

Phil could make a run for it. Even with a wounded shoulder. Even with the big cop dragging him toward two more deputies. Run back the way he'd snuck in.

Those enormous men closed in, too, their wings visible.

Wings?

Angels?

Impossible.

The big deputy wrenched Phil's cuffed arms behind him. "To jail with you."

Phil didn't hear anymore. The muzzle of the other deputy's gun was so close he could smell the lubricant.

Boy stepped in front of Phil. "Bad Daddy." He pounded him with the mop.

Phil was defenseless.

An angel picked up the boy and held him higher so he could reach Phil's head.

Over and over, the kid clocked Phil with the mop as the deputies pulled him down the hallway.

"Ow! Stop it, kid!"

The deputies shook their heads.

"What kid?"

"He's right next to you." Phil growled, trying to point.

To the boy. "Stop hitting me."

The deputies glanced at each other. "Bea's the only—"

"Hallucinating." The big deputy handed Phil's gun to another. "We'll give him a drug test back at the department."

Phil stomped his foot. "He's right beside you. Angels, too."

"Whatever."

The angel set the boy down. He crossed his arms and stood by the nurses, as the deputies dragged Phil down the hall.

Phil looked back.

Something about that kid.

The angels bound the demon. Wrapped golden ropes around his arms and legs. Supernatural tape over his mouth.

Phil shook his head.

Seeing demons?

All the time.

Angels? Never.

And nobody else saw the kid.

Wait.

Bea saw him.

Katty held Bea tight. "Bea. Baby Bea." She rocked her back and forth. "Oh, Bea. I'm so sorry."

"Mommy?" Bea's eyes flickered open. "Did you know I have a brother?"

Lisha and Carol backed away, started opening doors, checking the residents.

Clarence hugged them both. "My girls." He wiped his eyes.

Carol opened a door nearby and Mrs. Bernadine appeared, pointing and babbling.

"A-a brother?" Katty almost swung her around and stopped. She checked her over. "Phil hit you. Where?"

Bea pointed to her head.

"It's bleeding." Katty couldn't stop the tears. "What was he thinking?"

Carol checked it. "I'll get a bandage. Take her to ER, just to make sure she's okay." She shook her head. "He really hit her."

Clarence pushed Mrs. T closer in her wheelchair. "She was waving at me to come see you. See Bea."

Bea wiggled out of Katty's arms and onto the floor.

"Can you stand?" Katty fussed. "Are you okay?"

"I'm okay, Mommy." She looked up at Mrs. T. "I have a brother."

Clarence lifted her onto Mrs. T's lap and Bea snuggled in.

"Oh, my Bea." Mrs. T kissed her. Bea's head came up to Mrs. T's head—both tiny girls. She closed her eyes. "Thank You, Father."

Bea lifted her head. "Did you see my brother?"

Mrs. T nodded. "I did. He helped you."

Bea leaned back against her, nodding. "He did." She must have seen Mark and pointed. "He saved me."

Katty knelt beside them. "What's she talking about—her brother?"

Bea looked back down the hall toward the utility closet. "There." She waved.

A little boy, in sweatpants and T-shirt, was peeking out of the utility closet and waved back.

Katty shook her head. "Baby, he's not your—"

Someone tapped her shoulder.

Mrs. T?

But Mrs. T was waving at the boy, too. Holding Bea with one hand and waving with her other hand.

Katty sat full on the floor and stared.

Something about that boy.

Bea's angel blew out a breath. Relieved.

Michael was, too.

Human lives didn't always end well.

This time, it had. Well, Bea's life hadn't ended, but she was safe. That was the end they had worked for, hoped for.

Bea looked to be okay.

Cops had apprehended Phil Daynton.

Katty had only drank one sip.

The boy.

Michael reached down and lifted him onto his shoulders.

"Good job, Buddy."

"When am I getting a name?" The boy looked doubtful.

"Don't you like the name Buddy?" Michael tweaked his hair.

"No. Well, it's okay." He scratched his head. "But it's not a real name." He looked into Michael's eyes. "Is it?"

Truth.

"No. No, it's not."

Poor kid.

Michael set him down on the floor.

Buddy sighed.

CHAPTER 32

Katty opened a can of paint. Every cell of her being lit up at the sight of that blue. The color of sky, of a robin's egg—no … brighter than that—of the spinning, round thing on her computer, of the big Welcome to Osceola sign painted on the retaining wall in front of the swimming pool. She could see the sign in her memory. The paint in her can was the same. The city of Osceola must have bought their paint at the same place she had. Same color exactly.

Odd night, tonight. She might be almost sober, but she couldn't sleep. Wide awake. With all that had gone on at Hillcrest that day, Katty was wired. So many images floated through her head. Right now they were all a mishmash, layer over layer: Clarence holding her down, Phil dragging Bea out of the closet —slumped over his arm—out cold, Mark and Guy laying down their guns.

Katty shuddered and almost dumped over the whole can of blue at that thought. That visual. Phil and Bea. Literally brought her to her knees.

Awful, awful memory. Bea in his arms. Helpless.

Tears dripped onto the newspapers and towels under her on

the floor. Emotions of pain, fear, and regret rose, buried deep within her soul. Some from years with her mom, then Phil. All mixed in with the pictures imprinted in her mind of Bea and Phil.

Sobs burst from her mouth. She leaned over, her hands on the floor. Tears and snot ran down her face. She hadn't let herself cry since Bea was born. Couldn't. She needed to be the mom, the strong one, the one with answers.

Well, she knew that was a pile of crap. She knew nothing except that *right now*, something had taken over her body, making it spew out things she had carefully and completely buried. She had no control. Total opposite of her normal. If she let herself feel the brutality, she'd die. She'd never get back up. She'd never be able to raise Bea past this day.

Finally, she let her head fall to the towels on the musty carpet, all bent over.

Hiccup.

Belch.

No.

For once—just for once—Katty cried out to be free. Free of the pain. Free of the booze and her body's desperate need for it. And free of the bloody memories. Why couldn't she just be free?

God. Help.

What did she deserve? Why would God listen to *her*? She'd been a part of terrible murders. Why would God even look her direction?

She knew there was a God. With all her heart. She knew. Katty believed. She just knew He wasn't there for her. He didn't listen to her prayers, her pleading. He never had before. Ever.

Maybe when she was tiny and before all the harsh abuse. But not now. She'd done too much. Drank too much. Let Phil kill too many. Why hadn't she run away back then? Before? Why?

Because where would she have gone? Who would have wanted her back then? Who would want her *now*? Phil's lies had done the damage. She had thought he loved her and would take care of her. Be kind to her.

She lifted, gasped for breath. Tried to stop the hiccups.

Breathe.

She tapped the lid on the blue paint can and sat back.

God, her face was a mess—wet with snot and tears.

Hiccup.

Exhausted.

As she sat there by the wall, Katty allowed—demanded, no dared—pictures, memories, triggers to float in and out of her mind. Visuals. Out of all the memories of her tough life, that one of Phil dragging Bea away might make her … or break her.

She knew she had abused Bea herself. She'd hit her. Sometimes bad. Clarence had caught her in the park that day they'd first met. Why Clarence had even cared to get involved back then was beyond her. But he had. He'd gotten involved to the tune of adopting them.

But she'd never seen anyone else hurt Bea—except Phil. He'd hurt Bea before—thrown her against a wall when she'd peed on his arm. He had been trying to kidnap her even then. Bea had gotten so upset, she couldn't hold it and peed on him and he threw her hard.

Katty was almost inviting those memories to send her over the edge. Like … come on. Either break the stupid addiction, that awful need to drink, or kill her trying.

Face off.

If she could only go back … if she could change going into that convenience store that night when Phil had set her up. If she could only make a different decision, take a different path. He'd lured her with beer and candy. If she had gone to a friend's house instead—only she couldn't let friends into her secret world of being abused, of her mom's scathing words.

She didn't have any friends.

She'd been at that convenience store because she had

nowhere else to go and no one she could trust who might help her.

Her hands clinched into fists. Either face the hard, awful facts, or die.

She belched. Stomach rumbled.

She slowly tipped her head side-to-side.

No.

Not going to drink. Oh, she had a whole line-up in the cupboard. Clarence had paid her the day before and she had filled in her little liquor cabinet, her stash. With clear bottles, and yellow bottles, and golden ones all in a row.

That image of Phil dragging Bea out of that closet was birthing a determination that she felt now, but could she hold out against those bottles tomorrow? Or the next day?

For right now, the torture seemed to be held back by something. Suppressed. Impeded. It wasn't totally gone, but just underneath the moment. Just underneath. Always there.

Interesting to think of the torment in that way. The thoughts, the pain, had always been full-on. Like someone always throwing water in her face. Or food at her. Both had happened. Mom had thrown a dishpan of hot soapy water at Katty as she walked into the kitchen. Mom had found her drawing pencils again. The day Mom found Katty talking to a boy outside of school. Mom had seemed so sweet. "Katty has a boyfriend." Sang it all the way home and into the house. Called Katty later, for supper, and as Katty entered the kitchen, Mom had slung a whole pan of hot macaroni and cheese at her. Then she made Katty clean it up.

But today, at this moment, the pain was just underneath all that. Katty hadn't even buried it. What was all this for … her life, the pain, the guilt, the shame?

The wind always blew in Osceola. Always. Some days it blew really hard, so that she had to grab hold of Bea's jacket to keep her from flying away. A person couldn't escape—the wind was everywhere, every corner, every turn, every road.

Other days, the wind caressed as one turned a corner or changed direction. Gentle.

But today was one of those days when a dominant memory stayed front and center, like a rotten meal. It remained like a brick in the stomach.

There.

Full-on.

The memories invaded, seeped into every situation and decision, like a disease—at first quiet and undetected—but soon becoming full-blown, painful symptoms. Those memories had become the underlying foundation that permeated every decision, every move, every visual. They infected everything in the physical world.

Katty rubbed her eyes and glanced up at the wall in front of her.

That tree.

Just sitting in front of that tree. Facing her past in such a strange way. But facing it. Not numbing out, although she could right now. Get stinky drunk.

Katty embraced that picture of Phil and Bea. It gave her such a determination that if she ever had the chance, she'd kill that man. Kill the father of her child. Kill Phil Daynton.

For now, that was her strength. She had to stay sober because if she ever caught Phil out free, she'd kill him. Pay him back for everything her mom had done to *her*, even. Pay him back for every torturous thing he'd ever done to Katty and now to Bea.

That was her strength. For now.

She knew the rest of the memories would be back, slowly weaving their way into her day, into her thoughts, to shove her over the edge again. To drink. Again.

But now, there was an unnatural peace, even with that visual layered in. Whatever this was, however it was happening, it wouldn't last. She had never experienced that kind of peace before, but if she knew her life and the patterns that had developed, that peace wouldn't last either.

She lifted the lid on the can and peeked at the blue paint again. Sighed.

So beautiful.

Gently, she placed the lid on the towel she'd laid out. Newspapers even. She'd made a terrible mess the first time she'd painted these walls. Not going to happen that way again.

She could almost watch the brush dip into the paint as if it was someone else doing it. Someone else's arm and hand holding onto the brush and watching it lift out, blue paint dripping back into the can.

Beautiful.

Deep sigh. Even the smell of the wall paint stirred her emotions.

How she was blocking the usual repercussions, the normal response, she did not know.

Maybe it wasn't her at all.

She made herself look up at the wall.

That tree.

Something about that tree.

Bea peeked one eye open. She never wanted to get up to go to the bathroom in the middle of the night.

Roll over. Close eyes.

Sigh.

It didn't work this time. Sometimes it did. She could fall asleep and wake up dry in the morning. Not this time.

Both eyes open. It wasn't dark. There was light. She sat up and looked outside.

Dark.

Back to the hallway. Light.

She struggled out of bed. Her covers tangled around her legs. Mommy always said she was like a little worm in her bed—all twisted and wound up—a bedtime burrito.

After she finished in the bathroom, there was still light down the hallway. To the kitchen. Maybe Mommy was hungry. Bea was hungry.

In the kitchen, Mommy wasn't eating.

"Wow."

Mommy was painting. More babies. Better babies. There were leaves on the tree. So pretty.

Bea yawned and sat on the sofa. She liked paint smell—made things feel and look new. Mommy was humming a song. Bea didn't know the song, but she knew that when Mommy was singing, Mommy was happy. Mommy liked to sing when she was happy.

Every line on the wall was so careful. Bea's eyes followed Mommy's brush and the lines it made. The baby she was painting looked real. Like someone Bea knew. Like a photo … photograph. Real baby pictures. The babies kind of looked like … her.

She blinked. Not all of them, but some looked just like her.

She tiptoed to Mommy's room and looked at her own baby picture. Just like her. She grabbed it and walked to the living room. "Mommy?"

Mommy jumped and almost knocked over the can of paint. "Bea. What are you doing up? Did I wake you?"

Bea shook her head. "I had to potty." She held out the framed photograph. "Look, Mommy, they look like me."

"Where'd you get that?" She stepped closer, brush in her hand. Brown paint.

Bea searched the walls. Where was brown? The tree. "Wow. Mommy. The tree is so pretty."

Mommy turned to the wall and looked at where Bea was

pointing. "That tree." She stood looking at it. "That tree … was a special tree." She sat down where Bea had been sitting.

Bea sat beside her, still holding the photograph. "Special tree?" She shook her head. "You mean it grows apples? That kind of special tree?"

Mommy smiled. Good Mommy was here tonight. Bea yawned again.

"You should go back to bed." Mommy looked at the stove clock. "It's just after 4:30."

"Is it time for breakfast? I'm hungry."

Mommy laughed a little. "You're always hungry." She jumped up and added paint to the tree. "It's not time for breakfast, but if you're hungry, you can eat." She wiped her brush off on the newspaper and closed the can of paint. "What do you want?"

"Peanut butter?"

Mommy said it with her.

"How did you know I wanted peanut butter?" Bea crossed her arms across her chest. "How did you know?"

Mommy laughed again. "You always want peanut butter."

"No, I don't." Bea thought a minute. "Sometimes I want cereal." She thought again. "Maybe I want cereal instead."

Mommy shook her head. She didn't even smell funny. She even looked happy—kind of.

"Mommy. Do you want some peanut butter too?" What was that on the wall? She ran to look closer. "Mommy? Is that Daryl and Dumpty?"

"Can't you tell?"

"It is! It is them." Bea tested the paint. Dry. "How'd you know how to paint them?"

"They're all over your room—your curtains, your bedspread. That's all you watch on TV." Mommy stepped closer. "You like? I drew first so I could get it right, then painted over the pencil lines." She sighed. "Actually, it's not half bad."

"I like them." Bea looked up at Mommy. "Now we're never painting over this."

Mommy nodded, looking at the new paintings.

"I'm getting my Daryl and Dumpty out, so they can see what you did." Bea took off down the hall to her room. Still dark outside. She'd never been up all night before. Well, she had under the rocker.

Bea dragged out Dumpty, then Daryl. She always hid them behind the books on the bookcase. Behind *their* books. Clarence and Mrs. T had given her the last book in that series. That one was still on her bed—right by her pillow—because she slept with it. The others were all lined up on the shelf and that's where she found them now. Other books started to fall from the shelf, so she tossed Daryl and Dumpty on her bed.

She had quit hiding them for a while, but when those bad men had broken into their trailer, she started hiding them again. Before the bad men, it was Mommy. Mommy had told Bea that if she wasn't good, she'd take all those books and stuffed Daryl and Dumpty away.

She scooped them in her arms and sniffed them. They always smelled so good. Even when she'd dropped spaghetti on one, she'd just licked it off before Mommy could see. The spot was almost gone. She sucked on it every once in a while to make sure. If Mommy got mad at her for getting them dirty, she'd take them away for sure.

Just the thought of that made her squeeze them against her chest.

Back in the living room. The tree on the wall was so big—as big as a real tree. "Mommy? Did your tree fall?"

Mommy turned. "Fall?" She looked back at the tree, then at Bea again. "What do you mean, fall?" She added a few more brush lines, then back to Bea.

"Your tree is … the leafs." Bea pointed to one yellow one.

"They turned yellow and orange. That means the tree is fall." Bea scratched her head.

"Oh. I get you." Mommy nodded and tried not to laugh. Bea could tell. Mommy's mouth moved funny. "Hey, go back to bed. They said at the ER that you should get rest." She leaned over and checked Bea's head. "Your head looks okay. The scab is still there, but you need to be careful and not scratch it. Let it heal, okay?" She brushed Bea's hair off the scab.

"Mommy? Who is the little boy, the one in that closet with me?" Bea laid down on the sofa, still cuddling the stuffed toys. "He said Phil is my daddy and his daddy, too."

Mommy covered Bea up with a coverlet and sat down beside her. "I don't know. I've never seen him before. Mrs. T said he looks just like you, but I didn't see him all that much." Mommy stopped combing Bea's hair with her fingers and looked at the wall. "He looks like ... he looks—"

"Like those babies." Bea looked at what Mommy was looking at. "He looks like those babies on the wall. The ones you painted, Mommy."

Bea didn't say anymore. Just looked at the babies and the tree. The clouds. "Mommy?"

Mommy didn't answer.

"Mommy?" Bea pointed at the tree. The leaves were floating.

"What, Bea?" Mommy still watched the wall.

"Are those babies moving?"

CHAPTER 33

Katty opened her eyes. Was the wind blowing? What was that sound?

She looked at the clock.

9:37 a.m.

A dim light outlined the shades. The time on the clock must be right. They'd been up most of the night. She rolled over and pulled up her covers. It was getting colder outside. Soon they'd be getting heating bills again. That always gave her anxiety. Heating a trailer house and paying for those bills gave her nightmares.

Breathe. It wouldn't be for a month, maybe.

Quiet.

What was she hearing?

She listened again.

Bea.

Bea was singing in her sweet little voice. "Daddy. Daddy."

Katty gagged—almost threw up. No. That little girl better not have gotten attached to Phil. How could she when he had just tried to abduct her, and he had definitely hit her on the head with a *gun?* Katty shivered. What if Mark and Guy hadn't gotten there in time? What if someone had gotten shot? Well, Phil had been shot. What if Phil had shot that old lady … Mrs. Bernadine?

She sat up.

Or Bea.

"Daddy, you love me." Bea sang.

Katty jumped out of bed too fast and tripped over the coverlet. She caught herself by the side chair and sat on it. Damn.

She was not good.

She must have caught a bug.

Stupid girl.

That was a lie, and she knew it.

Why was she going back to the lies?

Three little shooter bottles on the bedside table answered her question. She stood up and peeked under her pillow. Two more.

No.

When had she drank all those? What had she done? They had been up painting during the night. What time was that? After 4:30? She must have drank after … after … they had seen the tree move. And the babies float. She must have been drinking before she painted. Then seen the babies floating and moving across … Bea had seen them, too.

She moved slower this time and stepped carefully to the bedroom doorway and listened.

"I love you, too." Bea sang.

What?

After all Bea had gone through yesterday being kidnapped at the nursing home? What was this 'I love you' crap, all of a sudden, when Bea had suffered all that yesterday—at her daddy's hands?

Katty slipped into the hallway and whipped past the bathroom door, even though she should have used it herself. She was almost at Bea's open door when she heard, "I will shine for you,"

Katty peeked into the room. Bea faced the window. The blinds were open, and the curtains pulled way back so the whole window was visible.

Little sparkles framed Bea's face.

The curtains were open, but the sun wasn't shining in—wrong direction.

A breath caught in Katty's throat.

Those lights.

Angels?

The soft light revealed Bea on the floor, on her knees.

Katty choked.

With every word Bea spoke in her soft, sweet voice, something in Katty broke. Warmth and sweetness poured into her, over her, with each word.

Where had Bea learned to pray?

"And Daddy, please help Mommy get better again."

Bea couldn't have possibly seen Katty peeking around the doorjamb.

Katty blinked the tears back and wiped her eyes. She slowly slid to the floor and let the tears fall.

"Daddy, I love you."

Each word Bea spoke brought more tears.

And each tear opened the wounds that Katty had so carefully covered up. With every humiliation she had suffered at other people's hands and words, every brutal pain she had endured, every accusation she had inflicted upon herself, she felt them all washed away somehow.

She knew it wasn't magic.

If only. If only. If only this time. This time, she could quit. If this time she could be free. She'd cried out so many times. Something was happening, but things had happened before.

God, if only.

She knew that her years of self-abuse and child abuse, of drinking and drugging, would take time, but somehow, she also knew that she was being affected by Bea's simple, sweet words.

Bea's prayers.

Katty was being changed and affected.

And … it had begun now.

Today.

Did you like Revealed? Want to continue on with Katty's Story in The Great Escapee Series?

Grab the next book, Redeemed, in Katty's Story and continue the adventure!

The voices inside Katty's head become clear:
The evil ex-boyfriend and father of her daughter, Bea, is all she deserves.
Her mom was right about her—she is a slut.
And the babies she aborted all hate her.
There is only one place she deserves to go and that ain't heaven.
But there's one person who sees …

Get Redeemed, Book 5 in The Great Escapee Series, Book 2 in Katty's Story www.bonnielacy.com

AUTHOR NOTES AND ACKNOWLEDGEMENTS

This book, Revealed, is book four in The Great Escapee Series and as I remember back when I wrote books 1-3, I did not know that books 4, 5, and 6 were on the horizon. I did not know what they might be about, or that they even existed somewhere in God's timeframe and mine.

I know those first three books had Katty and Bea in *parts* and that Katty had lived a very rough life with her evil ex-boyfriend—drugs, booze, abuse. I had hinted that he kept her drugged and drunk—mostly by him, but partly by her own addictive and abusive response to *being* abused, herself. And that he had aborted their babies—whether by taking her to clinics or doing it himself.

I know. Gruesome.

But one thing I'm learning. If I can imagine it—good or bad—it has happened.

Her boyfriend's actions were extreme, but those things happen.

This was written mostly in year 2021. We have been living with COVID-19. Learning way too much of some of the evil in this world. We knew it was here, we just didn't realize that leaders, media, and countries could suck us into it. Hook, line, and sinker. I was pretty sick in January and February 2020, but was it COVID? Could have been. I didn't go to the doctor. I stayed home, like I always do, used essential oils and rested, wrote and read. (Sounds like a vacation, now.)

That's when these books, Katty's Trilogy—as I've called them before I had titles—that's when I plotted them and fleshed them out.

My life didn't change all that much. I work from home anyway. Very blessed and thankful for a husband who drives a truck. He has worked hard as one of the many essential workers in this COVID nightmare.

Again, thankful for him.

Thankful to God for His provision and blessings. Grateful.

Have you seen the movie Unplanned? Seeing that movie with my sister was a kick in my hesitative backside. (Yes, that's a word, even though Auto Correct doesn't agree! I looked it up!)

Back to the movie. Was I being lazy? Putting off writing this important story?

No.

It terrified me.

Still does.

Terrified.

If anyone reading this has any experience with alcoholics, you'll know that just when you think they have conquered the booze, they fall again.

No condemnation.

Just hopefully, truth.

The ending to Revealed is hopeful, as I pray all my books are.

But sometimes God needs to take us *deeper* to heal *more*.

And that's what is happening in the end of Revealed—and onward to the next book, Redeemed—the next book in this series.

Please know that I am praying for you and your loved ones who still struggle with alcohol: from where Jesus sits at the right hand of the Father, and from the Cross and the Resurrection! I am praying for you!

I love writing about the supernatural—the blending of worlds— the layering of our physical world with whatever invisible realms there are. Angels. Demons. What are they doing while we are writing, working, living life on Earth?

I'm not too good at writing all that ... because, well, I can't see that realm—yet. So if what I write about them doesn't agree with what you know or have been taught, then teach me!

Any links I share in my books or website might be affiliate links: you don't pay more, I just receive a percentage if you purchase through my links. References I used: *Demon: A Memoir* by Tosca Lee, *The Screwtape Letters* by C. S. Lewis, and *The Fall of Lucifer* by Wendy Alec.

Yeah. The Bible.

All fun reads. Fun ... and disturbing, because as a human, I am still learning how the angels and demons operate in that realm. I'm still learning how to be who and Who's I am meant to be.

More: *Angel Armies* by Tim Sheets, *Angel Armies on Assign-*

ment by Tim Sheets, *Unplanned* by Abby Johnson, *The Jericho Plan* by David C. Reardon, *I Had a Secret for Seventeen Years* by Tori Shaw, *Unexpected Choice* by Patti Giebink, MD, *Tilly* by Frank E. Peretti, and *Survivor* by Claire Culwell.

There are many good places to get help with addictions, abuse, and surviving abortions: Teen Challenge, https://www.rachelsvineyard.org/, Alcoholics Anonymous, are just a few. I am compiling a list for following books. We have direct experience with Teen Challenge and AA. More to come! If you know of any places or resources, please go to www.bonnielacy.com and to contact. Thank you.

Disclaimer: the basement at the old Opera House, owned by Monson Antique Trading Co., is *not* a creepy place. To be quite honest, it is one of my favorite old basements and buildings ever! Remember Phil Daynton, who spent time down there, is evil!

Using my hometown, Osceola, Nebraska, is fun. I make things up. I stretch the actual buildings or park or nursing home to fit my story. This *is* fiction. So disclaimer again: any business or building that I reference and use for my story is not what the actual would be. There are great people working there. There are great owners, who are community minded people of integrity.

That includes anyone who might be a part of Osceola, Nebraska, in the future.

Disclaimer: and about the nursing home, Hillcrest Homes … er … Good Samaritan Society. I have stated in every book I've written about Clarence that the nursing home and staff in the books differ greatly from the real ones here in Osceola. We see Hillcrest Homes (I made the name up!) through the eyes of an eighty-year-old ex-con! And a four-year-old ice cream monster, Bea!

Besides, what would you do with an eighty-year-old man who gets kicked out of prison? Send him to another prison? The nursing home is a prison—in *his* mind. Remember, he is an angry, stubborn old man when we first meet him in Book 1, Released!

Disclaimer: Words either thought or said by Clarence—but mainly by Phil, and sometimes by Katty—are naughty. But then Clarence spent sixty years in prison—he ain't your white-washed, little old man. And Phil? He's a piece of work all by himself. He is evil. What words do *you* think he'd use?

Just know—even after reading the ending in Revealed—that there is always Hope.

Please remember that.

The story might get darker.

You know my stories. Even my grandsons read my books, so I'm not saying it becomes a horror story or anything like that.

We all should allow ourselves to go back through our past and ask the hard questions: have I opened that heavy door to the ugly and let God air it out, or like Clarence—have I found myself back in the prison of _______ (you fill in the blank), where it has gotten uglier?

We all want the happy ending in our lives and it's there. You might have already found it. But sometimes it's just on the other side of _______ (you fill it in, again.).

In the next book, Redeemed, Katty goes back to the addictions. It's hard to write. I want even my created characters to thrive and be happy! But if Katty hasn't let Jesus flush out those areas of her life with His love and with His Blood, then she is only putting a Band-Aid on it.

And it'll get filled with pus, nasty under that Band-Aid, until it erupts again from some other trigger.

Katty needs Jesus, and she knows that.

She's almost there.

But she has always been told she's a slut (sorry), that she's just a scab on her mother's life.

Until she kicks those lies out and embraces Jesus and His truth … well …

Thank you to many people who prayed for me while writing this book. You hold me up. You keep me. When I am ready to quit, one of you calls or emails or texts. I can write another day when you do that!

Please keep the prayers coming. There are two more books in Katty's Story!

And thank you to Jennifer Werth, Laurie Schmitt and Laurie Evans for counseling me. This trilogy was difficult to write, and I wanted to be sensitive and supportive and honoring to all the people who have been through this kind of loss: through abortion, miscarriage, untimely death of a child, alcoholism. These women (and others) gave me courage to press in and write the hard parts when I wasn't sure how to proceed. To seek Holy Spirit for discernment.

That reminds me … I want to thank Jeff Gerke, the editor who edited Redeemed, book *five* in The Great Escapee Series. He hasn't read this one, Revealed. But he edited Redeemed and what he taught me about writing and story stopped me cold. I knew from his input in book five that I needed to go back to book four—this one, Revealed. I had been a chicken. I didn't want to take Katty to the really hard places that we all need to go in order to heal. I had pushed it out too fast. He, without knowing, helped me see that I had to pull Revealed from wherever it was for sale and revise. It *hopefully*, became a stronger book, a better story. And that's what being a writer is all about—crafting a good story. You also introduced me to Steve Rzasa, the editor for this book, Revealed! Thank you, Jeff.

Thanks to my sister, Jan. And Penny—readers who gave their time to proof my work, making sure it's way more readable than it was before! If it shines, it's them!

Thanks to my cover designer: Jane Dixon-Smith! She has done every cover and I hope many more to come! She put up with a lot for this book. It was a struggle for me. Did it matter more than all the others? Not sure. I was difficult.

Thank you, Patrick O'Donnell. Writer and retired cop. I asked him to edit Revealed to keep it authentic to Deputy Mark's life. How does a deputy check in on his shift? Well, let's just say that I got a lot of things wrong and Patrick did a great job of setting me straight! His books are online and he has a great podcast, Cops and Writers Podcast. You'll love it!

Thank you to Steve Rzasa, who edited this book, Revealed. I so appreciate him making time for this book. Just took it on. Where it makes sense, it's him!

Thank you to Pastor Al and Ella Hazelton, who are such great friends, but are those stalwart warriors—always faithful. You heard my heart for this book.

As always, thank you to Dearly Beloved, who is my provider, my personal car consultant. To my kids and grandkids —my source of encouragement and support and joy! I love you all so much.

And to God, the Eternal, my Father, my Source.

This is really where it's at for me. Have you, Dear Reader, asked Jesus to be your Savior? It's really simple. Lots of people make it out to be more difficult than it is. Just tell Him you're sorry for your … stuff, you know … your sins. You know what they are. So does He. Even if all you say is, "I'm sorry, Jesus. Help,"

He is there.

He forgives.

And he loves.

So much.

You can email me if you have questions. There's a contact page on my website. Not that I'd know every answer, but I know Someone Who does.

THANK YOU, READER!

Thank you for reading my books! If you have a minute, would you consider leaving a review anywhere you purchase books? It is a huge help to any author! Ask for them at your Public Library. Even though you get to read them for free, I get a little kick-back, too.
It's not all about the money. But it helps when I pay an editor or book cover designer.

If you remember in my last book, I promised Katty's Trilogy. This is it! Katty's Story!

There is more to come—two more books for Katty and Bea. (This is how weird I am—as I typed that, I saw them taking a bow!)

There is a trilogy for Clarence and Harold, too, and The Timmelsen & Dexter Agency—a detective agency. Michael is in it. Katty and Bea. Noell appears, too.

Yeah, Phil is jumping up and down. "What about me?"

Ugly, evil man.
But what if …

Noell is drawn to that pool in Rescued, Book 2. What are her other gifts? She goes to strange places in her own trilogy!

If you want to keep up with my characters (literally!) go to: www.bonnielacy.com. Scroll down and you'll see "Get Your Free Copy." There you can fill in your info and hit the subscribe button. There's always a giveaway. I won't blow up your inbox, for sure … just keep you up on releases, maybe a doodle, and excerpts from my daily journals. You'll be added to my email newsletter list, but you can unsubscribe anytime.

Keep in touch.

Be Blessed!

ALSO BY BONNIE LACY:

Fiction:

The Great Escapee Series:

Released

Rescued

Restored

Revealed

Nonfiction:

Rage Rising: My Walk Through the Dark Tunnel of Anger

Cash Envelopes: You've Never Had So Much Money

Cash Envelopes: You've Never Had So Much Money Workbook